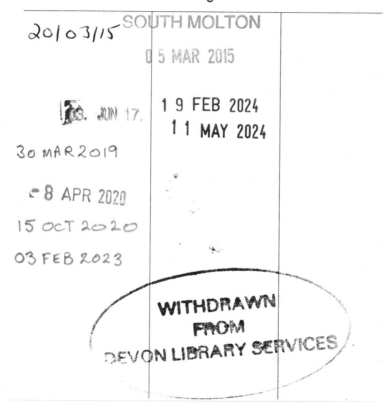

Maxwell's Ride

M J Trow

First published by Hodder

This edition first published in 2013 by:

Thistle Publishing
36 Great Smith Street
London
SW1P 3BU

ISBN 13: 978-1-909869-33-2

CHAPTER ONE

The blue Lincoln was moving too slowly as it turned tight onto Houston. The girl saw the crowd's faces reflected in the polished bodywork now that the sun had come out again after the rain. The colours of that day flashed onto the screen, the snapping red, white and blue of the flags, the sharp, shiny grey suits, the hideous pink of the First Lady's suit. No, she's not lovely, the girl thought – her eyes arc too wide apart, her mouth too big. And what about him? Wasn't he supposed to be the youngest ever President of the United States? He was ancient – easily as old as Bill Clinton. What was all the fuss about?

The buildings blurred by in the background, flying past the motorcycle cops with the sun dazzling on their white helmets, their black leather. The sound had been slowed down, distorted, the roaring crowd blending now with the purr of the motorcade's engines.

'Mr President,' the voice-over was gravel, 'you can't say that Dallas doesn't love you.' Love you. Love you. They'd just left Love Field. But the faces of the crowd didn't show any love. Now that the camera was slowed down, she could see them, the silent watching crowd. There were no smiles now just rows of sullen faces. Middle-aged men in fedoras, women in dark glasses and headscarves. And their eyes. Their eyes were empty, dead. They'd all turned out to cheer their president. But they weren't cheering. They were watching. And waiting.

The First Lady turned to beam at the camera, then turned back as a gust of wind threatened to take off her pink hat. She didn't see the man opening and closing his umbrella along Elm Street. Nor the man having a fit at the corner of Houston and Elm. She certainly didn't see a rifle in a sixth-floor window of the Schoolbook Depository.

1

Frank Zapruder's fuzzy film filled the screen now, the Lincoln with its radiator grille ablaze with sunlight, the stars and stripes on its wing barely stirring in the breeze. The girl had seen this before and had time to take it all in – Will Greer with his hands firmly on the Lincoln's wheel, the Secret Service agent whose name she didn't know beside him, out of condition, relaxed, switched off. There was talk they'd been partying the night before. Behind them, the waving Governor John Connolly, waving his white hat and looking tense, trying to grin, hoping to convince the President of what he'd just said – that Dallas loved him. Next to him, his wife, annoyed, the girl bet, that the First Lady had upstaged her – younger, better hairdo, better suit.

An animated clock appeared in the screen's left top corner. There was the crash of a rifle shot. What idiot had put that road sign there? The girl had thought that before, the first time she'd seen this film. Now she was furious. Her subconscious had expected somebody to move it.

The film blurred as the cameraman jumped. Zapruder should have stuck to dressmaking. The President wasn't waving now, but drowning in his own blood. His head faced forward, both hands came up, in the inevitability of slow motion, to grab at the hole in his throat, just to the left of his tie knot. She saw John Connolly half turn, first to his right, then to his left. Then his shoulder went down and his face contorted in the pain, his jacket billowing with the impact of the bullet.

The President's hands were still in mid air as he wrestled with death and the First Lady leaned towards him. The animated clock had recorded six seconds and she had heard the ricochet of four shots. Will Greer had still not put his foot down. What was the idiot doing? The girl was tapping her Biro on her desk, irritated, unbelieving. Was the man blind, deaf? The President was dying and the car had nearly stopped.

The girl couldn't feel the tension in the classroom for the tension in her own brain. She could barely hear the television for the thudding of her own heart. The President was slumped to his left, the First Lady steadying him, watching the blood pump over her sleeve.

Then the girl's Biro snapped with a crack louder than anything in Dealey Plaza. There was an explosion of glistening red, bright corpuscles in the November sun as the President's head lurched backwards and down. An actress's voice-over was screaming 'Oh, no, no, no. Oh my God, they've shot him. They've shot my husband.' Then quieter, as agent Clint Mill sprinted across the gleaming space between his car and the President's, 'I love you, Jack.'

The girl was still half out of her seat as she saw the First Lady scramble back over the Lincoln's boot, scrabbling for the safe hands of Clint Hill, scrabbling for the piece of her husband's skull that had been blown away and had bounced onto the limousine's bodywork. She would hold that jagged piece of skull in her hand all the way to the Parkland Hospital, as her husband's brain seeped into her lap.

The clanging of the bell shattered the moment. Miss Montague, of the pleated skirt and lace-up brogues, switched off the television and clapped her hands to bring her class to the here, the now. Thirty-six years, a million words, a thousand theories later.

Who would know, the girl asked herself as she trailed the gloomy corridor towards the Biology labs. It came to her as a light in the darkness, as a flash of inspiration in the murk of ignorance. There was one man who would know. One man in all the world. And that night, when her mother was on the phone to him, she gestured to her to pass the receiver and she asked him outright.

'Uncle Max?'

'Niece Tiffany?'

'Where were you the day they shot Kennedy?'

On the day they shot Kennedy, Peter Maxwell was sitting in the Blue Boar, in the market town of Cambridge, Cambridgeshire, sipping a pint. He couldn't yet afford the tipple that would become his favourite. Five Southern Comforts a term and he'd blow his grant entirely. He had more hair in those days, much of it around his chin. People who reckoned him and wanted to borrow money, likened it to 'Honest Abe' Lincoln; those who didn't saw a pale reflection of Manfred Mann. He was in hot debate over the recent

Viking finds in the good ol' US of A, debunking forever the glory that was Columbus. It was nearly half past seven and the landlord had quietened everybody down in the rowdy front bar and turned up the radio. It crackled distortion across the stilled room as Ed Morrow struggled with the words – 'I can confirm that the President is dead. John Kennedy died at 1 p.m. Eastern Standard Time today.' Some people looked at their watches; others at each other. In the far corner, a girl with a bee-hive hairdo burst into tears. Camelot had crumbled; and men in darkness muttered 'Arthur is gone . . .'

That was a long time ago. A lot of water, a lot of bridges. Peter Maxwell wasn't a student any more, idling away his Granta days, punting on the Cam, wandering through the golden fields that stretched towards Haslingfield and Coton. He was a teacher now, a Head of Sixth Form. More than that, he was Mad Max, with heart of gold and lungs of bronze. He did his fair share of shouting and banging and roaring and bawling, but he no longer sailed in amply billowing gown. The damn thing got too covered in chalk and caught on too many door knobs. Now it hung in his wardrobe like a neglected bat.

He looked across at his niece. It had been three weeks now since her mother's call. It was a crisis, Maxie. When, with Sandie, was it not? Kenneth had been sent suddenly to Beirut. Not exactly her idea of bliss, nor his. But that was the Diplomatic Service for you, kicking you from one bloody pillar to another bloody post. And it wasn't for long, really. Three weeks at the most. Just a holding exercise, until the new man arrived. But of course, they couldn't take the girls. Tiffany could have boarded, but not little Lucy. She was sensitive, going through a difficult time, coming up in thirteen. Great. Just what Maxwell needed, a neurotic delinquent at home to outweigh the three hundred or so he habitually clashed with at school.

'Well, that's Miss Montague's theory anyway,' Tiffany was saying, sweeping her long blonde hair away from her face and lucking her bare feet under her bum on Maxwell's settee.

'Miss Montague,' Maxwell was rubbing a lazy finger around his glass rim, feeling mellow as the Southern Comfort warmed his cockles, 'Head of History?'

Tiffany nodded. 'The Gauleiter from Hell.'

Her uncle nodded too. When Maxwell had last visited his sister and her family, he'd seen the school photograph, one of those long ones where, the urban myth had it, it was possible to appear at one end and trot round the back to appear at the other. Miss Montague was a mannish lass, steel-rimmed specs over her steel-rimmed eyes, darling of the Dachau guards' quoits team.

'She's a lesbian.' It was Lucy's contribution to the debate.

Tiffany's eyes rolled with all the bored sophistication of a fifteen-year-old, 'When you find out what that means,' she said, waving a fluffy-ended Biro in the air, 'we might just pay some attention.'

'I know what it means,' Lucy didn't look up from her copy of *Nineteen*, 'Samantha Cosgrove in Upper Four B is one.'

'Oh, right,' Tiffany yawned, 'with train-tracks like hers, she's never going to have any choice.'

'No, honestly,' Lucy persisted, 'she told Janet Stallybrass she couldn't stand boys and that she'd do anything for her.'

'Not a bad idea,' Maxwell found himself playing Solomon – and not for the first time since the girls' arrival.

'What?' Lucy frowned at him. 'Doing anything for Janet Stallybrass?'

'No,' Maxwell got up and stretched. 'Not standing boys.'

Tiffany gave him an old fashioned look.

'Now, I promised your dear Mama – blessings and peace be upon her – that I'd get you two to bed by ten every single night. It's now – Jesus – half past twelve.'

'Oh, Mummy was just kidding, Uncle Maxie,' Lucy trilled, flashing her slightly outsize teeth at him.

'Well, I wasn't,' he growled. 'Tiff, we'll go over the JFK thing tomorrow, all right? But just for the record, it wasn't me. And if you give me a few months, I may be able to find a pub-full of people who'll vouch for that. Now, hit the hay, you two. I'll be round to check on you later. In the meantime, I want a fair bedtime – no gouging, no kneeing, no bitching. Got it?'

'Yes, Uncle Maxie,' they chorused. Even after two days, the silly old duffer had got into an appallingly boring routine.

A sort of peace descended on Number 38, Columbine as Maxwell's clock chimed the witching hour plus one. He sprawled on the settee watching the glow of the lamplight on the ceiling and heard the familiar thud and patter as his lodger hurtled through the cat flap downstairs and took the lounge by storm. Metternich's tail was like a loo brush and his ears were flat on his head as he noticed Maxwell looking at him. He huffed on his claws and hopped onto the pouffé.

'Gentlemen fight their duels at dawn,' His Master's Voice reminded him, 'not at one o three.'

Metternich didn't frankly give a damn. He was named after the Chancellor of Austria, the coachman of Europe. Revolutions could topple him, but names could not. He'd taken jibes from the old bastard before; his back was broad. Besides, Maxwell had his place. He bought the food and paid the vet's bills, so, hey? The cat raised his head, scenting the air.

'CK, Count,' Maxwell answered the unspoken question. 'Calvin Klein. Although personally, from the smell of it, he ought to have stuck to acting. And yes, your deductions are perfectly sound. The girls are still here and they will be for a little while yet. And why am I here, I hear you ask? Easy – I live here. It's half term; Mr Diamond, the Headmaster, is in his office and all's well with the world.'

Maxwell kicked off his slippers and shuffled for the stairs that went up to the next level. 'Tomorrow, Count, I am taking your teen-aged cousins on a visit to a Theme Park, whatever that is. We'll be out of your fur for most of the day, so just be grateful.'

He paused on the stairs and turned back to the coiled black and white bastard on his pouffé. 'You know,' he said, 'it's that comedian I feel sorry for – that Eddie Izzard. He thinks you cats are human.'

CHAPTER TWO

'It was the French who invented the queue,' Maxwell told his nieces, plus anyone else who cared to listen in the long, tortuous line that wound its way through the leafy glade, 'although if you've been to that benighted country, you'll find that hard to believe.'

'We used to live there, Uncle Maxie,' Lucy reminded him. 'When Daddy was based in Paris.'

'Of course.' Maxwell smiled at the memory of his brother-in-law. 'Hitler's occupation, wasn't it?'

The girls ignored him. Uncle Max was as mad as a snake. They both knew that. Still, he had brought them here, shelling out the coach fare and the entrance money. True, he'd gone pale both times, but they attributed that to his age.

This was what Whitsun was all about, the little lull in the academic year of a teacher, that meant you hear the birds singing before the bombardment of the exams begins. That little time fragment when English teachers realize they've been teaching the wrong texts for the last two years. What Whitsun was not about was what Maxwell saw before him now, a giant rocket blinding white in the late May sunshine, dark doors at its business end thrown scarily back. And into the darkness, a steady stream of chattering people wound its way, following some demonic piper of the park.

He'd already forced down the indescribable elevenses at the Burgermaster fast food outlet where an acne-smothered teenage counter-operative had waited patiently while Tiffany translated the menu for Maxwell. There were no seats, not even a space to lodge your elbows. This was food on the hoof, grub to queue by.

Behind them, a large lady from the West Midlands was doing admirable Jasper Carrott impressions, which were quite droll for the first half an hour. When Maxwell read the sign that told him he still had twenty minutes to wait from this point, he lost the will to live. Lucy's face was buried in candyfloss, the only thing Maxwell vaguely recognized from his own childhood. Whatever sophistication the little madam affected on a daily basis had vanished at Magicworld. She was a kid again, laughing, joking, splashing in the fountains and pulling faces at her uncle. All that surprised her was that he was pulling them back.

'Jesus!' Maxwell felt the iron bars slide down over his shoulders. Several signs had already warned him that anyone with a heart condition shouldn't really be doing this. He felt his chest thump as the car shuddered into motion. He glanced to left and right. Lucy and Tiffany on one side were nattering together, the woman from the West Midlands was demolishing a toffee apple. Ahead, in the pitch dark, silver points of light were hurtling like small supernovae on a projection screen. Maxwell knew his feet were dangling over the dark void and as the stars burst bigger and louder, the 'oohs' and 'aahs' of his fellow cosmonauts increased.

'Are you holding on, Uncle Max?' Lucy wanted to know.

'Yes, darling,' Maxwell patted her arm. 'No need to worry about your . . . Christ!'

The ship shook and juddered as if hit by a broadside. A siren was pounding in his ears, the whole capsule pulsing red. A gaping hole was torn in the rocket's nose and Maxwell found himself lurching forward, his feet flying up so that his heels hit the seat. A toffee apple flew past his vision and hysteria filled his ears. He was a public schoolboy. Shouldn't he be taking charge or something? His stomach came up to hit him at the same time that the West Midlands woman perforated his eardrum with a scream. He daren't let go to protect himself and he knew his knuckles were white on the lion frame.

Lucy and Tiffany were screaming too, their hair flying back in the slipstream. Maxwell couldn't hear them above the noise he was making and he tried to focus on the neon electronic figures whipping past on his left. It registered, at terrifying speed, the thousands of miles they were falling through the earth s atmosphere, out of space. He tried to clear his mind, to catch his breath, to shut out the suffocating pain in his throat. Films, his first love. Think of that. But all Maxwell could think of was David Bowie in *The Man Who Fell To Earth*. Not much comfort, really. Lights were flashing all around him, hells ringing. A robotic voice screaming 'Impact! Impact!'

Then it stopped. Ahead the scene was a peaceful, sunbathed earth, the sea silver and safe. He knew his body was the right way up again and that the girls were still there, laughing with the relief of it all. Rigor mortis had set in on the face of the West Midlands woman, her lips peeled back over her teeth. Maxwell was wiping toffee apple off his shirt.

'Bloody Hell!' He'd barely glanced ahead again when the rocket ploughed into the sea and a spray of freezing water hit him full in the face.

'So how come you're both bone dry?' Maxwell wanted to know as they tagged onto the end of yet another twisting, chattering, excited line.

'We've done this before, Uncle, dear,' Tiffany winked at him. 'Feel up to The Cauldron, then?'

It looked innocuous enough. Walt Disney stuff, really. They were wending their way into a vast black cooking pot resting on massive concrete logs. A green concrete slime was oozing from its rim and Maxwell couldn't help reciting the mantra 'Hubble bubble'. Tiffany clapped her hands over her ears and shut her eyes.

'Macbeth,' Lucy chirped, ever delighted at her sister's discomfort. 'The Scottish play. Tiffs doing it for GCSE.'

'Not Miss Montague?' Maxwell checked.

Tiffany had dropped her hands. 'Do pay attention, Uncle Maxie. Monty's history. It's worse,' she moaned. 'Ms Frensham.'

'Ah, Ms.' Maxwell's face fell ominously. 'That says it all, my dear. On the shelf and hideously embarrassed by the fact.'

'She's a lesbian,' Lucy contributed to the conversation.

'Oh course,' Maxwell nodded. 'Oh, God.'

The savage sun had gone and they stood on the edge of Hell. Fires flared here and there and their ears were assailed with groans and cries. He shepherded the girls into a car and moulded restraints slid down over their shoulders. The woman from the West Midlands had gone, probably with the men in white coats, and she'd been replaced on his left by a rather dismal looking man with weasel eyes. He didn't seem to be with anyone and looked utterly bored by the whole experience. What struck Maxwell as being particularly odd was that the man was wearing a three-piece suit.

'Now, I'm not going to get wet this time, am I?' Maxwell checked with the gormless girl who was ushering them into their seats.

'Not unless somebody chucks up on yer,' came the reply. She'd obviously graduated from the Liam Gallagher Charm School. An impossibly deep electronic laugh sent shivers up Lucy's spine. At sub-Paul Robeson levels, it even brought tears to Maxwell's eyes.

'Is it me?' he whispered in the sudden pitch darkness, 'or are we spiralling upwards?'

Weird howlings and rattlings of chains filled their ears now, and writhing things coiled from the shadows to leer at them, snarling and slavering like demon wolves. Lucy's eyes were wide in the dim, misty red light and Tiffany, for all her sang froid was leaning as close as she could to her uncle.

Something cold and clammy parted Maxwell's hair. By the screams, it was happening to other people too. At least, he could still feel his feet on a hard surface this time. Nothing to this one. A little sub-Exorcist head rotation, a few things going bump in the night. Piece, as Maxwell's 11C would have it, of piss.

It may have been Lucy who screamed first. It may have been Tiffany. Come to think of it, it was Maxwell. The car had stopped, dangling it seemed by the slenderest of spider threads over a yawning precipice. Far, far below, the flames of Hell crackled and roared and sharp-fanged monsters rose from the abyss, snapping at their heels, swinging now over the sheer drop.

'Oh my . . .' But Maxwell hadn't time to finish his sentence. His head tilted forward, his knees came up, his stomach had an out of body experience. The noise was deafening, the rush of terror in his ears as the car plunged vertically down into the hellfire. None of them would ever be the same again.

It didn't help that Maxwell could remember when this place was still the home of the Duke of Somebodyorother. It had a great house, now demolished and graceful follies where the said Duke played bezique with his friends and dallied with the maidservants. A boating lake was as racy as it got when Maxwell first moved to Leighford. But Leighford Hall was ruin and the then Duke had death duties and an expensive wife and sons at Harrow. So he'd thrown open his gates to the public and sold hot dogs and burgers and things on sticks. He'd had the Doctor Who exhibition with the BBC corridor faithfully reproduced in the Orangery, the sleek racing cars of yesteryear Brooklands on show in the Old Stables. At least then there'd been a semblance of Old World Charm.

Now it was Magicworld, a cacophony of piped music, shrieks and screams, the smells of the Subcontinent. Maxwell made for the only familiar sight in the whole boiling, a sow roasting on a spit, reminding him of Merrie England by way of Errol Flynn. Pig on the bone. Grand.

Tiff and Lucy of course had other ideas. Clutching their multi-coloured purses, they tottered on their fashionable heels to join the line for the doner kebab house. The grey glistening thing twirling under the striped awning had more to do, Maxwell thought, with the Donner party, but it wasn't his place to say so. He settled for an appalling coffee apparently made with meths and looked wistfully at the way out.

'Montezuma's Revenge, Uncle Maxie!' Lucy tugged at his sleeve, pointing with all the glee of a five-year-old to the huge, concrete gaping mouth of a particularly vengeful- looking Aztec.

'Been there,' Maxwell was drawing a metaphorical line in the sand, 'done that. Something restful now, I think. Something redolent of Cambridge summers and Grantchester and strawberries and cream. "Stands the church clock at ten to three?"'

Lucy was looking around. 'I can't see it, Uncle Maxie,' she said. 'I make it half past one.'

His look said it all. 'Wild Water,' he said. 'It may not exactly be punting, but it can't be as wild as all that.' He missed the knowing glance between his nieces, failed to catch their momentary smirks. All he saw was the black rubber ring of the car, like a large version of what old men with piles sit on. It had high plastic yellow sides to it to make the public think they were getting value for money. That solitary weasel-eyed man was ahead of them, getting into one all by himself. Lucy slid past the barrier.

No,' the man said, reaching out to stop her. 'Get the one behind, will you?'

Lucy frowned, surprised by the request. Tiffany was standing next to her now, both of them staring at him.

'What's the trouble?' Maxwell asked.

The weasel-eyed man was steadying himself against the jetty, clinging on to Lucy's arm for a moment, 'No trouble,' he said and pushed himself off the planking so that his car swept away on the eddying ripples, Number Four gleaming in silver on its sides.

He obviously wants to be alone,' Maxwell shrugged, his Greta Garbo utterly lost on the girls. Ah, the callowness of youth. Their bums hit the soft rubber seating simultaneously and the car swirled to the right, spinning away from the slippery planking in its carefully controlled current. They glided around, the craft sliding effortlessly past polystyrene rocks and mock cacti, chaparrals surprisingly high for Hampshire. In the crags concrete cougars crouched for attack, granite grizzlies growled. Maxwell leaned back, his arms spread over the cool black shoulders of the car. In the distance, screams told them that Montezuma's Revenge had claimed another set of victims, hanging upside down like pupae about to hatch. This was

more like it, Maxwell mused. Tranquillity, just him and the girls and
the coolness of the water.

He was just leaning forward to say something inconsequential
to Tiffany when the first buffet hit. He lurched across the car, missing the girl's lap by inches.

'I wouldn't move about, Uncle Maxie,' she suggested. 'It is
called Wild Water, you know.'

Maxwell knew. But he'd seen Deliverance, not once but several
times. If Jon Voight could do it, he could do it. Besides, his legs
were longer than Burt Reynolds's. And he still had his own hair.
The car spun in a sudden vortex, the rocks hurtling past in a blur
of grey. 'Jesus Christ!' Maxwell felt his face whipped by an instant
wind, the G force flattening his features as he did his best to grin
reassuringly at Lucy. She was laughing, throwing her head back as
the car bucked and jolted, sliding downstream now at an impossible
speed. Maxwell grabbed at the craft. There was nothing to grab.
Nothing to grip. He slid sideways, crushing Tiffany again and rolling backwards.

Everybody was screaming, laughing, trying to catch their breath,
trying to be nonchalant. Only Tiffany was staring ahead, watching
the car in front, the end of the ride. Maxwell's knuckles were white
again, rather like his face and his knees came up for the umpteenth
time as he tried to steady himself. Water was buffeting the car, soak-
ing him for the second time that day and no one was more delighted
than he was as the car slowed to a crawl.

There was pandemonium in front. Maxwell glanced backward
to the car behind, where a party of underprivileged schoolchildren
were still sliding and shrieking, making life unnecessarily hellish
for the poor bastard of a teacher who had given up his holiday, like
Maxwell, to do his duty. Faithful unto death.

'Uncle Max, what's happening?' Lucy asked.

'It's just the end of the ride, darling,' Maxwell told her, wondering at the naïveté of the question. But it wasn't. From nowhere,
under the shadow of the jetty, uniformed Magicworld staff were
scurrying backwards and forwards, ashen-faced. Maxwell saw one of

them turn away quickly and vomit over the side, her heaving shoulders held by the friend who steadied her.

They were converging on the car in front where the weasel-eyed man had been sitting. But the car seemed empty. Maxwell's craft hit it amidships and bounced away, sending an arm flailing over the side. Then the screaming started. First Tiffany, then Lucy, then several of the park staff.

'Get out,' a pale-faced boy in a company coat was jabbering to Maxwell. 'There's been an accident. We have to stop the ride. Get out. Please.'

Maxwell hauled his nieces upright and got them onto the water-splashed planking. It was cool here and dark after the May sunshine. He screened the girls from the car in front and the old Toyota advert filled his brain – 'the car in front is a coffin'. He half turned to see the weasel-eyed man slumped in the watery bottom of his craft, his mouth open, his eyes staring at the rubber seat, as though in disbelief.

'Shut it down,' he heard a voice hiss over a walkie-talkie. 'For fuck's sake. We've got a dead bloke down here.'

'Uncle Maxie . . .' Terror was etched on Lucy's face.

'Sshh,' he hushed her, encircling them both with his strong, safe arms. 'It's all right. Everything's all right.' And he led them away, glancing backwards over his shoulder. Staff were shepherding away the underprivileged children, away from the car. Away from the corpse. Dead man floating.

CHAPTER THREE

Credit cards. AA membership. A cheque book. A set of keys to the dark green Peugeot left in Car Zone C at the end of another day at Magicworld. The contents of a dead man's pockets. The contents of a dead man's life. DC Jacquie Carpenter catalogued them before popping them back into the polythene bag. Around her, the incident room was coming to life, officers carrying files, VDUs, rainforests of paper, display boards. In deference to the proprietors of Magicworld, Leighford CID had set up its Incident Room off site, in the community centre at West Meon. The Chief Constable himself had been contacted. No fuss, please. No bother. Magicworld was a family institution. Uniforms all over the place would do it no good at all. Besides, the owner of the park played golf with the Chief Constable.

The community centre had been the village school in the days when Thomas Lord, he of the cricket ground, had lived there. Jacquie had come in that morning under the lintel that still bore the carefully chiselled 'Boys' to remind the world of the days of Political Incorrectness and sexual segregation. Well, why not? Jacquie had the vote, for God's sake. She even smoked on and off, from time to time. And sure as Hell, she was doing a man's job.

She felt his eyes boring into her back; metaphorically, he was twanging her bra straps. She turned to face him. DS Frank Bartholomew, who thought he looked like Laurence Dallaglio, stood there, smirking.

'What've we got, then, Jacquie?' he sat on the chair across the desk from her, letting his eyes rove over the cleavage under the pale peach blouse. Jacquie Carpenter was probably twenty-eight. Her eyes were pale and grey and they sparkled as she spoke. Her chestnut hair was swept up on each side and there, Bartholomew pondered, was a mouth he'd like to get closer to.

'Larry Warner,' she told him, her eyes as cold as her voice. 'He was forty-eight. A chartered accountant. Lived in Portsmouth.'

'Well, I suppose somebody has to. Have we got an address?'

'Twenty-four Cadbury House. On the way out to Southsea.'

'Governor got somebody on that?'

'I don't know, Mr Bartholomew, as I've only just come on duty.'

'Frank.' He leaned towards her as though over a candlelit dinner for two. 'I've told you to call me Frank.'

She managed a smile that would freeze Hell over. 'I'd rather keep it professional, if you don't mind.'

'Suit yourself,' Bartholomew winked, leaning back in his chair. 'Where is the guv'nor?'

'Morgue.'

'What's this?' Bartholomew's roving eye had found the computer print-out on Jacquie's desk.

'It's a witness list,' she told him. 'Everybody on or near the ride at the time of Warner's death.'

He flicked down the dot matrix. 'Right, then. That's our morning mapped out. You ready?'

She nodded. When it came to working with Frank Bartholomew, short straws were the order of the day. And she always drew them.

Who's first, then?' he frowned at the list. 'Peter Maxwell, thirty eight, Columbine. Right.'

She paused by the coffee machine. 'I think we should start with the park staff,' she said. 'They're the ones in the know.'

Bartholomew gave her an odd look. 'I'm sure they are,' he said. 'But you see, Jacquie, this list is not as new to me as I made out. I had sight of it last night and I did a little cross checking. This Mr Maxwell is on file. At the station. Not form, exactly. But I found his name under 'P'. That stands for Pain in the Arse. I'll drive.'

Like West Meon village school, they'd built Leighford Mortuary in the nineteenth century too. It was dwarfed now by Leighford General, a monolith of concrete and steel built over the old cottage hospital. A grim place where old ladies lay on trolleys in the corridors waiting patiently for new hips, and regretting having voted for Frank Dobson at the last election.

Chief Inspector Henry Hall had never liked mortuaries. There was that indefinable smell, one that had never left him since DC, that antiseptic abattoir aroma that coated his nostrils and permeated the clothes. It was cold and metallic and sweet and sickly all at the same time. And there wasn't a chrysanthemum in sight. Henry Hall was a graduate, a fast-track promotion candidate who'd done only six months on the beat rather than the customary two years, plodding at the time-honoured two and a half miles an hour. That changeable May morning he was in his thirty-sixth year. He'd done well; collars and commendations to his credit. The Chief Constable liked him, even the Lord Lieutenant knew who he was – and after the fifty-odd years of alcohol abuse that man had suffered, that was quite an accolade. But Hall wasn't what you'd call a happy man. There were too many knives in his back, too many old timers on whom it grated to call him 'sir'. Then there was his family. A wife and three kids, when he'd last looked. The eldest would be starting at Leighford High in September. Where had the years gone?

At that moment, he was following the information given to him by Jim Astley, police surgeon, pathologist and professional bastard. Hall had been in this position before, his back to the morgue wall as the good doctor went about his business. Astley was, what, fifty-four, fifty-five, old enough, just, to be Hall's father. Except that Hall's father was a retired civil servant growing dahlias in the West Country. The doctor was dressed up all in green, ho, ho, bending over what used to be a person and occasionally he'd reach over to adjust his microphone or stretch to alleviate the constant pain in his back. In his weaker moments, when his wife had gone to bed with her Gordon's and a Catherine Cookson, he sprawled on the sofa alongside the red setter and knew he was too old for all this. A dead man was reflected in his glasses.

'A well nourished male,' he was saying, for the benefit of Hall, the court and criminal posterity. 'Caucasian, as we pathologists are obliged to say these days, mid-forties. Not overly endowed with hair.' His eyes ran the length of the body. 'Come to think of it, not overly endowed. Slight bruising to the arms, right and left. Forearms and upper. Large yellowing bruise on left shin. An old scar, probably a childhood injury, on the left side of the torso.' He fumbled with his tape. 'Nearly two centimetres long. In the thoracic region.' Hall stood upright, waiting for the rest, like that moment in the Chancellor s Budget speech when he stops burbling bollocks and gets on to the relevant bit about screwing Joe Public with road tax, petrol, alcohol and cigarettes. 'A large bullet exit wound, er . . . three centimetres left of the sternum mid-line, measuring two centimetres by . . . one and a half. Donald.'

His assistant reached over and the two of them rolled the corpse onto its side and then onto its front. 'Still showing signs of lividity,' Astley noted, slapping the dead man's buttocks with a fine disregard, 'which I would expect at this stage. No signs of bruising anywhere. A bullet entry wound to the left side of the midline by . . . four and a half centimetres, nine centimetres below the nape of the neck.'

Astley stood upright. 'Take him, Donald, would you?' He straightened, pinging off his rubber gloves and turning to Hall. 'How are we, Henry?'

'Marginally better than that poor sod.' Hall watched as the assistant rolled his man back and slid him onto the steel trolley ready for his drawer. He was appalled to note once again that they really did tie luggage tags around cadavers' big toes, like something in Jeffrey Dahmer's bargain basement.

'You've got a marksman on your hands.' Hall followed Astley into his office as the doctor busied himself hauling off lie. mask and cap and scrubbing down, instinctively using his elbows on the specially adapted taps. 'What's the score?'

'I've got a Press Conference later this morning. Chief Constable insisted on it. I don't remember a killing as public as this.'

'Who was he?'

'Larry Warner. A chartered accountant.'

'Ah, well, there you are.'

'Sorry?' Hall lowered himself into Astley's spare chair, leaning his head against the wall.

'Chartered accountants. Parasites, all of 'em. They're in the Bible, you know.'

'Are they?' It had been a long time since Henry Hall had dipped into the gospels. He was a different generation from Jim Astley. Hall had got comparative religions at O level, Islam and Buddhism, with a hint of Ba'hai. Astley was of the Old School and the New Testament; he could have retraced St Paul's missionary journeys in his sleep.

'"Tax gatherers and others",' Astley quoted smugly, wrenching paper towels from the dispenser.

'I thought that meant prostitutes,' Hall frowned.

'Oh ye of little faith,' Astley shook his head. 'Nothing wrong with a little healthy prostitution. Madame Sin of Golden Calf Road, Damascus. No, no, the unmentionable in society. The lot the Jews cleared out of the Temple. The profession – and I use the word guardedly – that dare not speak its name. You mark my words, Henry, for this one you'll have a list of suspects as long as your arm. It's the root of all evil, it makes the world go around. And I'd be prepared to bet it put a bullet through Mr Larry Warner, who probably had it coming.'

'What kind of bullet?' Hall wanted to know.

'Oh, now you're being picky!' Astley scolded. 'Robert Churchill's the gun expert I'm not. Still, you buy me a cup of coffee upstairs in what we still laughingly call a hospital and I'll give you the benefit of my years of speculatory wisdom.'

The rain set in mid-morning, sending those who thought spring had sprung scurrying for cover, forcing them to spend a few minutes extra in the Leighford Asda or, God forbid, the Leighford library.

Peter Maxwell was lolling back in his modeller's chair at the top of his town house, his gold-laced Crimean forage cap at a jaunty angle on his head, a paintbrush at a jaunty angle between his teeth. Before him on his desk, under the glare of the lamp, was scattered plastic arms and legs, 54 millimetres of careful reconstruction. Bored with watching the rain, the Master Modeller leaned forward again and took up the white head.

'What did you really look like, Albert Mitchell, Private, 13th Light Dragoons?' he asked it, focusing on the standard plastic features under the magnifying glass. 'Any ideas, Count?'

The menfolk at 38 Columbine had, it must be admitted, retreated upstairs to Maxwell's Inner Sanctum. The people he allowed this far into his private world were few indeed. And every one of them had gazed in awe at the plastic horses and their riders on the huge diorama under the skylight and the triangular roof. Three hundred and forty-eight Light Cavalrymen ready to ride into the Jaws of Death, the Mouth of Hell. Albert Mitchell would be the three hundred and forty-ninth.

'Count?' Maxwell repeated. 'Look at me when I'm talking to you.'

The cat called Metternich flicked an ear. It was the nearest in acknowledgement that Maxwell was likely to get. 'Ginger, you think? Well, it is possible, I suppose. Bit of a bugger, though, paint-mixing wise. But no, you're right. I've done too many with saddle-brown hair. It is a bit of a cop-out.'

Downstairs, Maxwell's nieces were working their way through his vast video collection. It was just as well for Will Smith that *Independence Day*'s president of the United States just happened to be an ex-USAAF pilot, or the world would already have come to an end. Maxwell had calmed them down after the bizarre events at Magic world, dried Lucy's tears, taken them all out for something repulsive at the local Thai restaurant. Escapism now. That was the order of the day. He'd do them some soup for lunch, then hit them with *Babe*. No nightmares there.

And in the meantime, there was a little male bonding and plastic bonding to do.

'Mitchell sailed for the Crimea on board the *Culloden*, Count.' Maxwell had ditched his paintbrush and was smearing the soldier's neck with glue. 'Had a horse killed in the Charge. Bay, do you think? OK. He reached sergeant eventually – Mitchell, that is, not the horse.'

Metternich ignored him. There was a time he used to listen to his master's interminable ramblings. But not now. Too much verbiage under the bridge. Too many thermometers up his bum.

'Ended up a copper of all things, Instructing Constable to the Kent Force. 1885, if my extraordinary, computer-like memory serves. Oh, bugger!'

The doorbell shattered the solitude of the late morning. Metternich raised an ear as if to accuse Maxwell. What haven't you paid now, *untermensch*? If he had his way, it wouldn't be just Maxwell's water he'd cut off. In his more wistful moments, the cat wondered whether Maxwell knew what it felt like to be a neutered tom, blank-firing.

It was Tiffany's voice at the bottom of the stairs, 'Uncle Max, it's the police.'

It was. A broad-shouldered, dark-haired attitude, who eyed Maxwell as if he were Dr Crippen, was standing in his living-room.

'Hello, Jacquie.' Maxwell ignored him and took the policewoman by the hand.

'Oh,' the attitude said. 'You two know each other.'

'Ah,' Maxwell smiled, 'a detective. Constable . . . er . . ?'

'Sergeant,' he corrected him, flicking out the warrant card. 'DS Frank Bartholomew. I clearly don't need to introduce DC Carpenter.'

'Clearly not,' Maxwell agreed. 'Jacquie, it's been a while.'

It had. They trod a line, did Jacquie and Maxwell, always fine, often a hair's breadth. It was a line each of them knew they couldn't cross, wouldn't cross. Could they? Would they?

'I'd offer you both a drink,' Maxwell said, 'but I fear you're on duty.'

'That's right,' Bartholomew said, finding a chair. That meant that Jacquie would have to take the settee, with its Maxwell-shaped space next to her. In the event, he stood with his back to the dead electric fire.

'You're . . . let's see . . . Head of Sixth Form at Leighford High School. Am I right?'

If Bartholomew had been blindfolded and on the music-hall stage in *The Thirty-Nine Steps*, Maxwell might have been more impressed.

'Indubitably.'

'And these kids . . .'

'These young ladies,' Maxwell corrected him, 'are my nieces, Tiffany and Lucy Clarke. They're staying with me for a few days.'

'That's weird,' Bartholomew commented.

Tiffany and Lucy looked at each other. Maxwell crossed to them, putting an arm around their shoulders. 'The Maxwells are a weird family,' he smiled. 'We make the Addamses look like the people next door.'

Bartholomew thought he heard Jacquie stifle a chuckle, but he couldn't be sure and swept on. 'You witnessed the shooting at Magicworld yesterday,' he said.

There was an involuntary gasp from Lucy and Maxwell turned her away. 'Jacquie, could you take the girls into the kitchen and do us all a coffee? You know where everything is, I think.'

For a moment, Jacquie hesitated, then she gathered the girls up and shepherded them away.

'I'd appreciate a little more of the softly softly,' Maxwell rounded on his man. 'Lucy's only thirteen.'

'A man is dead,' Bartholomew reminded him, like something out of Clichés R Us.

'Yes, and as far as Lucy's concerned, from a heart attack. She didn't see the blood, thank God, and I've kept her away from the TV news. Typical of Henry Hall to send a bull into a china shop.'

'Mr Maxwell.' Bartholomew's jaw was flexing. 'Regardless of your niece's sensibilities, I have a job to do. You claim you witnessed the death.'

'No, I don't,' Maxwell corrected him. 'I was in the car behind the dead man's. All I saw was his body slumped in the thing as our car reached the jetty. I told all this to a constable yesterday before we left the Park.'

'Uniform,' Bartholomew muttered. 'Might as well talk to that sofa. I shall need a written statement, Mr Maxwell. From you and your nieces.'

'Yes, of course,' Maxwell said. 'But I must be there when you question them. And I want them questioned by DC Carpenter.'

'Really? Is there anything else you'd like? Wall to wall carpets in the interview room? A few canapés with the Ferrero Rocher?'

'What I'd like,' Maxwell leaned over the man, 'is civility from a public servant who is an uninvited guest in my house.'

'One with a statutory right of entry,' Bartholomew reminded him, standing up.

There was a clearing of a throat behind them. 'Mr Maxwell,' Jacquie Carpenter stood at the kitchen door with steaming mugs in her hand. 'Do you take sugar?'

Neither girl had ever been in a police station before. Maxwell had, not once, but several times. But he'd forgotten the smell, the dust, the piles of paper and the cups of tea. He hadn't forgotten the bastard on the desk, though, a tall, silver-haired sergeant who was presumably supposed to be the acceptable face of modern policing. Repressing the urge to scream 'institutionalized racist' at him, Maxwell merely smiled as the man ushered the three of them into an interview room.

'Uncle Maxie,' it was a very small girl who put her hand around the lounge door later that night, 'Uncle Maxie . . .'

'What is it, sweetheart?' Maxwell put down his glass on the coffee table and cradled Lucy as she cuddled up beside him on the settee.

'It's that man,' she was whispering as though the furniture had ears. 'The man at Magicworld.'

'Yes, poppet.' Maxwell brushed her hair away from her fore-head. His own Jenny would be way past this age now, had she lived, had she not gone to that party, had the roads not been wet and that police car in such a hurry. Perhaps with babies of her own. He put his head down to hers and took in the scent of her hair. It took him back. Back to the days when he was a young Head of Department, naive, strong of heart and head, shortly before Queen Anne died, and his own baby lay curled in his arms.

'He was shot.'

'Lucy,' he took her gently by the shoulders and sat her upright, looking hard into the wide, grey eyes. 'Are you all right?'

She nodded. And sniffed. 'I'm all right,' she said. She looked smaller in her scruffy tartan pyjamas, her feet encased in lurid pink fluffy mules. Miss Sophistication was Little Miss Muffet by night, Bolshy Spice turned into Thumbelina by the lamp's glow.

'I'm sorry about the police station,' Maxwell said.

'That's all right,' she smiled and leaned back against the sofa 'She's nice, your Jacquie.'

'My Jacquie?' he raised an eyebrow.

Lucy looked at him, wiser than her years. 'Uncle Maxie, you fancy her, you know you do.'

'Do I?'

She suddenly reached across and grabbed his glass, sniffing the amber contents. 'Southern Comfort,' she said.

'From the banks of the good ol' Mississippi,' he clicked his tongue and winked at her. 'And before you ask, no, you can't have any.'

'I'm a Malibu girl,' she said, tossing her long hair and putting the glass down.

'I'll have to have a word with your mother about you.'

'I'm sure you will.' Lucy could be as arch as her uncle when she had a mind. She even raised the same eyebrow. 'You know she's having an affair, don't you?'

'What?' Both Maxwell's eyebrows were raised now.

'Just kidding.' It was her turn to wink at him. Then she was quiet for a while. 'Why didn't you ever get married, Uncle Maxie?'

Maxwell looked at her. Clearly the girl didn't know. Her mother could never have told her.

'I did,' he said.

'Oh,' Lucy scowled, 'Divorce. It's very common these days. Brenda Pargeter's parents are going through one at the moment. Brenda doesn't mind. Can't stand her mum, anyway. She drinks.'

'Brenda or her mum?' Maxwell thought he'd better ask.

'We are allowed to, you know,' Lucy tucked her feet under her bum in what was obviously a family tradition and started playing with a cushion. 'Legally, drink that is, at home, once we're twelve . . .'

'It wasn't divorce,' Maxwell found himself saying. 'It was an accident. My wife and daughter. They were killed in a car crash. A long, long time ago.'

Lucy sat upright, then she felt her lip go and she threw her arms around her Uncle Maxie, crying bitterly into his shoulder.

'Now, darling,' he patted her head, 'I'm sorry. There was no need to tell you about it. Not now, anyway. Not today. Look, come on,' he held her at arm's length, fishing in his pocket with the other hand to find a handkerchief. 'I'll never forget my girls,' he told her, 'but this week, well, I've got two more, even if they are just on hire. Now, blow into this. That's it. Give us your world famous Poo Lorn impression.'

Lucy trumpeted as ordered, although she'd never heard of Poo Lorn and sat there, looking red-eyed and rather sheepish.

'Who shot him, Uncle Maxie?' she asked.

'The man in the ride?' He shrugged. 'I don't know, darling. I'm sure the police will find out.'

'But all the way home in the taxi, Uncle Maxie, you were slagging them off.'

'Was I?'

'I think your exact words to Tiff were "incompetent bastards". Then you turned to me and said "excuse my French". But the French for bastard is *bâtard*, Uncle Maxie. Celestine McCracken told me and she should know. Her mother's French and she is one.'

'One what?'

'A bastard.'

'Oh. Well, it's all relative, niece of my dreams. It's true I don't have much faith in the boys in blue. But sometimes they're wonderful. And occasionally they solve crimes.'

Lucy was quiet again. 'Have you seen *Cape Fear*, Uncle Maxie?" she asked him.

'The Robert Mitchum or the Robert de Niro?'

'I didn't know there was a choice,' she said. 'The Robert de Niro.'

'I have,' he nodded, 'though I think I preferred the original.'

'It scared me.'

'I'm not surprised,' Maxwell nodded. 'Robert de Niro can be a pretty scary bloke. However,' he put on his teacher's voice, '*Cape Fear* has an eighteen certificate.' The eyebrow raised again, 'Something you watched while sipping Malibu?'

She giggled. It was good to hear. Then she was serious. 'But the thing that scared me, is that Robert de Niro is out there, isn't he?'

'Out there?' He remembered the song – wasn't Robert de Niro waiting, talking Italian? 'What do you mean?'

'Well, he's like . . . in the school, on the street, he's everywhere. He comes for the girl.'

Maxwell reached out and took her hand. 'It's only a story, sweetheart. A sort of grownups' Hansel and Gretel. He gets his in the end, doesn't he? Just like the witch with the gingerbread house?'

'Oh, I never believed that one.' She shook her head dismissively. 'Or perhaps Mummy wasn't very convincing. I always knew Hansel and Gretel would be okay. But . . . well, Cape Fear was so real.'

'It was well done,' Maxwell agreed.

'And Magicworld,' Lucy's voice was small again, like her in the shadows, 'That's real too, isn't it? Somebody killed that man, murdered him. And he's still out there.'

'Like the truth,' Maxwell murmured, looking the girl full in the face.

'Can you get him, Uncle Maxie?' Her voice was scarcely audible and her eyes were like saucers.

'Get him?' Maxwell repeated.

'Can you get Robert de Niro? Like Nick Nolte in the film, can you get him? Stop him?'

'Sweetheart,' he squeezed the girl's hands, 'he isn't after you, poppet. Or Tiff. Or me. What happened yesterday was awful, but it's nothing to do with us.'

'Isn't it, Uncle Maxie?' she asked him in a way that made the hairs on his neck prickle. 'Isn't it?'

CHAPTER FOUR

He didn't like leaving the girls. But at least they were in good hands. Sylvia Matthews's hands, strong and kind and there. You couldn't define Sylvia. She was ageless, like Shakespeare's Egyptian queen. Steady as a rock, comfy as a blanket – but Maxwell's metaphors (or was it similes?) always did have a habit of getting away from him. Sylvia had been the School Nurse at Leighford High longer than either of them could remember, long before, certainly, the paranoia of Ofsted and the banality of the National Curriculum. Long before any grey at all had begun to appear in Maxwell's thatch of hair.

Now Sylvia Matthews knew things. And she had secrets. Secrets she kept from the world; that Tanya Blinstock had had an abortion in Year 10; Adam Price's dad wore women's undies at the weekend; Sarah Quarrie still, at twelve and a half, wet the bed. But her biggest secret was that she loved Peter 'Mad Max' Maxwell. He didn't know it. Couldn't know it. Three quarters of the staff at Leighford High and perhaps half the kids had a pretty shrewd idea – that half of the kids that could walk and chew gum, that is. But Peter Maxwell? He was ignorance itself.

And in that ignorance, he'd rung Sylvia that Wednesday morning and explained the situation. A man was dead, in police parlance. The girls were fine . . . well, fine-ish. Tiff seemed okay, but Lucy? Maxwell was worried about Lucy. Sylvia had called for them at eleven, that time of day that Tiffany felt able to face the world for the first time, after the daily zit check was over, nose to mirror, locked in the bathroom. Maxwell could have reassured her that all was well. Sylvia Matthews, with all her many talents, was the zit nurse too. He watched them drive off into the gilded weather, to do something girly in Guildford.

Then, heigh-ho for the open road. White Surrey was never in mothballs, even in the worst of weathers and the old Raleigh warhorse, named for the charger of the last Plantaganet, chain oiled, rat-traps dangling, spokes spraying silver in the sun, had carried his master now for long, long years. Maxwell hadn't sat behind the wheel of a car since the accident – the day the music died. He just tucked his trousers into his socks, remembering the Granta days and off he pedalled, in and out of season. Just another facet of being Mad Max.

He knew of course where Jacquie lived. But he knew she had neighbours and didn't want to make life difficult for her. He parked White Surrey against the wall of the Greasy Chip cafe and went in, ordering a coffee and a Danish. The window seat was taken by two fat ladies, wedged into their chairs, but beyond their bobbing heads and through the nets of the window, he could see the Victorian gates of Leighford nick plainly enough.

He unfurled his Guardian and when the scalding coffee hit his lips, pretended that the tears in his eyes were the result of some particularly moving editorial. He was in serious danger of making a giant hole in his meagre teacher's salary when on the fourth cup, he saw her, stepping out from the front door. He abandoned his paper, the crumbs of his Danish (which could well have been Viking from the taste) and left the door clanging in his wake. The enormous women in the window stared after him and wondered aloud what his generation was coming to.

She saw him then, jacket tails flapping as he hared across the road. Mr Subtle. She was in the car, belt on, head down. She wanted to be clear of the station before he pounced. Clear of the eyes at the window, the knives in her back.

'Should you be doing this?' He had sensed her mood, swerved right behind the hedge and had leapt into the passenger seat as she idled at the lights.

'No.' She slammed the thing into gear and they screamed away.

'No, I mean giving lifts to strange old men.'

'I know what you mean.' She was staring straight ahead.

'We have to talk.' He was sitting at an angle, watching her eyes flaming, her lips tight.

'Yes, we fucking well do. Put your seat belt on.'

He did as he was told, like a kid in one of his own classes.

'You couldn't have just crashed into the nick and said "Hello, I've come to pick up Jacquie. Where is she? Having a shower? I'll just pop in and join her, shall I? For old times' sake."'

'I needed to see you,' he told her.

She spun the wheel over, hurtled down a side street and parked under a lime tree, switching off the engine and turning in face him. 'Why?' she asked.

He undid his seat belt, wanting to slow down the moment, kill the speed. 'My nieces witnessed a murder,' he said.

'I know, Max,' she nodded. 'I was there, remember? I spent nearly four hours with them yesterday. I can recite their statements in my sleep.'

'I didn't have a chance to talk to you,' he said, 'without them, without your Sergeant Bartholomew, without protocol.'

'Protocol?' she blurted. 'What sort of protocol was it when you told me to make some coffee at yours yesterday? What sort of message did that give to that bastard Bartholomew – who is no more "mine" by the way, than you are.'

'Ah.' Maxwell's relative silence said it all. The verbal swordsman reduced to quietude.

'Oh, Max, I'm sorry.' She was quieter, calmer, her anger controlled, her fire out. 'That was unkind. You know . . . you know how difficult my job is. You've been . . .'

'In the way?'

'No.' She was quick to correct him. 'No, not that. But they don't understand. About you and me . . .'

' I don't understand about you and me,' he confessed.

She bit her lip, fighting off the army of emotions inside her. She looked at him, this man old enough to be her father. She felt, as she always felt in Maxwell's company, her legs turning to water, her throat tightening and her heart crying out to him. But this was new. This was different. Maxwell had been involved before, nosing, asking questions, the Sherlock Holmes of Leighford. Now, it was personal. It was family. For the sake of the girls, he was scared. Not for himself. But for them.

'One question,' he told her. 'Just answer me that and I'll go away. For good.'

'For good?' she repeated mechanically as though someone had just read out her death sentence before the firing squad.

He nodded.

'What's the question?'

'Larry Warner, the dead man . . .'

'Yes?'

'Have you got a motive?'

She looked to her right, through the windscreen, to where an old couple were trudging home with their shopping bags. And to her left, through the back window where the street was empty and the trees heavy with their May blossom.

'He was a forensic auditor.'

'You what?' That was a new one on Maxwell.

'An accountant. A financial adviser's financial adviser. That's what we're working on at the moment.'

'Why . . . ?'

'You said one question, Max,' she reminded him.

He looked at her. And he sighed. 'You're right, Policewoman Carpenter.' He hadn't called her that in a long time, not since they'd first met and she was a little afraid of him and he'd kept her at arm's length. Then he was out of the car and gone, trotting off down the blossomed avenue, remembering where he'd left his bike. He didn't look back. And as the tears started, she was glad of that.

He sat in the lounge, head lolling on his own sofa, pondering that he must do something about that crack in his ceiling. He heard the rattle in the lock, the whistling gypsy that was his cleaning lady pattering about in his hall downstairs.

'It's only me,' he heard her growl in a passable Harry Enfield.

'Afternoon, Mrs B.,' he called back.

'Oh, bloody hell, don't I know it. Sorry, Mr Maxwell, I'd have been here sooner, but it's my Wilfred's piles. You know how he is. Where's them girls you've got staying with you?'

'Of course you would. Don't I just! Out for the day.' He well was used to Mrs B.'s barrage. She was the Mrs Mopp of Leighford High School, probably quite an attractive woman once, but the years of scraping chewing gum off the furniture had taken their toll. Heart of gold was Mrs B., straight out of ITMA. She probably 'did' for Tommy Handley in any number of ways.

'Ooh,' she appeared at the top of his stairs, unwrapping several layers of clothes, for all it was a sunlit Whitsun day. 'You don't wanna let 'em go out, ducks. How old did you say they was?'

'Tiffany's fifteen, going on forty. Lucy's thirteen. But don't worry, they're with Sylvia.'

'What, that Sylvia Matthews?' Mrs B. was digging around in her overall pocket for the first of her many ciggies of the day. 'Well, that's all right, then.' She looked slyly at her employer. 'Somebody oughta make a honest woman of her, you know.'

'They should, Mrs B.,' he agreed and missed completely the moment as her eyes rolled heavenwards. For a bloke with a Cambridge degree, Mr Maxwell was pretty bleeding thick, really.

''Ere, what about this bloke, then?' She threw a newspaper at him.

'What bloke?'

'This whatsisface . . . Larry Warner. It's in there.'

'Yes, shocking.' Maxwell didn't want to mix it with Mrs B. or he'd have been there, swapping non sequiturs all day. He was wrestling with what he knew already, trying to sift the situation for himself. Her input would only cloud the issue.

'I only ran into him the other day.' She pottered off into the kitchen. 'Mind if I have a cuppa first? Only my bleeding feet are something else.'

Maxwell was with her, leaning on the doorframe, frowning. 'You did? No, not at all. I'm sure they are.'

'Well, of course. Up at the school. It's not every day you know someone what's murdered, is it?'

'At Leighford High?' Maxwell checked.

'Yeah.' She filled the kettle with a vicious burst of tapwater. 'Buggered if I know what he does there, but you must have seen him. It's in the paper, look. Have a look. You'll know him as soon as you see his photo.'

Maxwell did. He ducked back to the settee, rustled his way through the Advertiser's letters about the proposed new marina and the Tottingleigh Whitsun Carnival and found the offending article. He scanned it quickly, hoping his lips weren't moving at the same time. There was the photograph. A slim, weasel-eyed man with a small moustache.

'Course,' Mrs B. was clattering with the mugs. 'You probably wouldn't know him. You've usually gone by the time he's around. He's always with that Mrs Lessing, the cow.'

'The cow' was a fairly mild epithet for Deirdre Lessing. And to be fair, it didn't really do her justice. Devil-bitch from Hell, the Morgana Le Fay of Leighford High, She Who Must Be Obeyed, Maxwell's Medusa – not even these handles, all of them Maxwell's, could come close. She was the Senior Mistress at Leighford High School, with a brief to comfort hysterical girls. So in what context did she know Larry Warner? Had he perhaps, in the words of the late Noel Coward, been her lunch?

'Got to go, Mrs B.' Maxwell was already hunting for his cycle clips, the full dress ones he only wore when he wanted to impress. 'Can you feed Metternich for me?'

Who to?' she muttered when he'd gone.

They'd built Leighford High in the 'sixties, when all was optimism and windy corridors and flat roofs that collected the rain and the seagull shit. Kidbrooke was a flagship school and the Labour party was telling Mr and Mrs Nonetoobright that of course their little

Duane could go to Oxford. To be fair, the views from the Year 12/13 Common Room were magnificent, out over sleepy Leighford town to one side, the sweep of The Shingle and Willow Bay to the other. Due south, across the grey and shifting sea was Abroad, the 'bloody place' that Maxwell warned his A-level historians about. Not that there was much risk of them ever setting foot on the soil of France. When they travelled, it was either to Lanzarote or Orlando. Did American culture have nothing to commend it but Walt Disney? When they left school, of course, assorted A levels under their belts, they did the pilgrimage to Ibiza, the Twentieth Century's Grand Tour, to pray at the shrine of St Gazza.

Deidre Lessing was ex-directory, like all hated teachers.

She hadn't been, in fact, until that glorious day, about which Maxwell still chuckled, when a reprobate in Year 10 had made an obscene phone call, having reversed the charges first. Maxwell pondered long and hard whether to give the kid a bollocking or a medal. He knew she lived somewhere off the park, in the more civilized area of Tottingleigh, out of brick-range of the unspeakable Barlichway Estate, but that wasn't narrowing it down enough.

So Leighford High it had to be. He guessed the place would be open and he wouldn't have to use the side-door key no one knew he had. Schools in the holidays quickly become building sites, work-men in overalls wandering about calling incomprehensibly to each other 'einer liner', to which the impenetrable answer always seems to be 'burr'. Only now they do it with mobile phones.

One of them grunted to Maxwell as he leaned White Surrey on Leighford's steps and bounded up them two at a time to the foyer. Exam timetables flapped in the afternoon breeze and a pile of unsorted mail lay on the Reception counter. You couldn't get the staff any more. Already, there was a phone ringing. Probably some parent begging the school to reopen early. The door to the inner office was open and Maxwell knew exactly where Thingy, the girl on the switchboard, kept the private addresses of staff.

'It's half term, Max,' a voice like cold steel hit him in the small of the back. 'You're not supposed to be here this week.'

He turned, smiling. She'd saved him a trip. 'You know how it is, Deirdre,' he said. 'Just couldn't keep away.' He looked at his bête noire, the perfect cross in fact between Bette Midler and Bette Davies. Except she had Hitler's eyes, blue and ice – although where she kept them, no one knew. 'Doing a bit of senior mistressing?'

She ignored him, sweeping past like a galleon in full sail. 'The Theatre Bid,' she said.

'I'm sorry?' Maxwell wasn't fluent in Sanskrit.

'Surely you know about the Theatre Bid?'

'Dame Judi may be a bit long in the tooth,' Maxwell conceded, 'but "bid" is a little demeaning, don't you think?'

'I sometimes wonder if you're a part of this school at all, Max.' She picked up a fat folder lying on the secretary's desk.

'My dear,' he beamed, 'I *am* Leighford High. Don't you know the hymn?' And here he broke into baritone song. '"Peter Maxwell is our corner stone; on him alone we build."'

'I think that would be blasphemy in an earlier age,' she said.

'"Blasphemy, blasphemy",' he parodied the late, great Kenneth Williams, '"they've all got it blasphemy".'

'Why is it,' she turned to face him, 'that I don't always know what you're talking about?'

He looked at her carefully, searching the face. 'Alzheimer's?' he suggested.

She whirled away. 'See you next Monday, Max.'

'Actually, Deirdre,' he was at her elbow, trotting with her down the darkened main corridor, 'it was you I came to see.'

She paused, an eyebrow raised. 'Why?' she felt bound to ask.

'Your ravishing beauty, your womanly body, the heaven- scent of your . . .'

'Animal!' she snarled and slammed into her office.

Morgana Le Fay ought to have lived in a cave with writhing snakes and sulphur smoke and dead men's eyes. Instead, there was a desk, a VDU, some spring flowers in a vase and a rather awful cuddly toy.

'But seriously, Max,' she stood waiting, deciding whether to offer him a seat or the door.

'But seriously, Deirdre,' he took the former, lounging so that his cycle clips dazzled in the sun, 'Larry Warner.'

'Dreadful,' she shuddered. 'Positively dreadful.'

'I was there.' Maxwell's Max Boyce impression was utterly lost on Deirdre.

'When he was killed? My God.' She had sat down now, beyond her desk so that a few feet of County Hall compressed cardboard stood between her and Maxwell.

'How well did you know him?'

'Well, we worked on the Theatre Bid together – that is, the technical side.'

'I'm sorry, Deirdre, you're going to have to explain all this, I'm afraid.'

'Oh, really.' The Senior Mistress tossed aside a Biro like the discarded husk of a man. 'It was announced in the Weekly Bulletin.'

'Never read it.' Maxwell was proud of the fact.

'Discussed at the Year Heads' Meeting.'

'Fast asleep.'

'Aired at the Staff Meeting.'

'Wasn't there,' he confessed. 'Pressure of work.'

'Max,' she sighed. 'You're impossible.'

'Ah, but you wouldn't have me any other way.'

She narrowed her eyes. 'Don't flatter yourself, Maxwell, I wouldn't have you at all.'

'Touché, Senior Mistress mine,' he bowed in his chair. 'Now, Larry Warner.'

She sighed again. 'In the beginning,' she began, 'there was LMS.'

'London, Midland and Scottish – a fine railway company,' he nodded sagely.

'Local Management of Schools. Really, Max, if you don't want to know . . .'

'Sorry, Deirdre.' He raised his hands in supplication. 'It's been one of those half terms one way and another. Sniper's bullets whizzing all around one.'

Deirdre was horrified. 'How can you be so flippant?' she shook her head.

Maxwell was about to tell her, but he needed to know what Deirdre knew and in his experience, she was the sort who would suddenly clam up or change the subject. 'LMS,' he repeated. 'Basically, we have to find our own cash.'

'Basically, yes. Or at least be responsible for it.'

'And the supply budget is currently half a grand in the red and it's only May.'

'How did you know that?' she bridled.

He tapped the side of his nose. 'I have friends in low places,' he told her, 'and a wine glass held against the First Deputy's wall works wonders.'

Deirdre Lessing never knew when to believe Mad Max. It was a trump card he played again and again. 'We have to watch the pennies in the way County Hall used to in the good old days.'

'Ah, but Deirdre,' he smiled at her, 'a slip of a thing like you can't possibly remember the good old days.'

'All right, then.' She was on form this afternoon. 'Something my mother told me about. Has it escaped your attention that we are trying to build a school theatre?'

'Harold Wiseman,' Maxwell clicked his fingers.

'Exactly. He talked to the staff in January and to the sixth form in March.'

'Bit of a pompous old fart, I thought.'

'Perhaps,' Deirdre pursed her lips, 'but he's a rich fart and owns a theatre.'

'The Wyndham in Bournemouth. Ellen Terry played there.'

'So have a good many other people. Harold is a big wheel in Charts.'

'He sings as well?' Maxwell was impressed. Universal men were rare these days. In fact he thought he was the last of the breed.

'Not *the* Charts,' Deirdre fumed. 'Charts. Charity Arts – it's the Arts Council without the paperwork. Oh, really, Max, are you a *total* philistine?'

Maxwell smiled. He knew that Deirdre's alma mater was Salford. 'Total,' he sighed. 'So, Wiseman is giving us his expertise?'

'He is,' Deirdre enthused, 'and it's *very* exciting. You'll need to talk to David Boston about the plans. We may even, eventually, perform in the Millennium Dome.'

Maxwell would rather not talk to David Boston. The new Head of Drama had not really impressed the old Head of Sixth Form. He was too stereotypical, too limp of wrist. Not for nothing had Maxwell christened him Camp David.

'The PTA are doing all they can – coffee mornings, car boots, the usual stuff, but really big money comes from bids. We could have tried the Lottery, Council for the Arts, the Prince's Trust even. In the end we went for Charts, especially since David knows Wiseman.'

'Would that be in the Biblical sense?' Maxwell wondered aloud; but sensing that had just sailed unerringly over the Senior Mistress's head, changed tack. 'And Larry Warner?'

'Larry is one of the accountants Charts uses locally. It's a huge operation, Max, monopoly money, really. He's also been the school auditor since '96, so it all ties in rather well. I really can't get over this. The poor man.'

'I don't suppose he felt much,' Maxwell reassured her.

'What I can't understand is – what was he doing in that park in the first place?'

'Ah yes,' mused Maxwell, 'the "solitary mister". That's the sixty-four thousand dollar question, Deirdre.'

'Oh no,' she arched her back and her left eyebrow simultaneously, 'the sixty-four thousand dollar question is – what were you doing there?'

He looked from side to side, checking that they were alone. 'The usual,' he leered, in a perfect Lewis Carroll, 'exposing myself – to danger.'

CHAPTER FIVE

'How were they today?' Maxwell looked at Sylvia Matthews through the amber distortion of his Southern Comfort. She always looked years younger in shirt and jeans, without the pale blue orthodoxy of her nurse's uniform, school matrons for the use of.

'Fine,' she told him. 'They're lovely girls, Max. How are you is more to the point?'

'Me?' He leaned back, stretching his toes out along the settee. 'Same as always, nursie. Suicidal.'

She looked at her watch. 'God, Max, it's nearly midnight.'

'Ah, yes,' Maxwell looked at her in the lamp's glow. '"The lights burn blue. Give me another horse, bind up my wounds. Have mercy, Jesu!"'

She shook her head, laughing. Mad as a March hare. 'How did *you* get on?'

'In the Inner Sanctum, you mean? The white man's grave laughingly known as Deirdre Lessing's office? The bourne from which etc, etc? Well, the late Larry Warner was helping her out with some fund raising.'

'Oh, yes, the Theatre Bid.'

He sat up. 'Am I the only one at Leighford High not to have heard of this?'

'If you listened a bit, Maxie,' she scolded gently, 'read the paperwork.'

'Paperwork, schmaperwork,' he muttered. 'There are only so many hours in the day, Nurse Matthews.'

'Lucy didn't mention it at all,' Sylvia told him, 'the murder, I mean. Tiffany . . . well, it's difficult, Max, I don't know them.'

'They seem to have taken a shine to you, though,' he said, offering her another glass. She held her hand over hers and shook her head.

'I've seen kids in shock before. I think Lucy's all right, but Tiffany . . . I'm not so sure . . . I noticed her looking around, watching everything. She didn't stray very far. Neither of them ate very much – but that's teenage girls for you.'

'Right,' he nodded. 'What is that stuff they have for breakfast? It looks like budgie seed and sawdust.'

'That's Muesli, Max, as you very well know. Did Deirdre shed any light?'

'On Warner? No, not really. Mind you, she's a suspicious old cat – nothing personal, Count.' He threw a glance at the dozing animal on the pouffé. Metternich was about to offer to fetch this intruder's coat. He'd always sensed a certain chemistry when Sylvia Matthews was around. And his powerful nostrils could pick up oestrogen at forty paces. 'Wouldn't give me the time of day without checking why I wanted to know first. He lived in Portsmouth, but she didn't know where precisely. Drove a Peugeot – odd for a woman to notice that.'

'Careful, Max,' she warned him. 'Teensy bit of male chauvinist piggery seeping in there.'

'You're right,' he confessed. 'I've got the tie, somewhere; founder member of the club an' all. No, Deirdre was as forthcoming as a clam. Mrs B. put me on to the Leighford connection. When I saw Warner at Magicworld, he didn't look familiar at all. Just struck me how odd it was that a single bloke would be there, in his three piece and all. Square peg in a round hole.'

'Max,' she looked oddly at him, 'you're thinking again.'

'Right again,' he laughed. 'I really must stop it or the Secretary of State for Education will be demanding my resignation. Of course, we historians are a bunch of crypto-lefties as it is, denying children their birthright, mustn't mention the war and so on. Of course we should be grateful for an extra two grand a year, etc, etc.'

'Stop changing the subject,' she was leaning forward now, cradling her glass in both hands. 'What do you mean "a square peg in a round hole"?'

'It's an old English saying, nursie. Bit like "a rolling stone butters no parsnips" or "many a muckle mak's a mickle" – although actually, that's Scottish.'

'Max!' she screamed at him.

'Damn good Marge Simpson there, Sylv,' he had to admit. 'Why, I asked myself, did Larry Warner go to Magicworld? If he was a family man, he'd have gone with the family; with just the kids, maybe, to give the missus a break. If he was a single man, going for the thrill of the rides – sad bastard – then wouldn't he have gone casual – shirt, jeans, blue suede shoes? If he was a pervert, wouldn't he have worn a mac? Oh,' he smacked his forehead, 'There I go again, being Politically Incorrect about perverts – stereotyping them.'

'So what's your conclusion?'

Maxwell leaned forward so that he echoed her posturally, their glasses almost touching in the lamplight. 'He went there in a suit, Sylv, dressed for work. He was meeting someone. A client, perhaps.'

'At Magicworld?'

'A client who didn't want to meet him at his office. Didn't want an accountant traipsing all over his flowerbeds. I don't know. Somewhere neutral? Some bland, public territory where there'd be no advantage, no quarter?'

'He sounds like an agent,' she said, 'in one of those sixties films where they swap spies over the border.'

He nodded. 'The chartered accountant who came in from the cold.'

'You're getting involved in this, aren't you, Max?' she asked him after a moment.

'Me?' He held his heart in mock astonishment.

'I know you too well, Peter Maxwell,' she said. 'We've been together now . . .' But she'd said too much and her voice trailed away.

He stood up sharply, putting his glass down on the coffee table and offering his arm. 'Come on, then, my dear old Dutch, I'll walk you to your car.'

'Why, Max?' she stood up with him. 'Why are you getting involved?'

He smiled slowly, his eyes flashing in the half light. 'Because it's there,' he said. 'And because a little girl asked me to.'

He led her to the door as Metternich rolled over and launched himself onto her recently vacated seat. His sighing purr was the feline equivalent of 'Thank Christ'.

'Bloody Hell,' Chris Logan was on his fourth cup of coffee that morning, staring out of the window where the rain drove hard against it. Below him, in the back car park of the *Leighford Advertiser*, a figure he knew was parking his bike. 'I thought he was dead.'

'Yehudi Menuhin?' His oppo Keith Kershaw didn't look up. 'Yeah, he is.'

'Mad Max.'

'You wanna lay off that crumbly white stuff, Christophe, me ol' mucker. It's giving you hallucinations now.'

'Christ, he's coming up here.'

He was. Peter Maxwell had given his girls strict instructions. They were to stay securely in Number 38 Columbine.

They were not to answer the door, the phone, any question Chris Tarrant might put to them and above all, if either of them touched his beloved Light Brigade in the attic, he'd hang them both out on his rotary washing line and bore them to death by reading them chunks of Professor Trevor-Roper. Now he was standing at the *Advertiser's* front desk, steaming in the warm rain of the morning, water seeping into his socks.

The dim-looking woman opposite picked up the intercom aid it buzzed upstairs. 'Chris, there's a Mr Maxwell to see you. He says it's urgent.'

There was a muffled response in the dim-looking woman's ear.

'What's it about?' she asked.

'It's about an essay he owes me on Hitler's Polish policy,' Maxwell told her, straight faced.

'Foreign affairs,' the woman said into the intercom. 'We don't cover any of that, do we?'

There was another buzz in her ear, the only buzz, Maxwell guessed, she was ever likely to get.

'He's on his way down,' she told him. 'Won't you take a seat?'

Maxwell raised his dripping hat and paddled off to a corner where a retired colonel was scanning the microfiche to find something to complain about and a travelling couple were combing the small ads.

'Mr Maxwell,' the Head of Sixth Form didn't have to look up to recognize the nasal whine. True, it was over-larded with Fleet Street Speak and the outstretched hand spoke volumes for the Confidence Building For Young Journalists Course, but it was still, in essence Christopher Bites-Yer-Bum Logan, sub-editor of the school magazine, in the days when Leighford High still had a school magazine. He came down the spiral staircase like a ginger Gloria Swanson, if that wasn't too much of a contradiction in terms.

'Chris,' Maxwell stood up and shook his hand. 'It's been.'

'Must be ten years.' The hand-wringing ritual was exhausting, designed to assure his old teacher by his grip that Chris Logan had grown up in that time, was shaving now and quite possibly had had carnal knowledge of a live woman. He'd also thickened around the girth and wore contact lenses to replace the geek glasses that were once his trademark. His gingerness seemed to have diminished not one jot.

'Still hacking, I see,' Maxwell beamed.

'Oh, yes,' Logan nodded. 'Come back for a bit of a break actually. You know, after the hurly-burly of the *Sun*.'

'Quite,' Maxwell nodded, frowning, sharing for a fleeting moment what must have been the endless agony of the Murdoch years.

'What can I do for you? Looking up old pupils?'

'Shame on you,' Maxwell slapped the younger man's arm. 'That's illegal, you know.'

'Oh yes, ha, ha.' The braying laugh and delayed humour were still the same, despite a 2.2 in Media Studies from Salford and the years at the computer interface.

'No, it's about Larry Warner.'

'Ah,' Logan's grin had already frozen. 'Mavis?'

The dim-looking woman glanced up from her phone. 'Any chance of two coffees, in here?' he pointed to a dingy office.

'I've got the leader of the council on two,' she cupped her hand over the receiver.

'Well, that's one more vote than he'll get next time round,' Maxwell quipped.

'Hah, oh quite,' Logan grinned. 'Tell him I'm out to lunch, Mavis.'

Maxwell was quite prepared to believe that.

'Have a seat, Mr Maxwell.'

'Max'll do,' the Great Man said, removing past copies of the Advertiser and arranging his coat over a computer terminal.

'Max,' Logan sat opposite him. 'It seems strange after all these years. I remember when you ran the school magazine.'

'Oh no,' Maxwell corrected him. 'You were the driving force there, Chris. *Logan's Run* I used to call it, remember?'

'Oh yes.' Logan hadn't understood the comment then and he didn't understand it now. 'Now then, Larry Warner.'

'Right.' Maxwell got down to business. 'You covered the story.'

'That's right. It was my first murder for the *Advertiser*.' He leaned forward, sotto voce, 'Not exactly the cutting edge here, Max,' he confessed. 'I've actually been brought in as a sort of galvanizer . . .'

'Really?' Maxwell leaned back, impressed.

'Kick a bit of arse, you know.'

'Long overdue.'

'Well, it's all new marinas and chrysanthemum shows. Odd bit of lavatory cowboying is as risqué as it gets. Larry Warner was a godsend, really. I got in fast and networked it. The editor was well chuffed, I can tell you.'

'I'm sure he was. So what else can you tell me?'

Logan blinked. 'What can *I* tell *you?*' He launched into a very bad Nazi 'Ve vill ask ze qvestions'. And he brayed like a donkey.

'Absolutely.' Maxwell chuckled for old time's sake. After all, it was he who had told Logan what a Nazi was. 'But I have a special interest in the case.'

'Why?'

'Tut,' Maxwell scolded. 'There you go again!'

'Ha,' Logan giggled. 'Sorry, Max, occupational hazard, I suppose.'

'I was there.'

'What? When it happened? Excellent.' Logan reached for his notepad.

'Uh-huh,' Maxwell shook his head. 'No exclusives just yet. I wasn't alone.'

'Oh,' Logan's eyes widened. 'Anything Mrs Maxwell should know about?' He couldn't for the life of him remember whether there was a Mrs Maxwell or not.

'Nothing like that,' Maxwell said. 'I had my nieces with me. I don't want them involved any more.'

'Ah, Mavis.' The dim-looking woman popped her head around the door and brought in a tray with polystyrene cups and a single plastic spoon.

'You're spoiling me,' Maxwell beamed.

'Thank you, Mavis. Can you get the Warner file, please?'

'Well, it's nearly my lunch break,' Mavis whinged.

'It won't take you a minute, Mavis,' Logan insisted and she trudged off, wondering if she couldn't take the matter to the NUJ.

'I happened to be the first journalist on the scene. Oh fuck, that's hot.' Logan felt a rush to his head, not just with the pain of the coffee on his lips, but that he'd sworn in front of his old teacher. Funny how the old things still mattered.

'Who did you talk to, in the police, I mean?'

'DCI Hall. It's his case, apparently.'

'Ah.'

'Do you know him?'

'We've crossed truncheons before,' Maxwell nodded. 'It's always been . . . a pleasure.'

'He wasn't giving much away.'

'No, that's our Henry's way,' Maxwell commented.

'I'm following up on Warner this afternoon, funnily enough.'

'Really?'

'I've got an address in Portsmouth.'

'Really? Mind if I tag along?'

'Er . . . well, Mr Maxwell . . . um . . . Max, that's a little awkward.'

'Nonsense!' Maxwell scolded, drinking his coffee without a qualm. 'I know Portsmouth like the back of my hand. I'll be your navigator, shall I? I say, Chris, could I use your phone?'

It had been bad enough in the sunshine, but now, as the rain drove hard on their capes and flat caps, a struggling line of policemen were combing the rocky outcrops on the banks of the Wild Water. They'd been quite a tourist attraction in their own right for the past two days and the waiting crowds had queued for hours longer than usual to ride the spray, telling themselves that the car they sat in was *the* car, awash with a dead man's blood.

''Ere, our Trace,' an Essex girl shrieked over the roaring surge, 'This scratch 'ere – I'm sure it's a bullet mark.'

'Nah.' Her Trace was not impressed. 'That'll be where his head exploded. Like that melon in that old film – what was it, *Day of the Jekyll.*'

The rain, it was true, had driven the punters away. That and the fact that this was Thursday. Half term was drawing inexorably to a close and parental holidays were over. For the kids, it was back to the Playstations and the Gameboys, copping a crafty feel in the grounds of the old Fort and a spot of shop-lifting in the precinct.

DS Bartholomew turned his collar up again and looked at DC Carpenter. 'Shit a brick,' he muttered. 'Flaming June tomorrow. And here we are playing needles and haystacks. We'll never find the bloody thing.'

'Doc Astley's pretty sure it went right through him, no damage to bone at all, just punctured the lung and the heart. It should be in good nick.'

'A magic bullet in Magicworld,' Bartholomew was stamping his feet. 'Great.' From nowhere a raw wind was whipping up the eddying water, sending spray high into the air to mingle with the slanted rain that drove like stair rods against his anorak hood. Jacquie looked pinched and tired, trying to work out the trajectory, the angle of death. She'd ridden a car yesterday, shortly after she'd pulled herself together after that stupid business with Maxwell. She'd ridden it alone, as Larry Warner had on the Day in Question, sliding from side to side on the sloping black seat, rolling as the water buffeted and barged, snarling and growling underneath her. As the polystyrene rocks and tall spurges reeled in her vision, she tried to judge it, where the marksman had to be sitting to get a clear shot. Where he'd miss the car in front, where the Gordon family screamed, and the car behind, where Maxwell was brazening it out with his nieces. He must have been sitting, surely, or lying down, perhaps. A standing man was too visible. Someone would have seen.

'There's one thing.' Bartholomew must have been reading her mind. 'Whoever he was, he was one fuck of a good shot.'

Jacquie nodded. The killer's target was moving away from him, spinning round and round as well as bobbing up and down. This was no ordinary rifle club hit, with ear muffs and goggles and a ten foot stationary target. This was something special. And all they needed now, she scanned the sodden line of searching policemen again, was the tell-tale bullet.

The sun had come out again by the time Chris Logan's Rover purred along the Hard. To his left, Maxwell saw the tall spars of the *Warrior*, the gilded ironclad riding the sluggish swell in Portsmouth Harbour.

'State of the art in its day,' he told Logan. 'Thirty-six guns, its deck one hundred feet longer than any other ship afloat.'

'Superb.' Logan thought he'd better agree; he remembered Maxwell's obsessions. Seemed to remember he was more of a land-lubber though. Cavalry, wasn't it? Horses?

'Stop here,' the Great Man commanded. Traffic up his arse and hemming him in on all sides, it was a difficult manoeuvre for Logan to carry out. Not that such niceties ever bothered Maxwell. With all the instincts of a cyclist, he did what the hell he liked on roads. As other motorists gave Logan their views on his hasty U-turn, his old Head of Sixth Form leapt out.

'But this isn't Queen's Crescent,' Logan called after him.

'Right again, Horace Greely,' Maxwell winked, 'but they do a really mean chip at the bus station cafe. Join me?'

'Housekeeper?' Maxwell repeated, his hat still raised above his tangle of barbed wire hair.

'Yes,' the woman in front of him was the antithesis of Mrs B., manicured and hennaed to within an inch of her life, a positive lariat of pearls around her chelonian neck. 'And you are?'

'Relatively astonished,' Maxwell confessed.

'We didn't all die out with Victoria, you know,' she said. 'Mr Warner was a very busy man and had no interest in the basics. Thursdays and Sundays are my days off. I don't believe Mr Warner ate on those days.'

'I hadn't seen Cousin Larry for years,' Maxwell ruminated. 'Oh, forgive me, I'm Peter Warner. This is my son, Chris.'

A swift hack to the ankles reminded the newspaperman to close his mouth.

'When is the funeral exactly?' Maxwell asked.

'Look, you'd better come in. We can't discuss such things on the doorstep. I'm Juliette Pilgrim, by the way.'

'Charmed,' Maxwell all but kissed the woman's hand as she took them through the vestibule. Clearly, Larry Warner had done all right for himself. The address in Queen's Crescent was a large late Edwardian building with a tendency towards deco. The furnishings were tasteful, Heals at the very least.

'Do I gather you and Mr Warner were not close?' Mrs Pilgrim was making life easy for the Great Impersonator.

'Ooh, it really must be . . . what, must be twenty years since I saw him. You only met him once, I think, Chris.'

'Er . . . yes . . . er . . . Dad. I don't really remember all that clearly.'

'No, you wouldn't,' Maxwell beamed.

She showed the pair into an airy, high-ceilinged lounge with a vast bay window overlooking the street.

'And the funeral, Mrs Pilgrim?'

'Oh, we don't know.' She invited them to sit. 'The police won't release his body just yet. It's quite, quite awful.'

'It is,' Maxwell nodded. 'The police have been here, I suppose?'

'Oh, yes,' she told him. 'Whatever else they found, it wasn't a speck of dust, I assure you.'

'I'm sure not,' Maxwell nodded sagely. 'Er . . . whatever else did they find?'

She looked from one to the other, an intelligent woman with clear, grey eyes. 'May I be frank?' she asked.

You can be anybody you like, dear, Maxwell thought, as long as you give us some answers. 'Of course.'

'You knew your cousin was homosexual?'

'Well, I . . . let's just say, he was always into auntie's dressing-up box in a big way.'

'I won't beat about the bush, Mr Warner, I was not overfond of your cousin. Call me old-fashioned if you like, but a string of male callers . . . well, it wasn't healthy. I'm just a snob, I suppose, but it was the modern equivalent of Oscar Wilde's telegraph boys. Students from the local tech doing something called NVQ – I don't suppose it's even legal.'

'It shouldn't be,' Maxwell nodded grimly.

'The police took away a quantity of clothing, his computer and several disks, I believe you call them.'

'On the Net, was he?' Logan asked.

'If you mean, young man, that he surfed in search of electronic sex, I don't really know. I was his housekeeper with the flat above. I was not his mistress.'

'Quite,' Maxwell cleared his throat at the very thought of it.

'Was there any one young man?' he asked, 'Someone special who was here perhaps more than any other?'

'That's what the police asked,' Mrs Pilgrim said. 'You aren't a policeman, are you?'

'Good Lord, no,' Maxwell chuckled. 'I've got a degree. No, I'm a teacher.'

'I knew it!' She clapped her hands. 'My late husband was a teacher, Mr Warner, of geography.'

'Fascinating subject,' Maxwell lied. 'Er . . . the young man?'

'Well, there was one, funnily enough. Michael Somebodyorother. Mr Warner called him Micky. He made my skin crawl, I'm afraid.'

'Not your type?' Logan asked. Clearly, several years at the Interface had failed to hone his subtlety skills.

'And what do you do, Mr Warner?' she narrowed her eyes at him.

'Oh, I'm a rep . . .' He caught Maxwell's eyes burning into his soul, 'Repair man. DIY. That sort of thing, you know.'

'Charming,' she smiled politely.

'This Micky goes to the local tech?' Maxwell checked.

'I believe so.'

'Do you remember when you saw him last?'

'I don't snoop, Mr Warner,' she bridled, 'but I believe it was nearly a week ago – Friday.'

'He arrived at what time?'

'Afternoon, I think. Mr Warner had just arrived home himself. I didn't see the boy leave. Mr Warner, these questions . . .'

'I know, I know,' Maxwell sighed, holding up his hands in supplication, 'I just can't understand why someone should want to kill him.'

'Oh, I can,' Mrs Pilgrim stood up. 'Anyone with habits like his. He was a predatory homosexual, Mr Warner. People like him make enemies.' She suddenly shuddered. 'He brought the whole building into disrepute. Queen's Crescent, indeed. People have been very unkind.'

'You, however, have not been, Mrs Pilgrim. On the contrary, you have been kindness itself.' He shook her cold, limp hand. 'We'll see ourselves out. And at the funeral in the fullness of time, I have no doubt.'

She watched them go and they clambered into Logan's car parked in the street. As she did so, she picked up Warner's phone. 'Hello, is that Leighford CID? Yes. Yes. Sergeant Bartholomew please. I'll hold.'

In the car, Logan let his shoulders sag. 'For fuck's sake, Mr Maxwell . . . er . . . Max. I wish you'd told me you were going to do that.'

'Do what?' Maxwell was all innocence, strapping on his seat belt.

'Claim bloody kin.'

'Go with the flow, Chris, my boy. Learn a bit of sleuthing from the Master.'

'But we didn't have to do that. I've got my NUJ card.'

'Yes, and she'd have told us precisely nothing. As it is, we know that the late Mr Warner was not as other chartered accountants and that he probably surfed the net for porn and his boyfriend was a local lad called Micky. I think that's a pretty good haul for ten minutes work.'

'What now then?'

'Portsmouth Technical College, Christine. I'll dream up some ploy or other as we go.'

'Yes, Sergeant Bartholomew.' Mrs Pilgrim had her man on the other end of the line. 'Greying hair, silly shapeless hat, green coat. Said he was Mr Warner's cousin, which is a lie. Mr Warner has no family since his mother died. And that he was a teacher, which is possible – he had a rather 'Leftie' persona, I thought. Quite nice looking though. Early fifties, I'd guess. The fellow with him, posing as his son, had rather carrotty hair and freckles. He'd be late twenties, claimed to be a repair man which is nonsense. How do I know? His hands. Never knocked a nail in in his life. They've just left, the younger of them driving a dark blue Rover, registration number K173 HMN. Well, you did say if anyone called to see Mr Warner . . . or for any other reason, I was to ring you. Oh, yes, I've just remembered. A silly thing, I know. The older man's trousers, they were screwed up at the bottom, as though he'd got them wet and usually wore cycle clips or tucked them into his socks.' Mrs Pilgrim laughed brittly. 'I'm flattered, of course, Sergeant,' she said, 'but I think in all honesty I'm a little old for a job on the Force.'

CHAPTER SIX

What was it about Technical Colleges? They were like larvae longing for the day they'd grow into the butterflies that were Universities. Paint was peeling everywhere, black scuff marks etched the floors. There was an air of decay and a smell of squandered finances. Scraps of paper pinned by one corner only, because of cuts, gave a whole moving horde of Liam Gallagher wannabes the information that lectures were on hand that day for Hewing of Coal (Mr Bennet L23 10.00 a.m.) and Drawing of Water (Mr Webb L4A Mezzanine 11.30 a.m.). Everywhere else seemed to be Leisure and Tourism and Health Care. But then, Maxwell knew the hard way that life for everybody under twenty-two was one long round of leisure and tourism. And as for health, well, nobody cared anyway.

'Yes, please, your NVQ lists for the current term.'

The girl on the reception desk looked a little confused. 'Where did you say you were from?'

'The DES,' Maxwell lied. 'Just a routine enquiry.'

'Right,' she flicked buttons on her keyboard and her VDU screen performed a series of Bill Gates miracles. 'You'd want hard copy, I s'pose.'

'The harder the better,' Maxwell growled, winking at her.

'I've got one somewhere,' she assured him. 'Only, it's nearly going home time and it'll take a while to print one out. P'raps our Mrs Winters has got one.'

'Your Mrs Winters?'

'Our Personnel and Student Liaison Officer.'

'No, no,' Maxwell fussed. 'I wouldn't dream of bothering her – as you say, at going home time. Haven't you got one in a cupboard somewhere?'

'Well . . . oh, hang on.' She disappeared into an inner office while Maxwell looked suitably from the Ministry and Logan was shitting himself. Chris Logan was not really an investigative journalist; he hadn't the fire for it, nor the brass neck. Subterfuge left him worried and jumpy.

'Here you go,' the girl was back in a rustle of her tight leather skirt.

'Excellent,' Maxwell slid the folder under his arm.

'Can you just sign here . . . Mr . . . er . . . ?'

'Woodhead,' Maxwell beamed as he flourished with his Biro. 'Chris Woodhead. Thank you, my dear, you've been most helpful.'

The Black Horse had taken a direct hit the night the Luftwaffe came calling. The snug had ended up in the cellar along with a lot of beer, some sawdust and enough broken glass to patch up the Crystal Palace had it still been standing. It had been the end of civilization for some people.

Thatcher's children haunted it now, frittering away their student loans on nasty lager from Belgium. Maxwell and Logan had fought their way through the milling bodies to the far side of the circular bar which announced to a grateful generation that Murphy's was permanently reduced. A bank of amusement machines winked and nudged each other in neon flashes in the corner, the one-armed banditti of yesteryear gone electronic. What they laughingly call Live Music was taking a merciful break in the recess where the payload of the Junkers 88 had once landed. And an ageing rocker was giving his picking hand a break by sliding it around the breasts of a girl half his age. Everywhere was leads and mikes, but not the Mike that Maxwell was hunting. He was sitting, or so the pair hoped, facing the door, like Wild Bill Hickok on one of his more sensible nights.

Maxwell pulled a chair up and sat facing the lad. He was . . . what, nineteen, twenty perhaps, with hard, almost Nureyev features, high cheekbones and chiselled nostrils. Only his appalling woolly cap marked him out as a child of the 'nineties. That and the attitude.

'Who the fuck are you?' he asked.

Logan still stood dithering at Maxwell's elbow.

'Press,' Maxwell said. 'Well, he is.'

Logan thought he'd better join the conversation, so he took a spare chair from the corner and flashed his NUJ card.

'What d'ya want?'

'A story,' Maxwell said. 'That's if your name is Michael Lloyd.'

The lad looked at his mates, one on each side, like Horatius at the bridge. 'It might be,' he said.

'Great,' Maxwell beamed. 'That's just earned you a drink. Chris, what's the man having?'

'A whale of a time,' Logan grunted, seeing the lit-up grins on the lads' faces.

'Fair enough,' said Lloyd. 'Three Stellas – pints.'

'Is there any other measurement?' Maxwell smiled and thrust a tenner into Logan's hand. 'I might run to another if the answer to my next question's right.'

'Oh yeah,' Lloyd leaned back. 'And what's that?'

'How well did you know Larry Warner?'

'Who?'

Now, Peter Maxwell had been around. He knew kids like the back of his blackboard, when they lied and when they told the truth. He watched the eyes first, that's where the smart ones let themselves down. It was only slight, just a flicker really, but it gave the game away every time. It was one of Maxwell's favourite films – *My Friend Flicker*. The not so smart ones mottled crimson from the neck or licked their lips or said 'No', in that belligerent nasal way that teenagers have. Micky Lloyd was a smart one. The eyes had it.

'Chris,' Maxwell caught Logan's arm as he was making for the bar. 'Got your mobile?'

'Sure,' Logan reached into his jacket pocket.

'DCI Hall, Leighford nick. I think we've got our man.'

'Now, just a fucking minute . . .' Lloyd's eyes were blazing. 'What the fuck is this?'

'This,' Maxwell leaned forward over the hubbub, 'is a cosy little chat about your career as a male prostitute.'

Pins don't usually drop in Portsmouth pubs, but one did at Micky Lloyd's table that night. Lloyd's defences dropped, his eyes flickered left and right.

'Do you want me to take him outside, Mick?' one of his mates asked.

'No, no, it's all right.' Lloyd was focused on Maxwell now.

'No, you know,' the mate insisted. 'Out the back, y'know. Kneecaps.'

'No, I don't, Kevin,' Lloyd bellowed.

'Well . . .' Kevin was a little crestfallen.

'Look, you and Gringe piss off now, yeah? I'll see you around, mate.'

'Yeah, right.' Kevin and Gringe scraped their chairs and loitered before retreating to the door, eyeing Maxwell as they went. 'See you then, mate.'

'Whatever,' Lloyd leaned forward, suddenly becoming confidential. 'Look, who are you, really?'

'Really?' Maxwell leaned back and let the philosopher in him take over. 'Who are any of us really? I'm here to talk about you.'

'Why?'

'Because Larry Warner is dead and you might know something about that.'

'Oh, no, mate,' Lloyd said, 'you're not pinning any of that crap on me. No way.'

'Have the police talked to you yet?'

'No,' Lloyd frowned, sitting bolt upright, 'so how did you get onto me?'

'Don't worry your fluffy little head about that,' Maxwell waved a sheaf of paper under the boy's nose. 'College lists. You're the seventh Michael we've seen tonight. And the only one who's lied about knowing Larry Warner.'

'What makes you think I lied?' Lloyd was on the defensive now, ready to brazen it out.

'Years of experience,' Maxwell sighed. 'Ah, can you manage all three yourself?' Logan had returned with a tray of lagers.

Lloyd folded his arms. 'What if I don't want to drink with you?'

Maxwell dipped his lip into the froth. 'What if you killed Larry Warner?'

'What?' Lloyd felt his pulse racing. Logan saw the boy's eyes widen. 'Why should I do that?'

'Well, let's see.' Maxwell clasped his hands over his pint and rested his chin on them. 'There are a number of possibilities. He hadn't paid you for your last session. You were tired of that kind of life and wanted to go straight, so to speak. He was making unnatural demands – well, even more unnatural, I mean

'Leave it out,' Lloyd roared, 'he was my fucking meal ticket, wasn't he?'

'Ah,' Maxwell nodded, 'student loans don't go far, do they?'

'Fucking right they don't.'

'So why did you do it?' Logan asked.

'I didn't fucking do it! Look, look,' Lloyd tried to marshal his thoughts, rallying his fingers to help him disentangle the chaos of his brain. 'They said on the telly that he'd been shot, right. And the *Echo* said it was a high-powered rifle.'

'Oh, the *Echo*!' Logan scoffed. 'Well, it must be right, then.'

'Now where am I going to get a shooter, eh? Get real.'

'Got any form, Micky?' Maxwell asked.

'You what?'

'Are you known to the police? I mean, if my colleague and I turned you upside down and shook out your pockets, would we find any incriminating substances? Is there a file on you in Pompey Vice?'

'Fuck off,' Lloyd snarled.

'Well,' said Maxwell, 'it's only a matter of time. We found you. So will they. Especially when my friend Mr Logan here telephones his editor.'

'All right, all right,' Lloyd folded like a pack of cards. 'What is it you want?'

'Let's start with a little thing called the truth, shall we?' Maxwell asked, 'and see where that takes us.'

The truth took Maxwell to a sad man who habitually wandered the parks. He was an easy mark for Micky Lloyd, always on the hustle and not particularly fussy how he made his money. They'd met one sunny Sunday in February, in the public toilets under the giant shadow of Portchester castle. A quick bit of business in one of the cubicles and then it was a nice Peugeot ride to a snobby building along Queen's Crescent. Some frosty old cow of a housekeeper had looked down her nose at Lloyd, but there was nothing she could do. The boy ate well there, drank, watched videos, mostly imported Dutch stuff and went off to college with a wad of cash in his jeans. He was happy, the old poof was happy. What could be wrong with any of that?

'But he wasn't the only one,' Maxwell was thinking out loud as Chris Logan dropped him outside 38 Columbine at the witching hour.

'What?'

'Micky Lloyd. Not the only toy boy of the late Mr Warner.'

'It's the gun thing,' Logan was tapping his steering wheel, frowning at the empty street ahead.

'I know,' Maxwell sighed. 'Disgruntled AC/DC – or just plain DC – boys might go for a punter with a knife or a hammer or their boots. But a high-powered rifle . . . Was the *Echo* right, by the way?'

'Ha, ha,' Logan laughed. 'There's an unwritten law in the news-paper game, Max – never admit the other guy's right. I didn't get that from the police press conference the other day. They must have inside info.'

'Who would that be from? Hall? Bartholomew?'

Logan shook his head. 'I doubt it,' he said. 'Don't you know anybody on the force? Somebody we can trust?'

'No,' Maxwell shook his head, a vision of a girl scowling at him, tears welling in her quiet, grey eyes. 'No. Nobody. Anyway,' he turned to Logan, 'What's this "we", white man?'

The newspaperman laughed. 'Max, I must admit – old teacher and all – when I took you along this afternoon, I was a bit, well . . .'

'Pissed off?'

'Well pissed off,' Logan agreed, phrasemaker that he was. 'But, well, watching you work . . .'

'It was a joy to behold, yes, I know. Thank you, Chris. Now, to save my blushes, I must away. It's long past my bedtime.'

'What happens tomorrow?' Logan leaned across as Maxwell was about to close the door.

'Well,' Maxwell pondered it, 'the sun comes up, assuming we can see it, about five . . .'

'I'm serious, Max. This morning the Larry Warner thing was just a story. Now . . .'

'Now it's a crusade,' Maxwell nodded. 'Watch it, Chris. You're starting to care. That's fatal, believe me.'

'I'm in,' Logan insisted. 'Ring me.'

'All right,' Maxwell said. Perhaps the geek had grown up after all. And he watched the dark Rover snarl away into the night.

Softly, softly, he put his key into the lock, treading over Metternich lying like a draught excluder inside the door. The flick of the tail was the furry bastard's shorthand for 'And what time do you call this?' He crept up the stairs to the half light of his lounge and all three of them were lying there, fast asleep, Tiffany curled tightly on the armchair, dreaming of Brad Pitt or, God forbid, Leonardo di Caprio; Lucy snuggled into the safe, enveloping arms of Sylvia Matthews, whom Maxwell had asked to babysit again. And Sylvia? Maxwell could never guess what she dreamed of. He poured himself a Southern Comfort and sat down on the floor, his knees under his chin, his glass against his nose. He'd wake them presently, tell them all was well. There was no sign tonight of Robert de Niro. And he blew a kiss to them. His girls.

Later, he couldn't remember how it fitted into his dreams, but it was probably the school bell, tolling the knell of yet another god-awful day. Then he realized it wasn't the end of a day, but the start of one and it was as black as pitch in the tip he called a bedroom.

'War Office.' Even at an impossible time in the morning, Max was quite Mad.

'Max, it's Sandie.'

'Sister mine, how the devil are you?'

'Well, things are a little hairy at this end, darling. Complications – I won't bore you with it all now. The upshot is, can you hang on to the girls for a while longer?'

'Longer?'

'Yes. No more than a week, I promise. Are they behaving themselves?'

'Of course.'

'Good. Good. Give them our love, will you? Sorry, it must be quite early over there.'

'Something like that,' Maxwell muttered.

'Sorry, darling. Any problems, let me know, will you? Tell the girls I'll ring them, there's a big bro.'

And she was gone, off to do whatever it was diplomats' wives do – Maxwell couldn't imagine. Presumably they had somebody else to make the cucumber sandwiches. 'Big bro' shuffled out of bed and opened his curtains. The sun was a ball of orange fire in the early mists wreathing the sleeping town houses. The Downs were just a line of pearl in the haze and he watched the street lights go out one by one. He heard the door open slightly and he didn't have to turn to see who it was.

'Morning, Count. Sleep well, did we?'

The black and white animal loafed onto the bed, starting his morning ritual, kneading the duvet as if his life depended on it.

'No dribbling, please,' Maxwell warned him and fumbled for his dressing gown. 'What'll it be for breakfast? Little bits of coloured concrete they're conning you are mackerel, tuna and salmon? Go-Cat over easy? Fine. And no,' he peered down at the monster as he rolled over onto his back, 'you can't have it in bed.'

Metternich watched the silly old bastard hunting for his slippers and disappear onto the landing. He waited for the usual 'Oh shit' as his Master caught himself a nasty one on the banister. Then he stopped rolling around cutely, hating himself all over again. The things a cat has to do to get some food around here.

'I can't ask you again,' Maxwell was in the kitchen, phone in one hand, slice of toast in the other.

'You haven't,' Sylvia said on the other end of the line, from her kitchen somewhere across town. 'I've offered. They're lovely girls, Max, you know that. Just . . . well, don't get in too deep, that's all. I don't want you getting hurt.'

'Why, Matron.' Maxwell was doing his Kenneth Williams again. 'I didn't know you cared. See you at ten.'

'No,' she whispered into the receiver as the line went dead. 'No, that's just it, isn't it?'

They took the M27 West, past Magicworld where the crowds and coaches of the last day of the school holiday were swarming, skirting the New Forest, no longer new and not much of a forest and drove into Bournemouth in time for elevenses. It had to be said that Chris Logan wasn't Peter Maxwell's first choice for a companion of a mile, but he had a car and perhaps his journalistic skills would find an outlet one day.

The Wyndham Theatre stood on the western slope of Ramsdown Hill, where the Avon looped into Christchurch and the only sound, apart from the roar of traffic on the A338 was the drone of the odd aircraft circling into Hurn. The place had been built as a Music Hall in the days when the Halls packed 'em in. Dan Leno had played there, along with the Great Vance, George Leybourne and Vesta Tilley. They knew a thing or two about cross-dressing, did the Victorians.

What struck Maxwell as he entered the deserted auditorium was the cold. All morning, they'd driven with the Rover's windows open, the sun roof atilt in the golden weather, Logan tapping his fingers on the wheel to the incessant babble from Radio Ga-Ga. But here, with the proscenium rising before him, it could have been midwinter.

'Hello!' Maxwell called, 'Anybody there?'

There was a noise off stage, a clattering of flats and a silver-haired figure in a cardigan stood there, looking over his glasses, a clipboard in his hand.

'Mr Wiseman?'

'Yes,' the silver-haired man said. 'Who are you?'

'I'm Peter Maxwell, from Leighford High School. We met last term when you spoke to my sixth form. If I may say so, I've never heard a better Terry Wogan!'

'Yes, yes of course, Mr Maxwell.' He came to the edge of the stage and shook the man's hand. 'And flattery, by the way, will get you almost anywhere.'

'This is Chris Logan, of the Leighford Advertiser.'

'Mr Logan,' Wiseman shook his hand too. He was younger than the silver hair let on. Perhaps Maxwell's age, with a wiry frame and twinkling eyes. He could have been Sir Ian McKellen in a funny mirror.

'Ah,' Wiseman sat on the stage, swinging his legs over the edge and cradling his clipboard, 'Is the Advertiser doing a piece on the Wyndham?'

'Er . . . not exactly,' Logan said, 'although it's possible, in the fullness of time.'

'Then why . . . ?'

'We won't beat about the bush, Mr Wiseman,' Maxwell said. 'I'm sure you're a busy man.'

'We've got *The Duchess of Malfi* opening next week,' the impresario said. 'Everybody else is at the Green Rooms, rehearsing. I'm waiting for the bloody set builders. Honestly, it's hopeless. We've only just got rid of one lot doing refurbishment.'

'It's about Larry Warner,' Maxwell said.

'Oh, dear God, yes. Isn't it tragic? Life's a bitch, Mr Maxwell and then somebody shoots you.'

'I was there when it happened.'

'Really?' Wiseman pulled off his glasses, searching Maxwell's face. 'My God. Did you see what happened?'

'No. That's just it. I had my two nieces with me, but all we saw was the result, as it were – a dead man lying in one of those car/float things they have.'

'Must have been a hell of a shot,' Wiseman was thinking aloud. 'The car bobbing around like that. I saw the place on the news. Do the police have any suspects?'

'God knows,' Logan said. 'Leighford CID are playing this one very close to their chests.'

'Have they been to see you?' Maxwell asked.

'In connection with Charts, yes.' He slipped his glasses back on. 'Apparently, they're following up all Larry's clients. He was very busy, I believe – a popular practice.'

'It's his other practices that interest me,' Maxwell said.

'Other practices?' Wiseman looked at the man over his glasses.

'"Predatory homosexual",' Logan said. 'That's how he was described to us.'

'Really?' Wiseman chuckled. 'What a quaint phrase. Smacks of Mary Whitehouse. Well, I can't say I'm all that surprised.'

'But you didn't know?' Maxwell asked.

'No, I didn't. In my game, you meet all sorts. It almost goes with the territory. Look, have seats, gentlemen. There are plenty to choose from.'

Maxwell and Logan lowered the plush seats, lay back and thought of England.

'No, Larry was . . . well, a loner, I suppose. He had a secretary, and I think a housekeeper. I believe that was all.'

'You don't know the secretary's name?' Logan asked.

'Pringle, Patricia, I think. Mouse of a woman, but loyal, I'm sure. Look, Mr Logan, I understand why you need to know all this, but Mr Maxwell . . .'

'Morbid curiosity,' Maxwell chuckled.

'Ah, that kills cats, I understand.'

'Not mine, sadly,' Maxwell said.

'You're a cat person. Marvellous. What have you got?'

'Fleas, probably. But if you're asking breeds, I'd have to say Heinz.'

'Ah, shame. I have two Siamese.'

'"If you don't please",' Logan quipped and immediately wished he hadn't. Too many years as a cub reporter doing the local musicals had left him indelibly imprinted with lyrics.

'This is perhaps rather a silly question,' Maxwell ignored his oppo, 'but did Larry Warner have any money worries?'

'I really don't know. Are you thinking of blackmail?'

Maxwell shrugged. 'In this day and age? I should have thought the 'nineties were too openly naughty for that. It's only in my profession that people still raise eyebrows.'

'Well,' Wiseman said, 'perhaps you're right. But there's a skeleton in every cupboard, they say.'

'They do,' Maxwell nodded. 'Mr Wiseman, the nieces who were with me that day . . . the younger of them is . . . well, not unnaturally, she's afraid. I want to iron this out. Put her mind at rest.'

'Isn't that what the police are for?' Wiseman asked.

'Do you know,' Maxwell smiled, 'I'm not really sure what the police are for.' And he stood up feeling the seat fold up behind him.

'My card,' Logan passed it to him. 'If you know anything,' he said, 'or if anything occurs to you on Larry Warner, give us a bell.'

'Oh, I will,' Wiseman promised. 'I will.'

CHAPTER SEVEN

'**G**ood of you to see us again, Mrs Pringle,' DS Bartholomew perched on the corner of the late Larry Warner's desk. They'd been all over the office already, bagging up rainforests of paperwork and taking it away.

'I'm not sure what more I can tell you.' Pat Pringle was the wrong side of fifty with rather more chins than God had originally given her.

'Mrs Pilgrim mentioned a number of young men friends that Mr Warner had . . .'

'I don't know what you mean,' the ex-secretary pouted.

'Is there anyone who came to the office, Mrs Pringle,' Jacquie Carpenter asked from her chair near the door, 'who wasn't a client, I mean?'

'I told you,' Mrs Pringle said. 'Mr Warner saw relatively few clients here. He was mostly on the road.'

'Yeah,' Bartholomew eased himself off his numbing buttock, 'or in parks.'

'There was a man,' she ignored him, 'who came a few times.'

'What can you tell us about him?' Jacquie had her notepad at the ready.

'Not much. He said he was an old friend.'

'Mr Warner's age?'

'No. Younger.' Pat Pringle flashed a look of defiance at Bartholomew, but he just smirked and looked out of the window. 'Perhaps thirty. Short brown hair. Could have been ex-army, something like that.'

'How often did he call?'

'I don't know, three or four times, perhaps.'

'An old friend,' Jacquie was thinking aloud, 'so he didn't have an appointment as such.'

'No.'

'So you don't have a name?' Bartholomew turned from the window and leaned against it.

Mrs Pringle shook her head. 'Oh,' she suddenly remarked, 'when he first came, he called himself Jeff.'

'That's all?' Jacquie checked. 'No surname.'

'No. Sorry.'

'That's all right.' Bartholomew kicked himself off the wall and strode to the door. 'By the way,' he hauled it open, 'has anybody been to see you about Mr Warner, anybody but us, I mean?'

'No,' Mrs Pringle frowned. 'Nobody.'

'Good,' Bartholomew jerked his head towards the door for Jacquie to lead the way. 'If they do, two men in particular, posing as his relatives, give us a call, will you?'

'Yes,' she told him. 'Yes, of course.'

They clattered down the wooden stairs to the entrance lobby. 'He hasn't got this far, then.'

'Who?'

'Your boyfriend.'

'You what?' Jacquie had turned to face him.

Bartholomew sniggered. 'Peter Maxwell, the Miss Marple of Leighford High.'

'You don't know it was him,' Jacquie fumed.

'Yeah, and I don't know there isn't a Father Christmas either. I just put two and two together. Now, I've been hearing tidings about you, Jacquie.'

'Really?' She turned and made for the front door.

'Really.' He was there ahead of her, 'Your Mr Maxwell gets himself into all sorts of scrapes, doesn't he? A real little Don Quixote. He's also, from what the lads at the nick tell me, well informed. Exceptionally well informed, in fact. Pillow talk, is it? While he's giving you one?' He softened his voice, 'Ooh, darling, you're so big tonight. Here's a little titbit from CID.'

Frank Bartholomew wasn't really ready for what followed. Jacquie spun on her heel and slapped him hard across the face, sending him staggering back against Larry Warner's front door. Instinctively he grabbed her wrist. But Joe Public was passing in a busy street and now wasn't the moment.

'You little bitch!' he hissed. 'I could have you up on charges.'

'You can do precisely what you like,' she told him coldly, 'but you impugn my professionalism again and you're on the carpet in front of Mr Hall and that's a promise. You're new here, Mr Bartholomew, so I'm making allowances. This time. Catch my drift?'

It was that time in the shift John Merrill dreaded. Cocoa time. When he was at rock bottom. The last nick he'd been in had been a bell-push job, manned only at certain times. Leighford was twenty-four hours and so, it seemed, was his shift. He was still on Fourteen Down in the Mail crossword and the skin on his cocoa was thickening. He checked his watch. Half past bloody one. What was that bloody word? Tee-something-en-something-ar. And the clue was 'copy powder'. What sort of sense did that make?

'Toner.' A voice made him look up.

'What?' Sergeant Merrill frowned, staring through the glass at what faced him.

'The answer to the crossword clue, it's toner. The black stuff they use for photocopiers.'

'Really . . . Mr . . . er . . . ?'

'Hamlyn, Neil, Lance Corporal.'

Merrill hadn't time to take in the pale blue beret, the flak jacket, the cold eyes. All he was looking at was the rifle in Hamlyn's hands, presented across his chest as if he was on parade. Instinctively he moved back from his counter, but that took him away from the panic button, panic driving him in the wrong direction.

'Now, then

'The Warner murder,' Hamlyn said, staring his man down. 'I'm the one you're looking for.'

'Just give me the . . .' But Merrill was silenced by the slamming of the rifle mechanism. Hamlyn took a step back and swung the muzzle to face him. The sergeant's hands were in the air now. 'Come on, son, there's no need for this.' There was an iron lump in his throat and he heard his own blood roaring in his ears.

'You're right.' Hamlyn uncocked the gun and unslung the strap from his elbow. With a speed that terrified Merrill, he reversed the thing and presented it to him butt first. 'Well?' he asked. 'Do you want this or am I going to have to smash the bloody glass?'

After the coppers in the siege of Sydney Street had faced the automatic Mausers of the East End anarchists in 1911, they had a cup of tea and went back to work. John Merrill was given a Valium and counselling and three weeks off and nobody had fired at him at all. It was a sign of the times – the softening of the century.

DCI Henry Hall had left his wife snoring softly under the new duvet. There was a time when Helen had got up with her husband, when he was a struggling detective making his way. But that was when the kids were small and it was all breast-feeding and nappies and odd hours anyway. Now, as they neared their teens, the Hall kids could fend a little for themselves. The terrible twos had given way and the nasty nineteens had yet to be. Margaret snored on.

Hall didn't shave; didn't even grab a tie. If John Merrill was rattled, it was for real. Men like John Merrill were the rocks of constabularies the length and breadth of the country. A maniac had dropped into Leighford nick and it looked as if another case was closed.

DS Frank Bartholomew grabbed the nearest shirt and rummaged on the floor for his trousers. His electronic alarm clock told him it was two fifteen, a time he'd forgotten existed. He looked at the girl still asleep in his bed, her peroxide hair splayed on the pillow, her breasts rising and falling in the half light. He saw her bra and knickers draped over the chair-back and half expected to see her teeth in a glass by the bed. He took his wallet and cheque book, just in case. Bloody one night stands.

DC Jacquie Carpenter hauled her tights on and fished in the wardrobe for her skirt. She'd been awake when the call came through from the nick. The girl on the switchboard had a quiver in her voice. Some bastard had pointed a rifle at John Merrill. Code red. She glanced at the Dorothy L. Sayers she'd tossed into a corner. Murder at the vicarage. Something sinister in the hamlet, with half-Tudor thatchery and cream teas and an aristo detective. Yeah, right.

'Mr Hamlyn.' Hall sat opposite his man in the lamplight of Interview Room Two. 'I am Detective Chief Inspector Hall. This is Detective Sergeant Bartholomew. Would you give me your full name, please, for the tape?'

'Neil Thomas Hamlyn, Special Air Service.'

'SAS?' Bartholomew wanted clarification.

Hamlyn nodded. 'You don't want to believe that Andy McNab bollocks, Mr Bartholomew,' he said. 'We're not all bloody John Wayne meets Arnie Schwarzenegger.'

Neil Hamlyn was a fit, wiry-looking man, perhaps thirty-one, thirty-two. Dressed as he was in full combat rig with the sand, black and white of Desert Storm, he could easily have been Wayne or Schwarzenegger. His biceps bulged under his rolled up sleeves and his dog tags caught the lamp light.

'You live at 25, Benington Street, Leighford?' Bartholomew checked.

Hamlyn nodded.

'For the tape, Mr Hamlyn, please,' Hall reminded him.

'Yes, that's correct.'

'Are you still a member of the Special Air Services?' Hall asked.

'Yes,' Hamlyn said. 'I'm on leave just at the moment.'

'And the gun?'

Hamlyn leaned back in the hard, upright chair. 'It's a Ruger Mini 14. I have a licence for it.'

'Why did you come here tonight, Mr Hamlyn?' Hall leaned back too, out of the lamp's glare, out of the line of fire.

'To give myself up,' Hamlyn said. 'I killed Larry Warner.'

'Why?' Hall asked.

For the first time, Hamlyn's concentration seemed to slip. His eyes flickered, as if he'd been asked the sixty-four thousand dollar question and he was stuck for an answer.

'Mr Hamlyn fails to respond,' said Bartholomew for the tape.

'All right,' Hall leaned forward again. 'Do you want to arrange some tea, Frank? I expect we could all do with some of that, couldn't we, Mr Hamlyn? Then we'll try another tack.'

The other tack they tried didn't work. Neither did the next.

All Corporal Hamlyn was doing was, in effect, giving his name, rank and serial number.

The unlikely trio sat in the police canteen, Jacquie Carpenter cradling her coffee mug with both hands. Henry Hall sat opposite her, the neon lights reflected in his glasses' lenses like some alien shapeshifter who had inhabited the body of a DCI. Frank Bartholomew was tucking into his bacon and eggs and a pile of something that, under the microscope, would probably turn out to be baked beans.

'Theories, Jacquie?' Hall leaned back in the uncomfortable plastic chair.

'You want my honest opinion, sir?' she asked.

'Of course,' he nodded.

'I don't think he did it.'

'Oh, come on!' It was a predictable response from Frank Bartholomew, delivered with a mouthful of full English.

'Go on, Jacquie.' Hall insisted quietly.

'He doesn't have a motive,' she said.

'He isn't giving us a motive,' Bartholomew interjected, 'no. But there's always a motive. There's got to be.'

Hall was looking at Jacquie. 'According to our information, Warner was homosexual,' he said. 'Is that the link?'

Jacquie shrugged. 'We don't know anything about Hamlyn yet,' she said, 'but even Warner had no form.'

Hall nodded. 'No,' he murmured. 'He was very discreet. The secretary – Mrs Pringle – you said she didn't seem to know about Warner's men friends.'

'That was the impression I got,' Jacquie told him.

'The impression I got,' Bartholomew was wiping his mouth with a paper napkin, 'was that she knew perfectly well, but didn't approve. Bit of a frosty, stuck up old cow, I thought.'

'Thank you, Frank.' Hall glanced at his sergeant for the first time. 'Your input, as always, is invaluable. Let's have your version of Hamlyn, then.'

The DS lolled back, happy to be the centre of attention, his coffee mug in his hand. 'He had the means,' he said. 'The rifle.'

'Assuming he can use it,' Jacquie countered.

'Well, I'm not going to hand the bloody thing back to him to find that out,' Bartholomew said. 'He was in the SAS. We're talking about blokes with talent.'

'He says,' Jacquie commented.

'Look . . .' Bartholomew started, but Henry Hall's raised hands blew the whistle for half time.

'The bottom line is, we don't have enough yet. It's early days. But Hamlyn bothers me. He's . . . a vacuum, a space. There's something missing.'

'A motive,' said Jacquie.

'Could he have got into Magicworld with the gun?' Hall was thinking aloud.

'Of course,' Bartholomew told him. 'Golf bag, large holdall. If that bloody thing strips down – and if he's in the SAS he knows all about that – he could possibly get it in a Wallace and Gromit backpack. All he has to do is pay his entrance ticket, follow Warner and pick his spot.'

'It was heaving with people,' Jacquie complained.

'So was Dallas,' Hall said, 'when they got Kennedy, Tel Aviv when they hit Yitzhak Rabin. Nobody expects an execution in broad daylight. It's the suddenness, the shock. Frank's right, Jacquie. Hamlyn could have done it.'

'Means and opportunity,' Bartholomew crowed, never a man to disguise how pleased he felt with himself.

'Which still leaves us without a motive.' Jacquie was sticking her neck out that morning.

'Frank,' Hall finished his coffee. 'Get onto Hendon. I want anything and everything on Hamlyn's gun. And I want it today.'

'Saturday,' Bartholomew sucked in his breath and shook his head.

'I don't care if it's Judgement Day,' his DCI told him. 'I want that lab open and working on this. Whatever else they've got, can wait. Jacquie, has Hamlyn asked for a brief yet?'

'No, sir.'

'Right. Let's keep it that way. We've read him his rights, but we'll have to move fast. Ring Bartlett.'

'Sir?' he caught her raised eyebrow, her enquiring look.

'There's something missing, Jacquie,' Hall said again. 'Perhaps Bartlett can find it for us.'

'Uncle Maxie,' Tiffany was mooching around the lounge, chewing the ends of her blonde hair in an effort not to bite her nails.

'Yes, darling,' the Great Man was in the kitchen trying to make sense of a recipe by Ainsley Harriott.

'I saw something.'

'Hmm?' Maxwell barely looked up. Why, why, why were all these measurements in foreign? It was all kgs and mls; whatever happened to good old lbs and ozs? And come to think of it, rods, poles and perches, guineas, half crowns and groats? And when had Peter Maxwell given Brussels permission to change all that?

'In the park. Magicworld. On the Wild Water Ride. I saw something.'

He looked at the girl, her staring eyes, her open lips. Perhaps Sylvia Matthews had been right. In her estimation, Lucy was okay. She was tough, resilient, could cope. But Tiffany? Sylvia hadn't been so sure about Tiffany. He grabbed the nearest cloth to wipe the flour off his hands and led her back into the lounge where Metternich sprawled on the settee.

'Manners, Count,' Maxwell said and upended the animal, who hit the floor with what dignity he could and sauntered into the kitchen. If there was going to be sobbing, he wanted out. Maxwell sat next to the girl, draping an arm around her shoulders. 'Tell Uncle Maxie all about it.'

'Well,' Tiffany was frowning, trying to remember, trying to make sense of it all. 'I've been having nightmares, Uncle Max,' she said. 'Dreams where we're on the car, riding the water. Mummy and Daddy are there too, but you're not. You're on the one in front, sitting with that dead man. And . . .' he felt her shudder, 'this is the horrible bit. He's already dead. He's sitting bolt upright, next to you. And you're talking to him. And you don't know he's dead. It's horrible. There's blood . . .'

He shook her gently by the arm, then cradled her head against his cheek, softly kissing her parting. 'Now, sweetheart,' he said, 'It was awful, I know. But it's over now. We're fine, aren't we? All of us. We'll be okay.'

'Lucy thinks he's still out there, doesn't she?' Tiffany looked up at him, eyes like her sister's, all hip sophistication gone.

'It won't be long now,' Maxwell assured her. 'Most murders are cleared up in a few days. They'll get him.'

But Tiffany was shaking her head. 'No, they won't, Uncle Max,' she told him. 'Not without you. I saw a flash.'

'A flash?' Maxwell frowned.

Tiffany was nodding now, gazing into the middle distance, letting memories flood back. 'High up, to our left,' she shut her eyes to focus more clearly. 'Up there,' her left arm waved around in the air, 'Above some rocks. There was a flash.'

'Like a gun going off?' Maxwell asked.

'No. Not like that. It was like. . . when Mummy and Daddy had some studio portraits done of us a couple of years ago. It was like a camera.'

There was a sudden hiss from the kitchen as Maxwell's milk boiled inexorably over the saucepan rim and hit the hot plate. The Great Chef leapt from his niece's side and sprinted away.

'How many times have I told you, Metternich?' he bellowed. 'Never leave your cooking unattended.' And as the smell of burning milk hit his nostrils, 'Oh, bugger!'

The bells of St Mary's were ringing out that morning over sleepy Leighford where Englishmen, Christians all, ignored them and washed their cars or drowned out the clanging with strimmers and hovers. Maxwell watched Miss Troubridge, his very own Neighbour From Hell (he had no need to watch the programme) making her way down her primrose path towards the everlasting bonfire sermons of Father Wainwright. Miss Troubridge was a sprightly old besom, Church of England through and through and the last time she'd missed a service was the day the doodlebugs came to Leighford, courtesy of Mr Hitler. She of course still called the lad with his collar back to front 'Vicar'. 'Father' was a threat too Papist for her.

The old girl peered over the communal privet, as she always did. Bras and knickers on Maxwell's rotary, so those girls were still there – unless of course, her worst fears were justified and her neighbour had turned. Maxwell saw her greeting somebody further along the road. That would be Mrs Brownleas, her companion of a mile, the chum beside whom she dozed during Father Wainwright's soliloquy and whose cheek she pecked during the Peace. But it wasn't Mrs Brownleas. It was a young policewoman in plainclothes walking down his path, making for his front door. He noticed the old girl break her stride and almost break her back looking over her shoulder to check on Mr Maxwell's doings.

By the time the doorbell rang, he was there, looking at the girl through the reedy fuzz of his door panel.

'Jacquie,' he bowed. 'Or is it Policewoman Carpenter?' She shifted uneasily from one foot to the other.

'It's Jacquie,' she said, not quite ready to look him in the face, 'if you want it to be.'

CHAPTER EIGHT

'Have the girls gone?' Jacquie asked, standing in Maxwell's lounge. This wasn't the first time she'd stood here, heart pounding, unsure of herself, like a schoolgirl again and hating herself for feeling that way.

'No,' he told her, 'they're still in bed. Disgraceful, isn't it? In my day, I'd already ploughed the lower meadow, fed the chickens and geese, built a windmill and been called to the colours by half past ten.'

'I've come to apologize,' she said.

He looked at her, the grey eyes clear, the head held high, its chestnut hair cascading over her shoulders. 'There's no need,' he said. The last time she'd stood here, in his lounge, on his turf, he'd leaned across and kissed her. Now she wanted it to happen again. But it didn't.

'PMT, I suppose,' she said.

'Ah, pre-Maxwell tension,' he nodded. 'That's biology for you.'

She fished in her handbag, the one dangling from her right shoulder. 'And that's for you,' she said. She handed him a video in a plain white cardboard box.

'Not *Dormitory Nights – The Director's Cut?*' he leered. 'You're spoiling me, my dear.'

Her face twisted into a half smile. 'I think you'll find this a lot more interesting,' and she sat down.

'Can I get you a coffee?' he asked.

'You can get me some answers,' she said, leaning back in the chair as he fiddled with the video.

'My generation put a man on the moon, you know, but I still have trouble with this.'

There was no preamble. No forthcoming attractions in which a sandpaper voice-over rasped 'at a cinema near you'.

'Max,' she stopped him before it started. 'If the girls come in, you must switch this off.'

'So it is *Dormitory Nights*,' his eyes widened.

It wasn't. A fixed camera looked down from a ceiling onto a spartan table. Two men sat facing each other, the glare from the bad light bouncing off the bald head of one of them. The other appeared to be in combat gear, sitting bolt upright, like a robot. At the bottom right of the screen was a date and logo and an electronic timer. Saturday night at the movies.

'The bald guy is Dr Richard Bartlett; he's a psychiatrist. The other one is Neil Hamlyn; he's just confessed to the murder of Larry Warner.'

Maxwell pressed 'pause' on his remote and sat down heavily opposite Jacquie open-mouthed. On the screen a band of white static crackled across Hamlyn's shoulders as he raised a hand to make a point. A man in the freeze-frame. 'Jacquie . . .' Maxwell began.

She held up a hand. 'I know,' she said. 'Should I be showing you this? No. Should I even have it in my possession? No. If anyone found out, would I lose my job? Yes. There,' she sighed, as if with relief, 'now we've got all that out of the way, let's get on with it.'

Maxwell looked at her, the remote still in his hand. This girl had put her career on the line for him before, and more than once. But in the past, he'd had to ask her, using all the old Maxwell charm, the public-school offensive. Now she'd come unsolicited, with classified information which could sink them both. 'You know,' he said softly, 'I have to ask why.'

She looked at him, biting her lip. What was she supposed to say? That she loved him? Was that why? Could it be that simple? And did she love him? More than the job that had become her life? More than that life? The other answer was easier. 'Bartlett's convinced – so now the DCI is convinced that Hamlyn did it. He's based his beliefs on this interview, taken yesterday.'

'Only one?' Maxwell asked.

Jacquie nodded. 'He says he's sure. Doesn't need any more.'

'This Bartlett – who is he? Some sort of Cracker?' He didn't look much like Robbie Coltrane.'

'He's a forensic psychiatrist, on loan to the force,' she explained. 'We don't, by and large, set much store by people like him. It's all a bit Quantico and the FBI. Psychological profiling is the darling of armchair detectives – oh, sorry, Max.' He beamed and bowed low. 'Hard-bitten coppers don't tend to buy it. It was all Frank Bartholomew could do to stop himself chucking up.'

'Hmm,' Maxwell mused. 'One of nature's gentlefolk, our Mr Bartholomew. Why are you risking your neck showing this to me, Jacquie?'

Would he never leave it alone? Get off the subject? Just play the bloody thing and be grateful. 'The chalk face,' she answered. 'You've been there, you told me, for ever. You know people, Max. How they work, what makes them tick. I'd like your expertise on this one.'

He nodded, the remote still idling. 'All right,' he said. 'Tell me about Hamlyn.'

'Neil Thomas Hamlyn,' she began, once Maxwell was sitting comfortably. 'Corporal, SAS.'

'Cool,' said Maxwell, in his best Bart Simpson.

'Are you impressed by that?'

'No,' he said. 'Fashionable things, regiments. And fashions come and go. No one had heard of the SAS before the Iranian Embassy siege, when you were a mere slip of a gel. Now suddenly they're everybody's idea of hard men. Then there was Two Para in the Falklands. No, I'll take the Light Brigade any time, thanks. Three feet of cold steel and three bloody miles of nerve.'

'Well, the point is, we don't know if he's kosher even there.'

'Won't the SAS talk to you?'

'Let's say they're evasive.' Jacquie gave him an old-fashioned look. 'Working with the army is never easy.'

Maxwell chuckled. 'That's what's so marvellous about this great country of ours, isn't it? We know the name of the chappie who runs MI5 – he even advertises in the paper; "Spies Wanted – For a Dangerous Time, Ring Whitehall 12345". But you try to find out any info on a serving soldier, a serving policeman or even Rudolf Bloody Hess and you're wasting your time.'

She nodded. 'So at the moment, we only have his word. We've been over his flat, though. His dogtags, his uniform, such paperwork as he's got seems genuine. And he appears to be a marksman.'

'Does he say what he used?'

'A Ruger Mini 14. He even brought it to show us.'

'I thought those things were illegal in private hands.'

'So's murder,' Jacquie told him. 'But it happens anyway. And if he is SAS, it's a moot point whether it's private hands or not.'

'Run the film,' Maxwell said.

'Tell me about Larry Warner,' Bartlett was saying on the screen, his right hand cradling a polystyrene coffee cup.

'He was a target,' Hamlyn shrugged.

'Is that all?'

'What more is there?'

'Why him?' Bartlett persisted. 'Why not me? DCI Hall? Your next-door neighbour?'

Hamlyn shrugged again. 'He was as good as any.'

'You followed him to the park?'

'Yes.'

'From his house?'

'No.'

'You saw him outside the park and you followed him in?'

'Yes.'

'Where did you fire from?'

'The Wild Water Ride. In the rocks.'

'Go back,' Maxwell interrupted the documentary unfolding like bad drama before him. He'd passed the remote to Jacquie so that he could concentrate. The heads jerked at high speed.

'You followed him to the park?'

'Yes.'

'From his house?'

'No.'

'No,' Maxwell repeated. 'Freeze it there.'

Jacquie stopped the action.

'Let me get this straight. He gets to the theme park, to Magicworld, how?'

'Car,' Jacquie told him. 'Hamlyn drives a clapped out Cavalier.'

'He's carrying the gun,' Maxwell was trying to get a handle on the whole thing.

'In a holdall. Apparently, the rifle strips down. It can be assembled and disassembled in minutes.'

'Seconds.'

'What?'

'If he's SAS,' Maxwell explained, 'and if he wants to get away from a murder scene, he's got to move quicker than that.'

'All right, then,' she conceded. 'Seconds.'

'So,' Maxwell went on, 'He's waiting outside the gates of Magicworld, carrying a holdall, when he spots Warner.'

'At random,' Jacquie added.

'Run it back again.'

She did and they heard the conversation for a third time. 'He was a target,' Hamlyn said.

'Is that all?' Bartlett asked.

'What more is there?'

'Freeze.' Maxwell was in full Dragnet mode now. He might as well have added 'Sucker'. But he didn't. 'A Hell of a lot, I suspect. "What more is there?" This Hamlyn,' Maxwell had turned away from the screen and was looking intently at Jacquie, 'Is he a Michael Ryan clone?'

'Ryan wasn't a member of the SAS.' Jacquie remembered the Hungerford massacre all too well. She had been a schoolgirl at the time, rather as she felt now sitting in Maxwell's lounge on a sunny Sunday morning, watching a man confess to murder. In a way, it was because of Ryan that she'd joined the police in the first place. One of those who had died in Hungerford was a family friend, Roger Brereton, a family friend who had driven the wrong way, into Ryan's line of fire.

'But he wore the gear and carried the guns,' Maxwell said. 'If I remember, he was a member of a rifle club.'

'Devizes,' Jacquie nodded.

'What about Hamlyn?'

'No record,' Jacquie told him.

'Ryan was a loner, a podgy, baby-faced shite with an attitude problem. I bet there are half a dozen teachers in Hungerford who weren't that surprised the day the bastard opened up on people. The same will be true of Hamlyn.'

'That's what Dr Bartlett thinks,' Jacquie said.

'Run it on.'

'How many shots did you fire?' the balding man asked, taking a careful sip of his coffee.

'One.'

There was a pause. The answer had clearly thrown Bartlett. 'You're that good?' he asked.

'I'm that good,' Hamlyn nodded.

'Self-effacing sonofabitch, isn't he?' Maxwell murmured.

'How could you be sure he was dead?'

There was another pause, while Hamlyn thought about that one. 'I'm that good,' he repeated.

'Rambo country,' Maxwell muttered, frowning.

'Have you killed anyone before?' Bartlett asked on the screen.

'No,' Hamlyn said.

'Warner was your first?'

'Yes.'

'How did it feel?'

'What?'

'When you killed him? When you saw him go down, a bullet in his head.'

Hamlyn shrugged. 'I'd done my job,' he said. 'And it wasn't in his head. It was in his back, about a foot below the skull.'

'Freeze,' said Maxwell. 'Is that right, about the bullet?'

'Near as damn it. Bartlett's trying to catch him out.'

'Clumsy,' Maxwell commented.

'You'd be amazed. I remember at police college we studied the Black Dahlia case.'

'Don't tell me,' Maxwell closed his eyes, struggling to remember. 'Beth Short, Los Angeles, 1947.'

Jacquie nodded. 'The LAPD were inundated with oddballs who confessed to that one. They were all eliminated by one question – what was forced into the dead woman's rectum?'

Maxwell winced. 'My, my, but you're in a nice job, Policewoman Carpenter,' he said.

'Tell me about it,' she sighed.

'What was?'

'What was what?'

'Forced into Beth Short's rectum.'

'Oh, no, I'm not telling you that. The case is still unsolved. You'd only go and confess to it.' She winked at him. For one glorious, fleeting moment, Jacquie Carpenter held all the aces. But with Mad Max Maxwell, that moment never lasted. He always had five more up his sleeve, in his trouser turn-ups, in the drawer with his socks.

'All right,' Maxwell conceded. 'So Hamlyn knows where the bullet went. Doesn't that clinch it?'

Jacquie got up and wandered to the window. The faithful would be returning from church soon. The aroma of roast lamb and mint sauce wafted along the leafy curve that was Columbine. 'Before he interviewed Hamlyn, the DCI asked Bartlett to give him a profile – the sort of man who would kill in the way Warner was killed.'

'And?'

Jacquie was remembering Bartlett's words. 'Driven,' she said. 'A mission-oriented killer.'

Maxwell looked at her. 'You mean Hamlyn hears voices? He's a cross between the Yorkshire Ripper and Joan of Arc?'

Jacquie shook her head. 'That doesn't come out on the tape,' she said. 'That's not Bartlett's conclusion.'

'All right,' Maxwell nodded. 'Run the thing through,' he told her. 'I won't stop it this time. Let's get a sense of our Mr Hamlyn. Find out where he's coming from, as we used to say in the 'eighties. See what makes him tick.'

Maxwell's clock ticked. Maxwell's cat came in, saw Jacquie and went out. She was simply one woman too many for Metternich at the moment. Hormonal overkill. Maxwell's nieces slumbered on past midday. And Maxwell's neighbour, Miss Troubridge, noted that Jacquie's car was still parked in the street, several hundred yards from Maxwell's house.

When the video had stopped, with an abrupt click, Maxwell sat back. 'Why does Bartlett think Hamlyn did it?' he asked.

Jacquie had been watching the Head of Sixth Form intently. She wanted answers. She'd settle for a miracle about now.

'For one thing,' she said, 'he's accurate on all practical counts. He knows where Warner was shot, both in terms of site and location of wound on the body. The gun could be right . . .'

'*Could* be?' Maxwell sensed a yawning loophole.

'We haven't found the bullet,' she admitted. 'The Wild Water Ride is a big area. Even fifty blokes on their hands and knees have had no luck. It's the DCI's guess the bullet hit the water and was washed away.'

'But wouldn't there be a spent cartridge?'

'We can't find that, either.'

'All right,' Maxwell mused, 'back to Bartlett. Why else is he convinced?'

'Attitude. What it comes down to in a police inquiry, Max, any inquiry, not just murder, is whether somebody's telling the truth or not.'

'And Bartlett thinks Hamlyn is?'

'Yes. But he's refused a lie detector test.'

'Good,' Maxwell bounced. 'Place gets more like the Bronx every day. I hope you people read Mr Hamlyn his Miranda.'

'Well, that's another thing,' Jacquie said. 'He doesn't want a lawyer. That works in our favour at first. You know we've got so many hours we can hold him, then it's walkies.'

'Ah,' Maxwell smiled, 'the wisdom of Habeas Corpus.'

Jacquie was less convinced. 'But there comes a point where we have to let a man have his phone call or we'd be accused of violating his rights.'

'Fair enough,' Maxwell nodded.

'He didn't, Max,' Jacquie explained. 'Not only did he not make a phone call, he didn't want a solicitor when we offered one.'

'So, he's going to defend himself?'

'There's no defence. He's admitted guilt. I doubt there'll even be a trial. Bartlett will just commit him.'

'Case closed,' Maxwell said. 'At least my girls will sleep easy.'

Jacquie looked at him. 'I hope so, Max,' she said, 'Because Neil Hamlyn no more killed Larry Warner than I did.'

'Convince me,' he said, sitting back and clasping one ankle.

She screwed her courage to the sticking place and launched herself. 'First . . .'

But he checked her. 'Please, Jacquie,' he said, holding her hand suddenly, 'no fingers.'

She found herself blushing in spite of herself and sat on her hands. 'Sorry, Max,' she said. 'First, the random target. Michael Ryan's first hit was Mrs Susan Godfrey, picnicking with her children in Savernake Forest. The place was secluded, in semi-darkness in fact because of the trees and the kids too little to stop him. He knew he'd get away with it.'

'Whereas,' Maxwell took up her thread, 'Neil Hamlyn opens up in broad daylight, blinding sunshine, in front of hundreds of would-be onlookers.'

'Precisely.'

'But he got away with it too.' Maxwell was good at Devil's Advocate.

'Second, rifle nuts like Ryan – and that bastard at Dunblane – aren't content with a single hit. They go berserk, shoot as many as they can. They carry Kalashnikovs and handguns. Often turn the gun on themselves, cheating the law in some sort of perverted triumph.'

'Whereas Hamlyn fires a single shot, then goes home to feed his goldfish or mow the lawn.'

'And he gives himself up,' Jacquie reminded him.

'Ah, but that'll be the fear,' Maxwell said. 'I almost had a nervous breakdown in '75 over a library overdue I had. For all chummie knew, you might have been about to feel his collar anyway.'

'Christ, Max,' Jacquie shook her head. 'We were nowhere on this one. No forensic, no sighting . . .'

'Sorry.' He shuffled his feet.

'Without Hamlyn, we'd be absolutely no further forward one week on.'

'Bartlett didn't follow up on the homosexual thing.'

'The what?'

'The late Mr Warner's proclivities.'

'Ah, yes.' Jacquie hadn't wanted to raise it. 'It was you, wasn't it? Who visited the housekeeper?'

'It might have been,' Maxwell affected mock bridle. 'But if Juliette Pilgrim – doh!' And he slapped his forehead Homer Simpson style. 'There, I've been and gone and admitted it.'

'Be careful, Max,' she suddenly pleaded, the eyes steady, the mouth earnest.

'Policewoman Carpenter,' he returned the gaze. 'You give me above top secret scuttlebutt like this,' he nodded in the direction of the screen, 'and you tell me to be careful? Am I getting mixed messages, or what?'

'Frank Bartholomew,' she said, 'I've known some shitty Detective Sergeants in my time, but he takes the biscuit. He's after you, Max. Seriously.'

'I wouldn't have it any other way,' Maxwell smiled. 'Can I keep this?'

She looked across at the television screen. 'Yes. It's a copy. Christ, they'll hang me as it is. If I'd taken the original out of the nick, God knows what they'd do.'

'Don't worry,' he caught her hands and winked at her. 'You can always retire early.'

'What do you think, Max?' she said, tightening her grip on his hands so that it almost hurt. 'About Hamlyn?'

'Hamlyn?' he blinked. 'Oh, he didn't do it, my dear girl. So it's our job to prove who did.'

He thought he saw her eyes fill with tears, but it might have been a trick of the light. Her head inclined forward and down and he leaned towards her, softly sweeping away a rogue lock of hair from her face. He held her cheek, smoothing it with his thumb. Her lips parted, so close to his. Then they jumped apart, the Head of Sixth Form and the detective.

'Uncle Maxie,' a still-sleepy Lucy stood there, all fluffy mules and tartan pyjamas. 'What's for lunch? I'm starving.'

CHAPTER NINE

It is a little . . . irregular, Max.' It was James Diamond talking, Leighford High's less than redoubtable head teacher. When he'd joined the school, only a twinkling ago by Maxwell's reckoning, the Head of Sixth Form had christened him 'Legs' in the fond hope that by giving him the sobriquet of a 'twenties Chicago gangster, the man might obtain some colour. Alas, the Head of Sixth Form had been mistaken. James Diamond remained as bland as the day he was born.

Maxwell found him now, in the early 'nineties banality that was his office. An indescribably awful painting of the school was pinned above his head, like the sword of Damocles utterly unknown to he at whose head it was aimed.

'I mean,' Diamond always felt uncomfortable when Max said nothing. Only a little less uncomfortable than when he said something. 'They must have schools of their own.'

'Oh indeed so,' Maxwell assured him, 'but,' and he held his fingers in the sign of the cross, 'we're talking Private Sector, here, Headmaster.' Only Peter Maxwell called James Diamond Headmaster. Again, in the fond hope that one day he'd become one. It hadn't happened yet. 'And the Private Sector, like all good schools, has not gone back yet. Thursday, my nieces assure me.'

'Thursday?' Diamond was horrified. 'Is that how long they'll be here, then?'

'They'll be here,' Maxwell blinked smilingly, 'for as long as it takes for their parents to collect them . . . with your blessing, of course, Headmaster.'

'So you're literally in loco parentis, then, Max?'

'In my case, just loco,' Maxwell smiled. 'Do I have a decision on this, Headmaster? Mr Prentiss, with the usual sadism of an exams officer, has put me on invigilation this morning. GCSE PE, whatever that may be.' And he stood up.

'Very well, Max.' Diamond knew when he was being hustled. This was the bum's rush and he was the bum in question. 'But you'll have to brief the staff concerned.'

Maxwell bowed. 'Your wish, as ever, Headmaster, is my command. Consider them briefed.'

And he left.

The winds that blew between A and C blocks, they cut him like a knife. For all the sun burned bright across Leighford High, dazzling off the chromework of the bike sheds and the staff car park, there was a distinct nip in the air. His nieces fell into step behind him as he fought his way through the main corridor.

'What's that smell, Uncle Maxie?' Lucy nudged him in the ribs.

'Seven B Four,' Maxwell said, 'either that, or it's my heartfelt advice not to touch the beefburgers for lunch,' and they swept into his office. For all they'd lived with the Great Man for over a week now, nothing could prepare Tiffany and Lucy for the inner sanctum that was the office of the Head of Sixth Form. His desk was buried in bits of paper, signed by his very good friends Doug McAvoy and David Blunkett. In the corner, piles of tottering exercise books, whose graffiti-worked covers proclaimed that the world should know that 'PL loves JA' and that '911 Are Cool' hid the cobwebs. But it was the walls that really held them. Giant posters hit them between the eyes, reflecting in glorious technicolor a misspent life. A terrified Lilian Gish clutched her baby and recoiled from the cruel hand of *Intolerance*; an over made-up Clark Gable and Claudette Colbert would have them believe that *It Happened One Night*, and Lana Turner and John Garfield looked hugely relieved that *The Postman Always Rings Twice*. In fact, Tiffany had seen that one, but she remembered the bloke as Jack Nicholson and the girl as Jessica Lange. And that version was old.

'Right, dears,' Maxwell sat them down. 'Between nine and four of the clock, this is where I live. If I'm not here, I'll be in the History Department, which is one floor above. H4 is my room. If there are any problems during the day, you'll find me here or there, so to speak. Tiff, it's only for a few days, so I'm putting you in Mr Macdonald's tutor group. He's the best of a bad bunch in Year Ten and even better news is that you'll be in Set Ten A One for History where your teacher is perhaps the finest brain in Tony Blair's Britain – me. Lucy, you've got Mrs Greenhow. Salt of the earth is our Sally, for all she's a Special Needs Teacher deep down. That way, you'll be in Eight B One where your History teacher is that same miracle worker of whom we spoke a few moments ago. Mr Irwin!'

His shout rattled glass and a rather dishy young man, all curls and smoulder, sauntered in.

'Mr Maxwell,' he beamed, eyeing Tiffany up like Freddie Starr with a hamster.

'Ladies, this is Mark Irwin. He's in my Year Twelve, that's Lower Sixth to you. He's a mean bass guitarist, whatever that is, shoots a decent amount of pool and if he ever does any work, may get to Exeter University in fifteen months' time. But his real asset is that he knows where your classrooms are and will take you there, won't you, Mr Irwin?'

'It will be my pleasure, sir,' the boy grinned.

'These are my nieces, Irwin,' Maxwell snarled. 'I will expect you to keep your hands in your pockets at all times.'

'That would be slouching, sir,' Irwin winked at him. 'Whereaway, ladies?'

'Mr Macdonald and Mrs Greenhow,' Maxwell told him, wondering again why each school generation only produced one public-school throwback like Mark Irwin. 'I've got to get you dears on roll, which means seeing a nice lady who understands the mechanical gubbins she calls a database. See you later.'

'See you, Uncle Maxie,' Lucy waved at him. Tiffany was already somewhere else and his eyes rolled heavenward as he heard Irwin purr to her, 'I'm sorry, I didn't catch your name.'

A certain peace descends on High Schools come the business end of the summer term. Those heady weeks when Year 11 have gone and Year 13 are about to go. It had to be said that Bernard Ryan, the Deputy Head in charge of timetabling, the calendar and all that makes the heart of a great school beat, had got it wrong that year. He'd spent months telling everybody that it was a computer glitch and the stand-up row he'd had with Maxwell in the staffroom was still imprinted on the memories of those who heard it – 'I don't know a megabyte from a Jacobite, Bernard, but I know what comes next after Wednesday. It's a pity you're a little lacking in that particular set of basics, isn't it?'

Peter Maxwell, one; Bernard Ryan, *nul point,* disappeared in confusion. So it was that the GCSE exam study leave didn't actually start until Wednesday and some of them were actually gullible enough to believe it. Maxwell would have to go on telling them stories until then.

'Gemma,' he cornered a gum-chewing girl in the first lesson after break, 'what, in your erudite and ever-welcome opinion, was the main problem facing the Weimar republic?'

Gemma looked blank, but at least she had the sense to stop her jaws working.

'Well,' Maxwell roamed the classroom, like a lion probing the defences of a herd of wildebeest. 'Was it split ends, I wonder? Broken nails? Perhaps jogger's nipple?' He thrust a litter bin under her nose. 'Spit it out, there's a dear. And when you get home tonight, write out a thousand times: "I've got ten days until my GCSE History; I must find out something about Adolf Hitler". Okay?' He watched the grey blob ping into the metal. 'Jolly good. Right,' and he spun back to the wary, milling herd, 'who's got a brain? Nobody. Well, never mind. Simon, you'll have to do.'

'What was the question, sir?' Simon felt his heart pounding.

'Ah,' luckily for Simon, Maxwell was feeling particularly generous that day. He'd let the boy live. He had reached the window and was looking at the staff cars parked below, 'What indeed?'

He kept an eye on them, of course, as only experienced teachers can. The school timetable told him where they'd be and he acted on it. 'Got any chalk, Ben?' he asked the Head of Science in whose class young Lucy was conducting an experiment.

'No, we use whiteboards here, Max,' the Head of Science was confused, glancing at the gleaming wall behind him, just to make sure.

'Of course you do,' Maxwell beamed. 'Silly me. I'll see myself out.'

He breezed down F corridor, past the mezzanine floor where they kept Business Studies, removing with deft swipes of his hand the misspelt posters that proclaimed that Acne were playing at the Dog's Head tomorrow night and that Melanie Stinks. He didn't want to hear Acne (he wasn't sure you could) and he already knew about Melanie anyway. He popped his head round the door of the French Department, where Tiffany had her head down over a book.

'Bonjour, Monsieur Maxwell,' chirped the head of Modern Languages, a reasonably pleasant woman in a bun, who shared that arrogant trait of language teachers everywhere that only their adopted tongue seemed to count.

'Bonjour, Madame Da Farge.'

The reasonably pleasant woman scowled.

'Got anything on the appalling performance of the Free French on D-Day?' he asked, 'Or how it was that 30,000 Germans could control the whole of France during the war?'

'Er . . . I'm afraid not.'

'Heigh-ho.' Maxwell smiled. 'Not to worry. *Au revoir*, Madame Guillotine,' and he vanished.

Lunchtime comes but once a day and unusually, Maxwell was spending it in the staffroom, that strange cluster of assorted furniture to which hapless teachers retreated as a last resort, rather like the 24th Foot behind their mealie bags at Rorke's Drift. Even more unusually, Deirdre Lessing appeared in her cloud of sulphur smoke to join him.

'Max,' she sat down to his right. 'Oh, my God, what's that?'

'Oh, I do apologize, Senior Mistress,' and he made great play in doing up his flies and pulling his sports jacket across his lap.

'I mean,' Deirdre Lessing had never let a little thing like levity spoil her morning, 'that thing you're eating.'

'Oh, that.' Maxwell studied it too. 'Well, Edna in the kitchen assured me it was a pizza slice, but having sampled it, I prefer to keep an open mind.' He winked leeringly at her. 'Want a bit?'

'Thank you,' she sat back, but upright in the chair. 'I think I'll stick to my yoghurt.'

'Very wise.'

'Max, I've something to ask you.'

'Oh?' A thousand possibilities sprang to Maxwell's ever-fertile mind, but a request to be allowed to commit hara-kiri loomed largest, preferably in the quad with the whole school's company forming hollow square.

'I have to go to a wretched Charts meeting tomorrow afternoon, in London. Could you come with me?'

Maxwell's pizza slice toppled inexorably into his lap. 'Well, I'm flattered of course, Deirdre,' he said, extracting slices of pepperoni from his gonadal regions.

She turned to him with her Gorgon stare. If only he'd brought his polished shield with him that morning. 'Don't be,' she said. 'James insisted.'

'Who?' For the briefest of moments, he was nonplussed. 'Oh, the Headmaster.'

'Why do you call him Legs?' she asked.

Maxwell could blush at will and he did so now. 'Please, Deirdre,' he whispered. 'It's personal.'

The staffroom door burst open and Tom Sugden, the Head of Technology stood there, fuming. 'Bloody Ten C Six,' he snarled at nobody in particular. 'You know, sometimes I think Hitler was right.'

'Only sometimes?' Maxwell was retrieving garlicky crumbs from his corduroy. Deirdre's glance failed to wither him. No sooner had Sugden sulked off to the coffee machine than Camp David arrived. 'Do you know what that new girl in Eight B One asked me a few minutes ago?'

No one in the staffroom did.

'"Are you homosexual?" I ask you!' and he minced to his pigeon hole.

'New girl, Ca . . . er . . . David?' Maxwell had to ask.

'Lucy something,' David growled. 'Stuck up little tart.'

'Absolutely,' nodded Maxwell. 'And no judge of character whatsoever.'

'How do you stand it, Uncle Maxie?' Lucy asked, lobbing dishes into Maxwell's dishwasher.

'What, my darling, the decay of civilization or yet another television mini series starring John Thaw? Although, come to think of it, one is a sign of the other.'

'No,' she said, 'Leighford High.'

'Hey,' he gave her his best Sly Stallone, 'Don't knock it till you've tried it.'

'I have tried it, Uncle Maxie,' she reminded him.

'Oh, yes,' he chuckled. 'Well, then, just thank your lucky stars that dearest Mummy and Daddy are loaded enough to send you elsewhere. And spare a thought, once you're back there, for your dear old uncle. Where's Tiff?'

'On the phone.'

'Oh, my God.' Maxwell paled. 'Not long distance?' And he bounced into the lounge on some pretext. Sure enough, Tiffany was curled up on his settee, winding the phone cord round her fingers as surely as one day she would wind some hapless lad.

'I don't know,' she was saying, 'I shouldn't think so. I'll have to ask. Why?' Her eyes widened and she laughed mischievously. 'Certainly not.' She covered her mouth briefly to giggle, then sat po-faced. 'Out of the question.' She snorted again, then said imperiously, 'Perhaps, but never on a first date,' and put the receiver down.

'Wrong number?' Maxwell asked, pointlessly straightening some books.

'Mark Irwin,' she told him. 'He's asked me out.'

Maxwell had never felt like this before. In one brief sentence he'd changed from Mr Pinko-Liberal to Mr Barrett of Wimpole Street by way of Attila the Hun. 'What?'

'Uncle Maxie,' Tiffany scrabbled up from her seat. 'You really should be careful, you know. You go a really funny colour when you're cross.'

'I'm not cross, dear girl,' he assured her, 'just careful. What, for instance, would your father say?'

Tiffany snorted again. 'He wouldn't even notice.'

'Your mother, then?'

'Mummy?' Tiffany thought about it, running a pensive finger through her golden hair. 'She'd give me a lecture.'

'Good,' Maxwell concurred.

'Then she'd give me a condom.'

'Jesus Christ Almighty.'

'No need to blaspheme, Uncle Maxie,' Lucy called from the kitchen. 'You can get flavoured ones nowadays.'

'Oh, joy,' Maxwell said, horrified to find himself a father again after twenty-five years – and the father of call girls at that. 'Just a minute,' he said to Tiffany, 'I didn't hear the phone go. Who rang who then?'

'I rang him,' she confessed, without a hint of shamefacedness.

'He gave you his number?'

'No. I looked it up in the book. Uncle Maxie, this is 1999. We don't sit around walls fanning ourselves any more in the hope that some bloke will ask us to do the gallop with him.'

'It is about riding, though, isn't it?' Lucy called.

Tiffany raised an eyebrow, followed by a languid middle finger. 'I thought he was rather impressive, Uncle Maxie – for a comprehensive oik, that is. Don't you?'

Maxwell had known a lot of comprehensive oiks in his time. Some he'd welcome like public schoolboys, at dances or shipwrecks. Some he'd trust to cross the road by themselves. There may even have been one or two he'd have trusted with his life. But leave one alone with his niece? Never. He grumbled something impenetrable and trudged upstairs to continue work on the plastic fifty-four millimetre Sergeant Mitchell of the 13th Light Dragoons.

'He's not going to let you go out tonight, you know,' Lucy said as her big sister swanned into the kitchen.

'No problem,' Tiffany said. 'It's tomorrow night he's asked me out. I'll have worked on Uncle Maxie by then.'

Uncle Maxie popped his head around the door. Neither girl had heard him come back down. He beamed at his elder niece.

'Tomorrow night?' he asked. 'Is that when Hell freezes over? Because that's when you can go out with Mark Irwin.'

By the time Chris Logan had watched the hot police video, it was late. He stretched on Maxwell's settee and rummaged for his shoes. The girls had long since shuffled off to bed, Tiffany to dream of her new love and Lucy wondering who she could annoy tomorrow. Metternich the cat was curled on the pouffé, happy at last in the company of men.

'Bloody Hell,' was Logan's informed and inestimably useful comment.

'Now, Chris,' Maxwell said, 'I don't have to tell you again that all this is highly confidential. There is no possibility of a story. I can't compromise my source.'

'You said you had nobody on the inside,' Logan remembered.

'I lied,' Maxwell smiled.

'So why did you show it to me, Max? I mean, I'm delighted you did of course. But I don't see how I can help.'

'I hoped you might know Bartlett.'

'The psychiatrist? No, I don't. Well, I did attend a press conference he gave in London. On the Critchley case.'

'The abattoir killings?'

Logan nodded. 'Very messy. I couldn't face goulash for a while, I can tell you. I was impressed by him.'

'What about this?' Maxwell wanted to know.

'Well . . . yes. I'd say he's got his man.' He caught a look in his old teacher's eye. 'Wouldn't you?'

Maxwell shook his head. 'Was A-level History all in vain, dear boy?' he asked sadly, disappointment furrowing his brow.

'Well, I . . .'

'Hamlyn,' Maxwell made the newsman focus, 'what about his performance?'

'Performance?'

'Yes. Yes, that's the only word for it. He's acting.'

'Acting?'

'If you'd just killed a man, premeditatedly gone out and put a high velocity bullet into him, then walked into a police station to confess, would you be as calm as this guy? Wouldn't you sweat a little? Shake?'

'Ha,' Logan stabbed the air with his finger, 'but I'm not a member of the SAS.'

'And we don't know he is, either,' Maxwell told him.

'Ah.' Logan had found his shoes and was slipping them on. 'Anyway, Max, we didn't see his face. He could have been showing any number of emotions.'

'Body language,' Maxwell said.

'You what?'

'Look at you, for instance.'

Logan did, quickly taking in his jeans, his Top Man jumper, his trainers.

'You're like a bow string,' Maxwell said. 'Taut as a pupil. Why?'

'Er . . . I don't know,' Logan said, but he secretly admitted it was true.

'Because you *are* a pupil,' Maxwell bellowed so that Metternich twitched an ear. What was the old fart going on about? Only he, the great Count, was allowed to leave blood on the mat. 'Oh, I don't mean it in an unkind way, Chris, but it's difficult for you. I told you what defenestration meant, for God's sake. Taught you the joined up writing. Now I'm treating you as an equal. You're sitting in my lounge, drinking my Southern Comfort, calling me Max and you can't quite handle it, can you? Oh, on the surface, you're fine. The firm handshake, the easy smile, the badinage. But deep down, I'll always be "Sir" won't I? Your body's screaming it at me.'

'Oh,' was all Logan could think to say.

'Now Hamlyn is another matter. Every answer he gave, every word he said is just like all the others. His head doesn't move. I've been fast forwarding this and rewinding it over and over since yesterday. Bartlett's bobbing about like a bloody cork on a wine-dark sea. But Hamlyn's like a rock. His shoulders are square, his back's straight, his voice is . . . well, dead in a way.'

'Yes,' Logan nodded, remembering it. 'Yes, you're right, Max.'

'Is he on something, do you think? Heroin? Mescalin? Christ, Chris, I'm out of my depth here. Ecstasy to me is half an hour with Jean Simmons or Doris Day. That's the kind of sad old bastard I am.'

Metternich raised his head to yawn. No surprises there, then.

'Maybe,' Logan nodded. 'Max, forgive me, but this takes a bit of digesting, a bit of thought. I couldn't borrow the tape, I suppose?'

'Sorry, Chris,' Maxwell shook his head. 'It's not me I'm protecting.'

'Say no more,' Logan was on his feet. 'I've been there myself. Look, let me sleep on it, will you? Do a bit of digging – don't worry, I'll be discreet. I'll ring you when I've got something.'

And he made for the door, worrying every step of the way what hidden messages his body was giving.

CHAPTER TEN

Maxwell stared out of the window, rushing along as he was, like troops in a battle. 'So why, Senior Mistress mine, did our great and worthy Headmaster ask me to accompany you on this jolly?'

'It is not a jolly, Max,' she assured him, stirring her Stagecoach coffee with one of those whippy, bendy plastic things which have replaced spoons on all public services. 'We are going to discuss plans for the new theatre.'

'Assuming the bid is successful?'

Yes,' she tutted, 'though I have it on excellent authority that it will be.'

'And my role is?' He bit deep into his Genoa cake. It tasted like a Star Wars figure, all plastic and crunchy.

'Tangential is as kind as I can manage,' she said icily. 'Here.' And she unfolded a sheet of paper on the table between them. 'This,' her gold-ringed fingers stabbed at a series of lines, 'is the proposed theatre. Stage, auditorium, green room, usual offices, box office. This,' she poked about next door, 'is that sink of iniquity, your sixth form block.'

'Good God!'

"Max, you must have seen this before.' Deirdre Lessing was at a loss.

'In point of fact, Senior Mistress, no. Still, it'll be handy to have a public urinal so close to my office.'

'Today is your last chance to object,' she told him. 'That's why I'm taking you along.'

'Oh,' pouted Maxwell, sitting back sulkily and kicking the padded seat opposite, 'and I thought it was just for the ride.'

They rattled north, through Guildford and Woking, past the desolation that was Clapham Junction where a whole new language was sprayed in bold overlapping letters on every flat surface, through the site of Vauxhall Pleasure Gardens, where the first Georgians had been forced to amuse themselves until they invented television and Playstations and theme parks. Then, it was Waterloo where the IRA had brought about the disappearance of rubbish bins and pigeons flitted about in the Victorian rafters, ready to drop on the buggers below.

On the tube escalators Maxwell was careful to keep to the right, although personally he always dressed to the left and had the unenviable experience of being at eye level with Deirdre Lessing's bum. Ferrets fighting in a sack. She nearly died when a huge Rasta with dreadlocks swept by and winked at her.

'We could have taken a cab,' he said.

'Certainly not.' She stood on her dignity on the escalator. 'Men masturbate in taxis.'

'Really?' Maxwell frowned. 'But it's not compulsory, surely?'

They'd built the Garrick Club in 1831 when London streets were thronged with riotous mobs demanding the immediate implementation of the Reform Bill – 'The Bill,' they had shouted, 'the whole Bill and nothing but the Bill.' And now *The Bill* was on telly every week. What had the world come to? The Club stood in King Street, Covent Garden, then, but they'd moved it to Garrick Street by coincidence in 1862 when Lord Palmerston was Prime Minister for the second time and beer was tuppence a pint.

A liveried flunky opened the heavy, black door.

'Mrs Lessing to see Mr Wiseman,' she said.

'And her monkey,' Maxwell peered cheekily around her shoulder.

'Ah yes.' The flunky let them in. 'I'm afraid Mr Wiseman couldn't make it this afternoon. Would you wait here please.'

Maxwell took in the oil portraits of the great and not-so-good in the worlds of the theatre and the law. Edmund Kean was giving them his best Richard III and Henry Irving, at least from his tartan, was rendering the Scottish play. The barrister Marshall Hall, a better actor than either of them, twinkled enigmatically from the spiral sweep of the staircase.

'Mrs Lessing,' a voice boomed from overhead, 'Deirdre.'

A man built like a wardrobe was thundering down the stairs, his dinner jacket stretched to breaking point over his paunch.

'Archie,' Deirdre extended a limp hand, 'how are you?'

'Now that I've seen you again, dear lady, positively effervescent.' And he kissed her hand. 'Who's this?'

'Peter Maxwell, I'd like you to meet Archie Godden. Yes,' her eyes shone and her voice trilled like an excited budgie, '*the* Archie Godden, music critic of the *Observer*.'

'Peter Maxwell,' Maxwell shook the man's chubby hand, '*the* Peter Maxwell, Head of Sixth Form at Leighford High.'

'Ah.' Godden didn't really approve of the man's choice of bow tie. After all, this was the Garrick. 'Do you play an Instrument at all?'

'I fiddle with my hair from time to time,' he beamed. 'Oh, strictly amateur, of course.'

Godden's smile faded and Deirdre fumed. 'Er . . . I'm afraid Harold's been called away,' the Critic said to the Senior Mistress, 'but the rest of us are here. Shall we?' And he led them up the glorious curve of the carpeted stairs into an ante-room. At the door, a white-jacketed waiter hovered like something out of Remains of the Day.

'Tea, Jonathan, please,' Godden said. 'For seven.'

'Yes sir,' and the waiter vanished.

'Everybody,' the Critic clapped his hands as though he were initiating the applause at the Proms. 'I think you all know Deirdre, Deirdre Lessing.'

The group draped around assorted leather furniture nodded and rhubarbed. The men stood up, the token woman stayed where she was.

'This is . . . um . . .'

'Peter Maxwell,' said Maxwell, smiling broadly.

'From the left, you'll know Anthony LeStrange from his television appearances.' Indeed, Maxwell did. He caught the man's hand. LeStrange was a magician of some repute, a rather cadaverous figure with a high forehead and long wavy hair, most of it, apparently, his own.

'Mr LeStrange,' Maxwell nodded.

'Robert Hart, this year's Booker winner.'

Maxwell was less impressed this time. He'd never yet read a Booker book he'd understood, much less liked.

'Mr Hart.'

The man was handsome in a nondescript sort of way, with short dark hair and scholarly glasses that seemed oddly flat, as though he wore them for the air of gravitas they gave him. Not a snappy dresser though.

'Hilary St John, fashion photographer.'

The man made David Bailey look quite dapper. He'd obviously put on a tie to get through the Garrick's front door and his moleskin trousers hung gracelessly from his female hips.

'Mr St John,' Maxwell smiled.

The grip was firmer than Maxwell had expected. Even so, he felt himself mentally undressed by the man. It was an unsettling experience. *Prêt a courir.*

'And last, but by no means least, Amy Weston, probably Britain's greatest poetess.'

The token woman drifted to her feet. Her age was tricky, perhaps forty, perhaps not. She had long sensuous fingers that curled around Maxwell's and eyes a man could drown in 'Mr Maxwell.' She didn't smile.

'Ms Weston.' Neither did he.

There was a warmth about her that held him briefly, but her eyes drifted across to Hart and she let her hand fall.

'Right,' Godden said, 'that's the formalities over. I've ordered some tea and I think I can speak for Harold in terms of theatrical input at this late stage. You understand, Deirdre, that we, at Charts, are not able to make a donation to Leighford High until next month. We've read your bid and I must say we are impressed by it. But of course, there are other worthy causes out there. Eton's asking again and Winchester . . .'

'Eton and Winchester?' Maxwell interrupted. 'Shouldn't they be offering you money?'

There was an uneasy ripple of laughter in the room, all except for Deirdre Lessing whose silent scowl covered the incantations she was muttering against Maxwell.

'Mr Maxwell,' Amy Weston purred. 'Sit here, won't you?' And she slid elegantly sideways to make room for him.

Deirdre unfolded the blueprints on the coffee table and then they all sat, six characters in search of an author, waiting for Godden.

It was in a lull in the briefing, when the little company had fragmented into splinter groups that she asked him.

'Tell me, Mr Maxwell, is there a favourite poet, for you, I mean?'

'Well, you of course, Ms Weston,' he beamed broadly.

'Flatterer!' she laughed so that even more of her teeth came into view. 'I suppose I meant dead ones.'

'Saw the film,' Maxwell murmured. 'Not bad, not bad at all.'

'But seriously . . .'

'Seriously? Rudyard Kipling.'

'Oh dear.'

'Yes,' Maxwell nodded. He'd trodden this road before. 'I know he's terribly un-PC these days, but hey, he'll become fashionable again when the Empire is reinstated.'

She looked at him oddly, as people often did at Mad Max. Then she laughed. 'Well, we all look forward to those days,' she said. 'But I'm talking about Kipling's poetry, not his politics.'

'Ah. Your turn to tell me, Ms Weston, who makes the earth move for you?'

'Among the world of dead poets? Oh, Rupert Brooke, every time. It's raw of course, because he was so young, but it has a magic all its own.'

'Bit of a miserable bugger, wasn't he? Doomed youth, failed love affairs and so on. Still, each to his own, as the French say.'

'What exactly is your role in this?' It was Hilary St John, the photographer, who had asked the question. Maxwell recognized the man's shaggy locks and sinewy forearms from the Sunday tabloids, where the man who made a living behind the camera was singularly often in front of it, usually on the arm of Koo Stark or looking snappier-than-thou outside the little Isle of Wight pad of Julia Margaret Cameron, doyen of early photographers.

'I wish I knew,' Maxwell smiled. 'Devil's Advocate, I suppose. The new theatre is earmarked next to my domain. If anybody's going to cut up rough, it'll be me.'

'What is it that you do?' Hilary St John could have patronized for England.

'Head of Sixth Form,' Maxwell explained. 'I wipe the bums and noses of seventeen and eighteen-year-olds who should know better. Tell me, do you give all your begging letters so much time?'

'We do what we can,' St John said, lolling back in his leather. 'It's rather akin to kissing babies and opening fetes actually. We've all done our fair share of that. Wouldn't you say so, Bob?'

Robert Hart was less worldly than the photographer. He wore a ghastly mustard-coloured jacket of corduroy and one of Frank Bough's old jumpers. He looked tired and was clearly a stranger to razor blades. Perhaps that was what authors were supposed to look like.

'I would,' Hart agreed and sat down alongside Amy Weston, finishing his tea.

'Working on the next blockbuster?' Maxwell asked him.

Hart's face said it all. 'I don't do blockbusters, Mr Maxwell. My art, no less than Amy's and Hilary's, is for its own sake. If I'd wanted to make money, I'd write some unbelievable tosh about serial killers who liked fava beans.'

'Yes,' Maxwell took up the theme. 'What are they, exactly? Sawney Bean I've heard of. Even Sean. Then of course, there's Mr . . .'

Nobody was laughing. Nobody was even smiling. It was like working the Northern clubs.

'I write about things that matter,' Hart told him. 'As does Amy.'

'Ah, the meaning of life, that sort of thing?' Maxwell could play the perfect oaf when it suited him. Working for ever at the chalk face had given him the edge.

'That sort of thing,' Hart nodded, as though it were an over-simplification. 'But then, life is never what it seems, is it?'

St John had wandered away, utterly bored by the whole thing.

'Indeed not.' Maxwell was reminded of Hancock's *Reunion*, where the great East Cheam resident had nothing whatever to say to his old oppos of yesteryear, inseparable chums though they'd once been. Except that Peter Maxwell didn't know these people and he didn't really want to know them. 'Been with Charts long?'

'Four years,' Hart told him.

'Tragic about Larry Warner.'

'Appalling,' Hart nodded. 'Still, if you lead that lifestyle . . .'

'Lifestyle?' Maxwell's ears pricked up.

Hart leaned across Amy's flat chest. 'Well known, I understand, in the gay community.'

'Ah. Yes.' It was Maxwell's turn to nod. 'Shame that in these enlightened times, that should still be a motive for murder.'

'"The love that dare not speak its name",' Amy murmured. 'A shame indeed.'

'Max, you were insufferable,' Deirdre Lessing sat down in a flurry of briefcase and chiffon as the eight thirteen rolled out of the station.

'Really?' Maxwell looked hurt. 'And I thought I was at my cutesiest.'

'Wrong!' She did her Big Ben impression.

'Well, they are a pretty weird bunch, Deirdre,' Maxwell rolled to one side as an enormous woman and her shopping trolley squeezed down the aisle past him. The tannoy announced gobbledegook and the Southern region train jolted forward, ready for its run to the coast.

'I thought you had a Cambridge degree,' Deirdre said.

'So did I,' yawned Maxwell. After all his years at the chalk face, he wasn't so sure.

'Then why are you afraid of intellectuals?'

'I'm not afraid of them, Deirdre,' he said calmly, watching the dying sun gilding the tall buildings over Vauxhall. 'They just get right up my . . . nose, that's all. A day's work would kill them all.'

Now, that's unfair, Max,' Deirdre insisted. 'Archie Godden's reputation is second to none.'

'Everybody's a critic, Deirdre,' Maxwell explained. 'Those who can, do and those who can't whinge about those who can. It's human nature, I suppose, but that pompous bastard gets paid for it.'

'He's also an author and philosopher of some repute.'

That's right,' Maxwell nodded. 'Didn't he come out with the pop-up version of *Mein Kampf* last year?'

'What about Anthony LeStrange?' she ignored him. 'Surely you can't doubt his ability?'

'No, I don't.' Maxwell shook his head, folded his arms and tried to find a comfortable position. 'But it's all so false. All done by mirrors and flashing lights. The whole dream team could be summed up by "Precious R Us".'

'Amy Weston seemed very taken with you,' Deirdre said archly.

'Really?' Maxwell yawned again. 'I didn't notice.'

'Liar,' she said flatly. 'I should warn you, though, Max. They say poetry is only her second love.'

'They do?' His eyes were closing now.

'Her first is men. She chews them up and spits them out.'

'Go on!' Maxwell nudged her in the ribs without opening his eyes, 'I thought that was you.' He raised his eyelids long enough to register the fury in her face. 'What are you reading?' he asked.

She showed him the thriller's cover.

'Oh, that.' He gave her his best Lee Marvin from *Cat Ballou*, but it was all lost on Deirdre Lessing. 'The private eye did it,' he told her. 'The dead girl was his bit on the side. ()ops, blown it for you. Wake me up at Leighford, will you?' And he suddenly turned to her, eyes open. 'And you won't tell anyone, will you, Deirdre?'

'What?' She fell right into it.

'That I'm about to sleep with a strange woman.'

It was already dark by the time Henry Hall got back to the West Meon Incident Room. The skeleton staff that was Ted Horner was sitting in the back area, almost invisible under the paperwork. Hall grunted at him and clicked on the kettle. As he waited, he let his tired eyes wander around the photo-covered walls. Larry Warner looked back at him in a number of guises. Larry Warner at a party, back in '82, a photograph that Mrs Pilgrim had found in a sideboard drawer; Larry Warner in a restaurant with three anonymous men; Larry Warner frozen momentarily in his passport mugshot; and Larry Warner frozen for ever by the bullet that killed him, one eye bright and staring – the other closed and dead. The morgue shots sent the same shiver through Henry Hall that they always did, the tangle of black hair pulled up over the cuts of the saw, the bluish signs of lividity at the corners of the mouth. Like an amateur actor, badly made up for Halloween.

His eyes passed to the frantic enjoyment of Magicworld and the polystyrene rocks and plastic reeds of the Wild Water. There were drawings of the yellow car and of Larry Warner's body lying in it in the position it was found, slumped forward and to the left. Alongside, the names of those who had known Larry Warner – his housekeeper, his secretary, the long, long list of his clients. And a string of anonymous young men, some with only Christian names or nicknames, others so blank that the CID had given them numbers. And the names of those near Warner when he died. And the one that burned into his brain at the end of another long day. The name he knew – Peter Maxwell.

The click of the kettle brought him back to the here, the now.

'Cup of coffee, Ted?' he called to the man in the back.

'No thanks, guv,' Horner said. 'It's coming out my bloody ears as it is.'

'Ah, Richard,' Hall had heard the door open. 'Coffee?'

'Black, Henry.' Dr Richard Bartlett looked different with his heavy-framed glasses off. Balder than Larry Warner, the two men might have passed for brothers in the watery neon-paleness of the Incident Room night. 'Are we going through?' He slipped his glasses on again.

'Have a seat,' Hall said, 'I'll be right with you.'

Bartlett sat himself down opposite Hall's desk in the make-shift space he'd turned into an office. From here, a computer linkup tied him with Leighford nick, HQ at Winchester and the Yard facilities called, rather optimistically, Holmes. There were filing cabinets everywhere, crates of bumf, VDU screens still flickering late into the night.

He took the coffee gratefully. 'Right,' he said. 'Schizophrenia.'

'That's it?' Hall sat down.

'In a nutshell.' Bartlett took off his glasses and began cleaning them. 'I won't bore you with the minutiae. It'll all be in my report and of course, I'm there for expert testimony in court if you need me.'

'So Neil Hamlyn, Corporal, SAS is two people.'

Bartlett smiled with the condescension only found in the medical profession. 'Multiple personality is not so easily explained,' he said. 'There's good and evil, if you like, in all of us.'

'Is he kosher?' Hall asked, leaning back and slurping on his still-too-hot coffee.

'Do you mean did he do it or is he really an SAS sniper?'

'Either,' Hall shrugged.

'As I told you, Henry,' Bartlett said, 'I'd already made up my mind yesterday. Today just confirmed it. As you know, I wasn't going to interview him again, but professionalism got the better of me – you know how it is.'

Hall did.

'The SAS are trained to infiltrate,' Bartlett went on. 'Work close to the ground. That's what Hamlyn's good at. That's what he knows. In Desert Storm, they went into enemy territory, deep and dirty. That's what he did at Magicworld. He'd have been in disguise. You've checked his flat?'

Hall nodded.

'Let's see,' Bartlett conjectured, 'you found a T-shirt, baseball cap, jeans?'

'I could find those in any flat,' Hall played Devil's Advocate yet again.

'Yes, but did you find them in Hamlyn's?'

'We did,' Hall had to concede.

'And something else,' Bartlett went on. 'A coat of some kind?'

Hall didn't know what to make of forensic psychologists. They were either brilliant and indispensable people, who pushed the barriers of crime-solving science further than anyone had a right to hope, or they were bullshitters of the worst water.

'Possibly,' he nodded.

'One he'd have worn on the way to the hit. Let's say he had it on as he went into the park. Once he'd made the hit, he'd take it off, stuff it in the hold-all and probably the cap too. Now, he's a different man.'

'A second personality?'

Bartlett chuckled and sipped his coffee. 'No, no, you're not following this at all, Henry. The Neil Hamlyn who went into the park and the one who came out one bullet lighter are the same one – a single, psychotic individual. The other one, the Neil Hamlyn who walked into your police station the other day and scared the shite out of Sergeant Merrill, well, he's somebody else entirely.'

Hall was still not convinced.

'Hence the blankness,' Bartlett said, leaning forward, enthusing. He'd spent his professional life so far winning over sceptical juries in court; a Detective Chief Inspector couldn't be much more difficult. 'He can't really understand what's happening to him, why he's done what he's done. But he knows he's done it and he knows it's wrong.'

'So he's fit to stand his trial?' Hall used the old legal jargon.

'Fit to plead?' Bartlett leaned back, sipping coffee again. 'I don't know yet. I'll need more time on that. Want to see the second video?'

'Not just now.' Hall was tired. He slipped his rimless glasses above his hairline and rubbed his eyes.

'What did you get today?' Bartlett asked him.

'Neil Hamlyn is on the DSS. If he ever was in the SAS, he's not now. And that's a whole different set of initials. Or if he is – and the army still won't tell us – it's the most complex DSS fraud case I've ever come across. He's showed up regularly for his giro and job seeker every week for nearly two years.'

'He gets a giro and he owns a Ruger Mini fourteen?' Bartlett was incredulous.

'The Queen Mum owns six houses and she can't make ends meet.' It was an unusually flippant remark from a man who played things by the book. 'It's just possible he has some political affiliations. National Front, British National Party sort of stuff – we're still working on that. The odd thing is his flat. Can you have a look at that for me?'

'Sure,' Bartlett said. 'Care to give me a clue as to what I might find?'

'Neatness,' was Hall's verdict. 'Fastidious neatness. There was only one gun listed in his paperwork, which is filed better than anything I've ever seen in any nick anywhere. It was kept under the relevant lock and double key.'

"But I thought weapons like that were banned?'

'Oh, they are,' Hall said. 'And perhaps that's where Mr Hamlyn's split mind comes in. It's as if he's following orders, by the book correctness. But they're somebody else's orders and they're obsolete.'

'That's the army for you,' nodded Bartlett. 'What did the pathology throw up?'

'No drugs,' Hall threw his hands in the air. 'I'd have put money on it. The slow blinks, the deliberation with his answers. But no. All the blood tests are clear. There's no sign that Corporal Hamlyn has ever taken so much as a glass of Coca-Cola.'

'Henry,' Bartlett leaned forward again, finishing his coffee. 'You've got your man. Trust me on this. I've been doing the job a long time.'

Hall let his man get up and watched him go.

'Motive,' he called after him. 'What about a motive, Richard?'

Peter Maxwell lost his balance as he got home. That was because his door was unlocked and slightly ajar and it opened under his weight. He flicked on the hall light. All was quiet. The girls were still at Sylvia's where he'd left them at the end of the school day, but on a whim, he'd gone home first, straight from Leighford station.

Refusing to be browbeaten, Deirdre Lessing had persevered with her thriller, only to find that Maxwell had been right – how that concept stuck in her throat. It was the private eye and the dead girl was his bit on the side.

'Thank you so much,' she hissed at him as they went their different ways in the car park.

'My every waking moment is filled serving you, dear lady,' he said, raising his hat. Then he pedalled like the furies into the darkness.

Why he'd turned left instead of right he never knew – away from the sweep of the coast and the coastwise lights, the ancient dynamo on White Surrey flaring as he crested the hill. He should have gone to Sylv's; she'd had the girls for six hours now, but he'd gone home instead, to Columbine.

Now Peter Maxwell had been burgled before. And Henry Hall had been in on that. The DCI had told him that burglars were usually kids who peed in vases and goldfish bowls and daubed shit over the walls. He took the stairs three at a time. Nothing. No furniture overturned as he switched on the light, no excrement dripping from the lampshades. His heart stopped. *The Light Brigade.* The building shook as he dashed up from the lounge to the bedroom and the bedroom to the attic. No sooner had he pulled the light cord than he started breathing again. All was well. His books, his photographs of the Granta days and above all, his beloved, half-finished Light Brigade, Lord Cardigan waiting impatiently at their head – they were all there. Even Sergeant Albert Mitchell lay at a rakish angle, his left leg in the air, his horse unsaddled on Maxwell's modelling table. 'And when,' the plastic soldier seemed to say, 'are you going to finish me?'

Maxwell went downstairs again. His bedroom was fine. No more of a tip than when he'd left it. The girls' room. He ran there, batting aside the door. The beds were okay, the window latch undisturbed. He checked the dressing table, the wardrobe, all their clothes seemed to be there and intact. Outside on the landing, he checked the linen basket, that pervert's paradise. Only his own Y-fronts looked up at him, accusingly, the pair he'd left there in an otherwise empty basket that morning.

It took him a while. The kitchen had not been touched – toaster, wine rack, tins of soup – all pristine and undisturbed. He heard the cat flap go downstairs and the black and white bastard galloped into view.

'Who was it, Count?' Maxwell asked, 'and what did they want?'

Metternich scented the air.

'Do you smell strangers, *mon vieux*? he asked him, 'of the criminal persuasion? Oh, Jesus.'

He might not know who had so carefully wandered through his house, but now he knew what they had taken. The coffee table in front of him was empty. That morning, on its corner, he'd left Jacquie's police video, the one of Hamlyn's interview with the police psychiatrist. The video that could lose her her job.

'Shit a brick!' He threw a cushion across the room and it landed near the phone, flashing to tell him there was a message. He pressed buttons, throwing off his hat and jacket.

'Max.' He heard a geekish voice. 'It's Chris. Chris Logan. Look, I think I'm on to something. I'm in London at the moment. It began as a long shot, but there's been developments. I'll call you tomorrow, after school. Bye.' And a double beep told him there were no more messages.

He picked up the phone, panic rising like a tide, stabbing the numbers furiously. 'Sylv? It's me. Look, I hate to ask you this, but something's come up. Keep the girls tonight, will you? And bring them to school in the morning. I'll explain all then.'

CHAPTER ELEVEN

There probably wasn't a day when Sylvia Matthews was truly alone. An endless stream of malingerers drifted down her corridor – and left again just as smartly. But she was Auntie to them all, the waifs and strays, the abused, Those Who Cannot Cope. She had sticking plaster and crepe bandages for the luckless in the gym or the just plain cack. She had advice to the lovelorn – especially to them – and cups of tea or coffee and morning after pills. Monday was a madhouse after a weekend of frayed tempers, late night bar extensions and unbridled passion in the shelters along the Front.

She'd just chalked up her bi-annual sighting of James Diamond on her school calendar – the man was obviously lost – when a face she knew appeared around the door.

'Sylv, are we alone?'

She looked at Maxwell and raised her eyebrows, then tapped on a side door and hauled out a particularly repellent member of Year 10.

'Come on, Mandy. See me at the end of the day if you have to. Maths now, isn't it?'

'I can't do it,' Mandy was a prey to her sinuses, a lump of a girl blessed by nature with acoustic catarrh.

'Neither can I,' Maxwell smiled at her, 'and total ineptitude with figures has got me where I am today – like the Flying Dutchman, doomed to wander the corridors of Leighford High for ever.'

Mandy looked at him. What was the mad old git going on about now?

'So,' Maxwell registered the look of utter bewilderment on the girl's face, 'if you don't do well in Maths, then you'll be here for ever. And you won't do well in Maths unless you get to the odd lesson now and again. By the way,' he stopped her in the doorway, 'has Mrs Wilkins seen you about that nose jewellery yet?'

'Yeah, she . . .'

But Maxwell couldn't wait for an answer. The girl could malinger for England. 'Later, Mandy,' he said and closed Sylvia's door.

'I was worried, Max,' the School Nurse said. 'I waited for you to ring back. What's all the mystery?'

Maxwell threw himself down on the plastic couch, and rested his head on his hands. 'Well, when I was six I used to wear my sister's dresses . . .'

'Max!' she growled, knocking his legs so that he swung back into a sitting position.

'Sorry, Sylv,' he said. 'I was burgled last night.'

'What? What did they take?'

'Nothing.'

'Nothing?' Now Sylvia Matthews had been around kids all her life too. She knew porkies when she heard them – even from a consummate porker like Mad Max.

'All right, an item I was looking after. For somebody else.'

She pulled a face. 'You can be a cryptic bastard, Peter Maxwell.' She shook her head.

'Thank you, Matron,' he said, bowing. 'You're most kind. The point is, Sylv, the game's changed.'

'What game?' Life was one long game to Peter Maxwell.

'The Larry Warner game,' he murmured. 'Do not collect £200, go to jail if you did it. Or, if I'm not mixing my metaphors, Corporal Mustard with the high-powered rifle in the park.'

'You've lost me, Max.' Sylvia's phone was ringing.

'If somebody can get into my house like you and I get into a paper bag, then the girls aren't safe, Sylv. Can they stay with you?'

'Nurse.' She'd already picked up the phone. 'Yes. Yes. All right. Give me a second.' She looked at the man she loved, sitting on her plastic couch, swinging his legs a little off the floor. 'Dan Roberts's ankle has gone again. I told him to keep it strapped up. You're not really worried, are you, Max? About the girls, I mean.'

'What was that god-awful Anthony Newley song in the seventies? Or was it Val Doonican?'

'Before my time,' she said, unfolding the school wheelchair from her walk-in cupboard.

'"When you're the father of boys you worry",' Maxwell was quoting, '"But when you're the father of girls, you do more than that, you pray." Just now,' he looked at her with those huge brown eyes, 'I'm the father of girls.'

'What will you tell them?' she asked as he held the door open for her. 'Why I'm having them, I mean.'

'That your lasagne is to die for,' he said. And the phrase left an oddly nasty taste in his mouth.

He waited as long as he could. All through break while young Paul Moss, the Head of History, was waxing eloquent over Saving Private Ryan, all through Lesson Three when Year 12 were delivering their halting, woeful seminar papers on the Enlightenment, all through Lesson Four when Maxwell was balancing on his chair, itself perched on his desk, charging with Seven A One as he and Prince Rupert's Bravoes of Alsatia drove Henry Ireton's Horse from the field. Then, when Ten Bee Two were silent, trying to make head or tail of Elizabeth's religious settlement as part of their In-Depth Study, he snuck out of H4 and slipped next door where the History Department kept Mr Bell's extraordinary invention.

'Jacquie?' he whirled away from the window where he'd just spotted that idle oaf Bennington sloping off early again, nipping past the Biology labs where he thought he couldn't be seen and out behind the oaks that fronted the staff car park. That would mean public castration for young Bennington in tomorrow's assembly – Maxwell's standard punishment for a second offence.

'Who's this?' Jacquie Carpenter didn't really want the answer. She was up to her ears in depositions and she'd had no lunch.

'Me,' he said, 'Maxwell.'

'Yes,' her voice was just as frosty now she knew. That was because she was staring across the West Meon Incident Room at Frank Bartholomew. Then his phone rang and she could turn her back. 'Max, you mustn't ring me here.'

'I know.' He was as sotto voce as she was, although only several past papers and a couple of hundred exercise books could have eavesdropped on him. 'I'm sorry, but I've got no choice. You didn't call at my place, did you? Get the video back?'

'What?'

'I thought not. Well, it's gone.'

'Jesus,' he heard her hiss, then louder. 'Are you reporting this, sir? I could send someone along.'

'Other than a busted lock, there's no damage. Nothing else has gone.'

'Where did you leave it?' She was whispering again, cupping the receiver with her hand. People seemed to be around her, here, there, everywhere, chattering, joking, putting the final screws in the coffin of the man who said he had killed Larry Warner.

'Out,' Maxwell said. 'On the coffee table.'

'In clear view?'

'Yes.'

'Well, if you aren't prepared to make a formal complaint, sir, I'm afraid there's nothing I can do.' And the line went dead.

Maxwell sighed. The brush-off, the cold shoulder. Jacquie knew the call would be logged – where it came from and when, who took it. That was a bridge she'd cross if she had to. Shit! She was chewing her finger nails again. Who knew? She looked at her oppos, blokes in shirt sleeves and hanging ties, girls in starched white shirts and unflattering flat shoes. Had any one of them noticed her slip into the video room at the nick? Seen her lift the interview tape out of the machine and back again two hours later? She didn't know them all. Men and women who were routinely drafted in from elsewhere at the start of a murder inquiry. It would only take one to be ultra-observant, nosy, up for promotion. And then it would be the Complaints Authority and investigation by another force. Suspension – with full pay of course. And the sniggering behind her back and the lack of trust. She slammed shut the open file and marched off to the loo. Just for a bit of peace. A bit of space.

Maxwell hit H4 like a Scud missile. 'If I have to leave the room for any reason,' he bellowed till the windows rattled, 'I do not expect to hear any noise at all when I come back. You people shouldn't even know I've gone. In there,' he tapped the cranium of the nearest hapless child, 'it should be 1559.' He sat down heavily at his desk. 'And I'm here to see that it is.'

Silence, along with Elizabeth I, reigned.

He saw them in his office as the battle-smoke of the day cleared and eleven hundred school-weary kids began the long trudge home. It was like the children of Israel on the march, going to the promised land of microwaved dinners and *Home and Away*. A few of them, those Year 11 students who had no intention of coming in to sit an exam, no one would ever see again. They'd slope off, smoking, swearing, 'forgetting' to return books and costing the school a fortune in wasted exam entry fees. Come the lazy, hazy, crazy days of summer, they'd start breeding another generation who would behave in exactly the same way sixteen years from now. Heigh-ho.

They didn't mind, Tiffany and Lucy. In fact, they were secretly very pleased. Sylvia Matthews was a laugh. And a good cook. And Tiffany of course had her own agenda, anyway. That agenda had swept past her in the corridor and had brought his sandwiches to eat alongside her in the dining hall; Mark Irwin, God's gift to women, a light in Tiffany's darkness.

'See you tomorrow, darlings.' And Maxwell cuddled them both before Mrs B. swept in, all fag ash and industrial strength stair cleaner.

'I just seen that Whatsisface Bennington down the town.' When it came to reporting skiving children, Mrs B. could shop till she dropped.

'Yes, he's on my list for tomorrow,' Maxwell told her, holding an exercise book at eye level and closing one eye to see if Susan Darby was purloining the History Department's stationery yet again by teasing pages from the middle to use to pass notes to her mates as to who said what to who and why.

'Ooh, before I forget,' she rummaged in the pocket of her County contract cleaners' overall, 'there's a message for you.' And she handed him a memo, plugged in her vacuum cleaner in his office and disappeared.

Maxwell reached for his phone. 'Thingee?' It was the closest he could get to the name of the girl who manned the switchboard. 'There was a message for me, from Chris Logan. Timed at 2.38.'

'That's right.'

'Well, why didn't you call me?'

'You were teaching, Mr Maxwell,' Thingee explained. 'I didn't like to interrupt.'

'Thingee,' Maxwell leaned back in his chair, as though explaining matters to a piece of chalk, 'I've told you – teaching is something I do in my spare time. I never let it interfere with my social life. What did Chris want?'

'He said you'd never believe it. That he was right and he'd be round tonight. About seven.'

'That was it?'

'Yes. I wrote it down.'

'Good girl,' Maxwell blew her a kiss over the phone. 'Getting better all the time.'

But Chris Logan didn't call at seven. He didn't call at all. Maxwell hadn't got his home number, but there was only one 'C. Logan' in the Leighford book and someone with Maxwell's research skills took such things in his stride. It was an answerphone, cleverly impersonating the reporter's voice.

'You've reached Chris Logan. I can't come to the phone right now. Please leave a message after the tone and I'll get back.'

'Get back, Logo,' Maxwell found himself muttering, in a vague memory of a Beatles' number, but he hung up as the thing bleeped at him and he reached for his cycle clips.

'Mountains, Count,' he swept past the dozing cat, 'and Mohammed. I'll explain that to you sometime. Stay well.'

He pedalled out past the flyover and skirted the Dam, that rolling open parkland where lovers wandered in the sun's embers and the professional vandals of Year 8 planned their night's escapades which always seemed to involve setting fire to yards of loo roll and writing 'Mr Ryan is a Wanker' somewhere prominent in permanent ink. White Surrey flashed pure silver as he crested Lantern Hill and joined, briefly, the steady traffic flow of the B2132 before swinging east towards Oakdene and the sea. Number 56 looked just like all the other houses in the street, opulent semis of a bygone age, when middle-class families could afford a live-in maid who may or may not have been given one by the master of the house. So 56 had a basement and an attic, but like so many of them, 56 was subdivided now into flats. All that remained of its former glory was the old brass bell-pull and the rusted housings of the long-gone shutters.

Chris Logan's name was printed above the ground floor bell, but there were no lights blazing, so near, as it was, to dark. Maxwell rang and waited. Nothing. He took the little concrete path past the side of the house, edging his way round the dustbins and a pile of building debris. There was another door here, leading to a porch and a second bell. He tried that too and there was no reply.

Most men would have got the message about then, cut their losses and gone to the pub. But he was not most men. He was Mad Max and there was something about Chris Logan and his messages that didn't feel right. He leaned on the porch door and it opened, creaking against his weight. There was a pair of green wellies standing sentinel by the back door proper and a folded umbrella. Maxwell glanced back down the long narrow strip of garden where a rotary washing line twirled slowly in the rising breeze, trailing a solitary white T-shirt. From somewhere a dog barked in the distance and a car pulled away – the sounds of suburbia on a summer's night.

Then his skin crawled and he felt suddenly cold. He reached to his right and his fingers curled around the umbrella. Not exactly a three-bar hilt, 1821 pattern cavalry sword, officers, for the use of, but it might give him a two and a half foot advantage in a crisis. The crisis yawned before him in the shape of an open door. The tell-tale marks on the frame said it all. He knew because his door looked the same. Someone had broken into Chris Logan's flat exactly as they had broken into his. He pushed the door open with the umbrella tip and let his eyes get accustomed to the dark. A passageway stretched ahead of him, with rooms off and open doors. The locked front door faced him, its fanlight letting in the amber glow from the street. From a side door came a faint glow, like the sort Mulder and Scully were constantly running into in their search for the truth, which was out there.

That was the room he took first. It was a study of sorts, with a desk and a computer, leads and wires like spaghetti over the carpet. The glow came from a fish tank in the corner, whose electrically-bright denizens of the deep darted here and there in their own watery world. Logan's answerphone was switched on and flashing red alongside the computer. Maxwell could just make out the buttons and played the tape.

'Chris, you old bastard,' a young male voice said. 'Where the fuck are you? Pick up, you turd. You owe me lunch.'

An older, gravel voice came next. 'Chris, where are you? The *Advertiser* might be small potatoes to you, but it's bread and butter to some of us. I allowed a day in London, but you're pushing it a bit, old son.'

Then the line went dead. And as it did, there was a thud from the front door, a series of sharp knocks.

'Who's there?' Maxwell heard a male voice through the letter-box. 'Come on, I know you're in there.'

He flattened himself against the wall, then ducked out of the lit room into the darkness. The beam of a torch through the letterbox was spraying light in erratic spears down the passageway. He heard muttered conversation outside and the rattling of keys in locks. The front door crashed back on its hinges and the lights came on.

Maxwell knew when his number had come up and sauntered around the corner, smiling broadly at the uniformed officer and the other bloke who stood there, filling the entranceway.

'So that's where the lights are,' he said.

'That's him,' the civilian was an overweight, pasty faced slob of a man. 'His bike's outside. Watch it, he's got an umbrella.'

'Could you put that down, please, sir?' the constable asked.

'Certainly,' Maxwell said. 'It's not loaded.'

'We've had reports of a break-in,' the constable told him.

'When?' Maxwell asked.

'Just now,' the constable said.

'Ah, well, that's interesting,' Maxwell leaned against the wall. 'You see, the break-in happened some time ago, I would say. Hours, days – I'm not sure. The back door was open.'

'Could I have your name, sir?' The constable still had not moved.

'Peter Maxwell,' Maxwell confessed. '38, Columbine Avenue. I'm one of those countless, faceless, honest citizens of this country who pay your, if I may say so, rather over-the-top salary.'

Maxwell regretted it as soon as it left his lips. It was textbook anti-police aggression, second only to 'Why aren't you out there catching real criminals?' But the deed was done.

'We've seen you before, haven't we?' The constable's face was set in stone. It seemed to be a night for swapping clichés.

'Possibly,' Maxwell said. 'I shop in Asda, except on payday when I run amok in Marks and Sparks. My route to and from work is within a mile of your establishment at Leighford Nick – and I'm available for bar mitzvahs and Police Revues.'

The constable was already talking into the gadget fitted to his shoulder, as Long John Silver might have chatted to his parrot. In this case, though, the parrot squawked back. 'I've got a car on the way, Mr Maxwell,' the constable said. 'Perhaps we can all sit down and you can tell us what you're doing here.'

The lights were burning long into the night at Leighford Police Station. Peter Maxwell was sitting in Interview Room Number One opposite a less-than-amused Frank Bartholomew.

'So,' the sergeant had finished wading through Maxwell's statement. 'Would you like to elaborate on this load of bollocks?'

'Ah,' Maxwell smiled, 'how wondrous the English language sounds when it drips from lips such as yours.'

'Cut the bullshit, Maxwell,' Bartholomew snarled. 'There's no fucking tape running now.'

'Hmm,' Maxwell recognized the moment. 'Rubber truncheon time.'

'You went to Logan's because . . .'

'He's an old boy of Leighford High. I like to keep in touch with my old charges.'

'We're talking about new charges on this one, sunshine.'

'Sergeant,' Maxwell leaned forward, 'I am at liberty to enter the house of a friend to ascertain whether he is in or not.'

'By the back door?'

'By the skylight if I so wish.'

'That's what we in the crime business call "breaking and entering",' Bartholomew faced his man. He should have known better.

'Yes, but the whole issue rests on the "breaking", doesn't it? As it says in my statement, the door was open. All I did was walk in.'

'I've got blokes going over the flat with a fine-tooth comb. If your dabs come up . . .'

'My dabs will be on Chris's answerphone button and perhaps the knob of the porch door. That's all. Oh – and the umbrella.'

'You listened to his answerphone?' Bartholomew's eyes narrowed. 'Why?'

'I want to find out where he is. I need to talk to him.'

'Why?' Persistent was Mr Bartholomew.

'Auld Lang Syne,' Maxwell often took refuge in Gaelic.

'You what?'

'Chris and I were arranging a reunion, kids of his generation. Class of '87 if I remember rightly. The *Herald of Free Enterprise* went down. Danny Kaye and Fred Astaire went to that Great Stars Retirement Home in the sky – oh, and a madman called Michael Ryan went walkabout in Hungerford.'

Bartholomew leaned back in his chair. 'Now why should you mention that?'

Maxwell shrugged. 'It happened in '87,' he said. 'And since my trip to Magicworld, shooting has loomed rather large for me.'

'And what's Christopher Logan got to do with all this?'

'All this?' Maxwell smiled at the Grand Inquisitor. 'Absolutely nothing. Am I free to go?'

Bartholomew leaned towards him. 'Then there's Mrs Pilgrim,' he said.

'Ah.'

'A man answering your description visited Mrs Pilgrim a week ago. The man with him could have been Logan.'

'Really?'

'It's a simple matter,' Bartholomew said. 'An ID parade. You in a line-up of other sad bastards. See if Mrs Pilgrim picks you out.'

'She might,' Maxwell nodded. 'But you know better than I, Sergeant, how notoriously bad eyewitnesses are. Do you know how many different descriptions we have of the man who was Jack the Ripper, for instance? Then there's the Hanratty case . . .'

'Look, you!' Bartholomew growled, his nose inches from Maxwell's. 'I'm not a helluvalot impressed by smartarses like you. From where I'm sitting, you're in deep shit, obstructing police in the pursuance of their inquiries . . .'

'Obstructing?' Maxwell interrupted. Then he smiled, relaxed and sat back. 'Sherlock Holmes never had this trouble.'

Frank Bartholomew would have liked to have thrown the book at Maxwell, followed by the chair, then the table. As it was, for the moment, his hands were tied. He kept him there as long as he could, waiting, wandering the Interview Room Number One. Then he had to let him go, to wreak whatever mischief the old bastard would. Frank Bartholomew knew how to wait.

Chapter Twelve

'So, the bottom line is, you don't know where he is?'

'Am I my reporter's keeper?' Maxwell recognized the voice from Logan's answerphone.

There was no real answer to that. Was the editor of a provincial newspaper in any sense responsible for what his staff did on their days off?

'But it wasn't a bloody day off, was it?' the editor had said. 'Chris Logan is on the company payroll, using company time and company funds. When you find him, tell him his days are numbered and I want to see him, on my carpet, forthwith.'

The editor wasn't built for the job any more. Too much of the sedentary lifestyle, too many convivial bevvies over lunch, too much linguini. His hair, along with his ace reporter apparently, had deserted him, and so had his sense of humour.

Maxwell felt the wind rush by him as the editor slammed out of the outer office into the bowels of the *Advertiser* where mysterious people did . . . no outsider quite knew what. The Head of Sixth Form just knew the man had on his desk the legend 'You don't have to be a surly bastard to work here and it doesn't help.'

'A martyr to his blood pressure, I would think, your editor,' Maxwell winked at the young hopeful hovering nervously by the aspidistra.

'Oh, he's not so bad. It's just as the deadline looms, he gets a bit tetchy. We all do. I'm Keith, by the way. Keith Kershaw.' He extended a furtive hand.

'Keith,' Maxwell took it, despising the way that media people have of instant chumminess.

'It's Peter, isn't it?'

'No,' said Maxwell and made for the door.

'Um,' Kershaw's whine slowed him momentarily, 'Can you tell me what Chris is up to, Mr Maxwell?'

'About five foot nine,' Maxwell smiled. 'Why do you ask?'

The grin had long ago frozen on the lad's face. He wasn't cut out for this game and he knew it. Chrysanthemum shows were okay, but the local magistrates filled him with terror and he couldn't look a councillor in the eye. 'Oh, it's just that Chris and I . . . well, we're a sort of team, you know, working together . . .'

A strange glint appeared in Maxwell's eye and he re- crossed the office floor. 'So you know where he is, then?'

'I know where he went, yes. An address in Bloomsbury. But . . . um . . . he didn't actually say what he was working on.'

Maxwell frowned, peering closely at the boy. 'I'm sorry, Keith,' he said. 'Did you think his going to London had anything to do with me?'

'Well,' Maxwell watched the lad's neck mottle crimson in the midday sun, 'I naturally assumed . . .'

'Never assume.' Maxwell shook his head, quoting a piece of Managerspeak he'd heard on a course once, just before he fell into a coma through boredom. 'It makes an ass out of you and me. No, I was helping Chris organize a school reunion. Nice to catch up on old boys and girls – who's screwing who, who's doing time, that sort of thing, you know.'

'Oh.' Kershaw looked a little crestfallen.

'Did Chris say why he was going to Bloomsbury?' he asked.

'No, not exactly,' Kershaw said. 'But he did mention you.'

'Really?' Maxwell smiled. 'How flattering. In what context, exactly?'

'Said he'd found something out.'

'Wait a minute!' Maxwell suddenly shouted so that the cub reporter leapt a mile. 'Gray Tollefer!'

'Beg your pardon?'

'Gray Tollefer,' Maxwell sat down with the shock of it all. 'Oh, not his real name of course. I'm afraid I can't tell you his real name.

Suffice it to say that Gray had the kindness to mention at the last
Baftas that he owed it all to me.'

'He did?' Kershaw asked.

'Nice, wasn't it?' Maxwell was hugging himself. 'I knew he was in
London, when he's not in Hollywood, of course.'

'Hollywood?'

Maxwell looked up at the man. 'Yes, you know, Tinseltown. The
film Mecca of the World. They've got studios and actors and things.'

'This Gray Tollefer . . .' Kershaw was desperately trying to sal-
vage some sense from the conversation.

Maxwell leaned towards him. 'Saving Private Ryan,' he hissed.

'Spielberg's film?' Kershaw asked.

Maxwell tutted, shaking his head. 'He's just the front man.
Tollefer made it.'

'No!'

'Yup! The English Patient?'

'Anthony Minghella?'

'Nope.' Maxwell shook his head. 'Gray Tollefer.'

'Why . . . ?'

'The man's a recluse. Makes Stanley Kubrick look like Mr
Goodbar. He was always like that. God, I've lost track of the number
of times I've fished that lad out of the History store cupboard.
Couldn't stand people, you see. Why he's become one of the world's
foremost film directors, I just don't know.'

'So Chris . . .'

'Was at school with him, yes. Right here in Leighford. Er . . .
you're not from Leighford, are you?' Maxwell suddenly checked.

'No. Devizes.'

'Bad luck. Chris must have found Gray's London address – the
one in Bloomsbury. Got it to hand?'

'Well, as a matter of fact . . .'

'Can I have it?'

'Well, I thought perhaps I . . . I mean, if I can get an exclusive . . .'

Maxwell roared with laughter. 'My dear boy, Gray Tollefer doesn't
give interviews. I believe he did talk once – to David Frost – but

insisted on seeing the thing first and then stopped the Beeb from broadcasting. That's how he is, I'm afraid. Still, I flatter myself, as his old master, I may be in with a slight chance.'

'Oh, yes. Yes, of course.'

'So, the address?' It was like drawing teeth.

'Ah, yes. Here.' He produced a notepad from his jacket pocket and Maxwell memorized the page.

'Gordon Square. Excellent. Thank you, Keith.' He got up and shook the boy's hand. 'Remind me to have a word with your editor about you. I think you've got a future.' He leaned towards the lad. 'One helluva future.'

'Oh, thank you, Mr Maxwell,' Kershaw beamed.

'Oh, no, dear boy. Thank you.' And he saw himself out.

Maxwell's answerphone was about to click in when he picked up, disentangling himself from the cord and the pile of tatty exercise books he'd just dropped all over the floor.

There. Metternich caught the moment. He'd done it again. Every time that damned ringing sounded, the silly old duffer picked up that plastic thing. There were scarier times though. Sometimes, when Maxwell wasn't there, that ringing sounded and people would start talking to him as if he was. Weird people, humans.

'Darling!' Maxwell recognized the dulcet tones from far Beirut. 'How the devil are you?'

'All is well, Max,' he heard his sister say. 'I'd hoped to catch you before we go up country tomorrow.'

'Up country?' Maxwell repeated. 'What's this, the Mem off to the Hill station for a spot of tiffin?'

'Don't be absurd, Max dear,' Sandie scolded him. 'It'll just be a day or two longer than I originally thought. Can you cope, dear boy?'

Maxwell smiled. He'd been to a good school. 'Does the Pope shit in the woods?' he asked, by way of an answer.

'I sincerely hope not,' Sandie shuddered. 'I'm sure there's an encyclical against it. Put the girls on, will you?'

'Ah, snagette there, soul sister.'

'Oh?'

'Slight crisis on the domestic front. I've palmed the girls till on a good friend.'

'What?'

'Trained nurse, divorcee, salt of the earth. No worries there,' Maxwell assured her.

'Is this one of your women?' Sandie wanted to know.

'How dare you!' Maxwell growled. 'If you must know, my cooker is on the blink. Can't function too well. Sylvia was the answer to a History teacher's prayer. She took the girls in like a shot. I can give you her number.'

'Later, Max,' she said. 'Give them my best. I'll have to go. Kenneth's . . . oh, all right. Just how many hands do you think I've got? Bye.' And with one click, she was gone.

Maxwell caught sight of the single bright eye looking at him. 'Well, what was I supposed to do, for God's sake? Tell the woman her daughters had witnessed a murder and the house where they are staying has been broken into? And her two thousand miles away? Right!'

He ferreted about for a change of clothes. 'If anyone calls, Count,' he was wrestling with a sock, 'just tell them I've gone north – tired of Southern Comfort. Well, actually,' he collapsed on the settee trying to get his shoe on, 'that's a lie. I'll be in London. Gordon Square. And if a man's tired of Southern Comfort, he's tired of life. Don't wait up.'

The philosopher Jeremy Bentham, he who had invented the felicific calculus as a sort of clapometer to measure people's happiness, had built the godless institution in Gower Street. He is there to this day, stuffed, as most philosophers have been, sitting in a glass case at the end of the main corridor. His femurs protrude through the frayed fustian of his breeches and he's looking rather waxy these days. That's largely because his head is a copy and the real one, probably quite nasty by now, is in a hat box between his feet. At night, of course, he gets up and wanders around, appalled by the prospect of modular degrees.

Around the corner is Gordon Square, at the heart of the Bloomsbury Academia. Maxwell watched the students as the twilight turned to dusk and the dusk to night, strolling home in twos and threes, debating the philosophical conundrums of their age group – was the beer best at UCL or King's? And how did the medics spell diarrhoea? A year or two ago, these same graceless oafs would have been sprawling in sixth form common rooms the length and breadth of the country. But they'd come on immeasurably since then; then, they had difficulty spelling shit.

'Yes?' a rather suave voice crackled over the intercom at the door of Number 239.

'Er . . . Peter Maxwell. May I come in?'

There was a pause. 'Who are you?'

'Head of Sixth Form at Leighford High School. I'm looking for Chris Logan.'

There was another pause, then a series of clicks and large, glass-panelled door opened. Maxwell found himself in a large, plush-carpeted hall, with subdued half-sunken lights glowing on the walls. A huge fireplace to one side was a reminder of more gracious days when Gordon Square had housed some of the finest families in the land.

'Come up,' a disembodied voice told him. 'The first floor.'

The stairs spiralled up like those at the Garrick, the brass hand rail smooth and polished. A door opened as he reached the first landing.

'Mr Maxwell? We've met, surely?'

'Mr LeStrange.' Maxwell had never admitted to being taken aback in his life. He wasn't about to start now. 'What a small world.'

'Indeed it is,' LeStrange caught his hand. 'Can I offer you a sherry?'

'That's kind.'

The magician showed the teacher into an opulent flat where top-of-the-bill posters plastered the walls and Anthony LeStrange

was shaking hands with the rich and famous in umpteen photographs. Trophies and awards gleamed in glass cases on either
side of an Adam fireplace. The whole room screamed fame and
fortune.

'Impressive,' Maxwell said.

'Ah,' LeStrange dismissed it with a gesture. 'Just baubles,' he
said. 'Dry?'

'Thanks,' Maxwell took the proffered glass.

'Your very good health.'

'Cheers.' They clicked glasses and Maxwell sank into a vast
chair. 'I really must apologize for coming unannounced.'

'That's all right,' LeStrange said. 'I'm not due at the Club for a
while.'

'The Garrick?'

'No. The Inner Circle. Shop, I'm afraid.'

Maxwell chuckled. 'Rather exotic shop, I should imagine.'

'All in a day's work, Mr Maxwell. I would imagine some people
would find a staff meeting pretty exhilarating.'

'Really?' Maxwell's eyes widened. Was this man taking the piss
or what?

Anthony LeStrange was handsome in a cerebral kind of way.
On television he looked taller and younger, but Maxwell knew
the lies of a camera, when the man was all stars and spangles and
dry ice.

'How can I help?' he asked the Head of Sixth Form.

'Yes.' It was time to come to the point. 'Chris Logan.'

'Who?'

'He's a reporter on our local paper, the *Leighford Advertiser*.'

'Yes?'

'He came to see you yesterday. Or possibly the day before.'

'He did?'

'So I've been informed.'

'I think misinformed would be a better word,' LeStrange said.

'You haven't seen him?'

'Never,' the magician shrugged.

'It's just that your address was in his address book.'

'My address?'

'Yes.'

'How odd. Wait a minute – the *Leighford* . . .'

'*Advertiser.*'

'You'd have to check with my secretary. Obviously I do an awful lot of interviews.'

'This interview would have been to do with Larry Warner's death.'

'Would it? How did this Mr Logan think I could help?'

'You knew Warner.'

LeStrange chuckled. 'I know a lot of people, Mr Maxwell. I met Warner, what, two, perhaps three times. Through Charts.'

'Can you think of any reason why anyone should want to kill him?'

'No, but the police obviously can.'

'Oh.'

'Ah.' LeStrange crossed to his tantalus to freshen their drinks. 'You'd have missed dear old Trevor Macdonald, trundling up from the coast as you must have been. Yes, it made the national news. The police have a suspect. The outside broadcast people interviewed a fellow called Hall, if I remember rightly. Same fellow who talked to me a few days ago.'

'Hall's got somebody?' Maxwell was playing dumb for Jacquie's sake. 'Did he say who?'

'Do they ever?' LeStrange grunted. '"A man is helping police with their inquiries".'

'I see. So he hasn't actually been charged, then?'

'That's going to happen tomorrow, apparently. Whatever some of us think of our constabularies, Mr Maxwell, they're not manned by utter buffoons. Hall will have his reasons.'

'Oh yes,' Maxwell said. 'I'm sure of that.'

Well,' LeStrange looked at his watch. 'If there's nothing else, Mr Maxwell?'

Maxwell knew a hint when he heard one. 'Quite.' And he downed his Amontillado. 'Many thanks for your hospitality,' and he shook the man's hand. 'Should Chris Logan get in touch, ask him to contact me, will you? It's quite urgent.'

'Yes, yes, of course. Let me see you out.'

'Bloody Hell, it's cold.' Tom Durrant stuffed his hands deeper into his pockets as he turned the windy corner underneath the Arches. Night beat was a bitch, but at least after dark, at three in the morning you could stick your bloody hands into your bloody pockets and not be afraid of being reported by some toffee-nosed old biddie.

'You got a rest day coming up?' WPC Jane Harperhay trudged beside him, the wind raw on her nose and lips.

'Monday,' he told her. 'One long glorious . . . oh, Christ.' Tom Durrant had stopped, staring straight ahead at the alleyway off Villiers Street.

Jane Harperhay flashed her torch into the darkness. 'Cat's Eyes' Durrant was rarely wrong and she'd learned to trust him implicitly since their first pairing three years ago. But this was cardboard city, that monument to Thatcher's England which Blair had done nothing about. Nameless people wrapped in filthy bundles, immune to wind and weather, people with just the strength to croak 'Got any small change?' as the busy, unseeing world passed them by. A sleeping bag, once pale blue, lay rolled up against the damp, green bricks of a chill spring night. She saw a cider bottle, its shattered neck like sparkling brown diamonds in the torch-beam. She saw a syringe, two – a third.

'Junkie,' she said. A naked foot protruded from the sleeping bag, white in the torchlight.

'No.' Durrant was moving forward, arcing in a circle, checking ahead and behind. His hands were out of his pockets and cradling the night stick, ready for anything. He'd been this way before, off work for three months with a broken collar bone. Painful price to pay for a commendation.

Jane Harperhay reached for her night-stick too, watching the bundle, the half-lit expanse of pavement, wet in the driving drizzle. Durrant's boot touched the white foot, gently at first, then hard. It didn't move, not even a twitch. He heard his oppo radioing in.

'Suspected incident at the southern end of Villiers Street, under the Arches.'

He heard the answering crackle of the walkie-talkie and eased back the bedroll with the tip of his stick. She saw him jump, crouching as he was, saw the helmet plate bounce as his hairline shot backwards. For an instant, Tom Durrant was upright again, fighting the urge to vomit. Then she saw him crouch for a second time, doing his job, getting on with it, investigating a death at the scene of a crime. Another reveller who would not see the Millennium.

Jane shone her torch full onto the upturned face of the dead man, his jaw and throat dark with congealed blood and his dark auburn hair matted over his forehead.

'We've got a corpse,' she spoke softly into the lifeline clipped to her shoulder. 'Male Caucasian. About thirty. Fully clothed except for shoes.' She watched as Durrant peeled back the sleeping bag and the body rolled out onto the pavement. He knelt on the wet tarmac and checked the heart for signs of a beat. Nothing. He lifted the cold wrist. No pulse. He could find nothing pumping in the neck because all the dead man's blood, it seemed, had left him, spreading like an evil over his throat, his chest, his shoulders.

'What appears to be a gunshot wound to the throat,' Jane Harperhay was talking to the station. As she said it, they heard the familiar whining siren. The ambulance was on its way, slicing through the minimal traffic in the Strand, swinging left at Charing Cross, bouncing with its lights flashing down the hill. And from nowhere, a squad car screamed around the corner under the bridge in a blaze of lights and sirens to angle itself under the Arches, where the body lay.

Tom Durrant stood up, holding the contents of the dead man's inside jacket pocket in his hand. 'Christopher Logan,' he said to Jane Harperhay. 'That's who he was.'

CHAPTER THIRTEEN

'He wasn't killed here,' DCI Ian Gallagher was emphatic about that. He hadn't shaved that morning, nor the morning before and he was beyond tiredness. Alongside Henry Hall he was a lump of a man, an unmade bed, John Prescott to Hall's Tony Blair.

'Ah.' Gallagher broke the silence as a constable walked in 'Coffee. Thanks, Des. You people take sugar?'

Jacquie Carpenter shook her head, praying that nobody would say 'She's sweet enough.' Nobody did. They were coppers. The rather dishy uniform put the tray down and swept out.

'Two, please,' Frank Bartholomew said and realizing nobody was going to do it for him, helped himself.

'So . . . er . . . Henry,' Gallagher eased himself into the well-worn plastic of the chair behind the desk at the fourth building in turn to take the name Scotland Yard. 'Tell me all about Christopher Logan.'

'We haven't got much,' Hall adjusted his glasses and took the folder that Jacquie slipped across to him. 'Working-class kid made good. Went to the local comprehensive in Leighford. Then to Salford University.'

'Graduates!' snarled Gallagher, slurping his coffee. 'Can't stick 'em myself.'

Jacquie and Bartholomew looked at Hall, the graduate. He ignored them all and carried on. 'Worked on the local paper there for a time, then on the *Sun.*'

'I didn't know the *Sun* employed graduates,' Gallagher frowned, reaching for a digestive to dunk. That was the way with Ian Gallagher – you took 'em or left 'em; please yourself.

'He was there for . . . what . . . three years. Then came back to work on the *Leighford Advertiser.*"

'Now, then,' Gallagher leaned back in his chair. He'd been in the business longer than Hall, the last of his breed, a dinosaur. Jacquie reflected for a moment how well he and Maxwell would have got on. 'Tell me, since I know Jack Shit about the *Advertiser* – is that promotion or demotion, after the *Sun?*'

'We could ask the editors,' Bartholomew suggested.

Both DCIs looked at him, but it was Gallagher, playing host at the Yard that wet Thursday morning, who answered him. 'Never ask an editor of a newspaper anything, son. You tell 'em. And if they ask you anything, well, that's when you stop telling 'em. Married?'

'Sorry?' Hall was losing the thread of this.

'Christopher Logan. Was he married?'

'No. We're trying to contact parents, but they moved away from Leighford some time ago.'

Gallagher was tapping a yet-undunked biscuit on the rim of his cup, narrowing his options, looking for jigsaw pieces in a shattered life. 'Anything known? Drugs? Sex? Money worries?'

'We haven't had much time on this.' Hall felt the need to defend his team, and himself. 'It'll take a while. What about the area?'

'Where the body was found? It used to be part of the Maryannes' Mile.' He leaned forward to Jacquie. 'For the benefit of you young people, that's an area frequented by homosexuals.'

Jacquie managed a smile that was only marginally weaker than the coffee.

'But that's a long time ago. Sort of thing you'd find on the eighth floor.'

'The eighth floor?' Bartholomew didn't mind making a fool of himself; after all, he'd been doing it for years.

'Black Museum, son. Hangman's ropes, death masks. Little mementoes of man's inhumanity to man. No, it's Wino's corner now is the Arches. Shame, really, I bet Flanagan and Allen are turning in their graves.'

Nobody except Gallagher smiled. Jacquie made a mental note to ask Maxwell who they were.

'There's a little drug trafficking goes on, but mostly, it's an extension of cardboard city. Derelicts and vagrants from Christ-knows-where, all of 'em with a hard luck story as long as your night-stick. We're making inquiries of course, but . .' His voice tailed away into a shrug. Everyone in the room knew the score. The flotsam and jetsam of a great city, like the debris washed up at low tide. They had no names, no past, no future. Just faces pinched and grey. Hope was a bottle of cider or a dirty needle.

Gallagher shook his head. 'Like the fucking living dead. We only talk to them if we have to and they never talk to us. One thing is certain – your bloke Logan didn't belong to any of that.'

"You think not?' Hall was trying to limit his horizons too. Alongside sleepy Leighford, the Thames Embankment was the dark side of the moon.

Gallagher shook his head, sipping again from his coffee. 'No needle marks, no glue stains round the mouth. No obvious stretch-ing of the anal sphincter . . . This doesn't bother you, does it, dear?'

Jacquie realized the DCI was asking her. 'No,' she said, with a head held high and a clear voice. 'Not at all.'

That's good,' Gallagher grinned. 'Only a few years ago . . . well, it's all changed now, hasn't it? So, I can't be certain of course, but I'm satisfied your man wasn't a user, a wino or a shirt-lifter. Somebody dumped him under the Arches like people dump an old mattress. He was just in the way. Stuff him in a dark corner and forget about it.'

'What's the forensic score?' Hall asked.

Gallagher chuckled. 'Henry, I don't know what it's like where you're from, but round here miracles take a little longer. As any far-tarsed crime writer will tell you, we haven't caught Jack the Ripper yet. Still,' and he winked at Jacquie, 'it's only a matter of time.' She couldn't help herself but smile.

'What about Maxwell?' It was becoming Frank Bartholomew's favour-ite topic of conversation. The rain had stopped by mid-afternoon and the traffic was building up on the M3 as they drove south. He looked at Jacquie's face through his driving mirror, but she was sitting in the back, staring out of the window, refusing to acknowledge him, refusing to be drawn.

'Maxwell?' Henry Hall was sitting in the back too, wrestling with the problem of the man under the Arches.

'He was at Logan's – remember?'

Hall remembered. And he rather resented Bartholomew's implication that he hadn't. 'What's your point, Frank?'

A more observant man than Frank Bartholomew would have seen the left corner of Jacquie Carpenter's lips curl for a second into a smile. Then it was gone. 'My point, guv . . . wanker!' he suddenly shouted to the BMW that purred past him like a bat out of hell, 'is that our friend Mr Maxwell knows a fuck sight more than he's letting on. I mean, it speaks for itself, doesn't it? We're called to what appears to be a break-in at a premises in Tottingleigh and the next day the owner of those premises is found with a bloody great hole where his voice box used to be.'

'Are you saying Maxwell did it?' Jacquie had come out of her shell.

Bartholomew straightened, checking his mirror, reading her face. Bitch. 'It wouldn't bloody well surprise me,' he growled. 'Tosser!' he suddenly screamed as an ambulance came from nowhere, bells clanging and sirens wailing.

'Can you just drive, Frank?' Hall asked, leaning back and closing his eyes. 'One thing at a time, I think. Jacquie, tomorrow I want you to have a little word with Mr Maxwell.'

'Is that both of us, guv?' Bartholomew asked.

'No, Frank,' Hall clasped his hands across his waistcoat. 'It's just Jacquie. You I want with your ear glued to a phone to Hendon. I want the ballistics on Logan. And I want it yesterday.'

'How did he do that?' Sylvia Matthews always found herself open mouthed watching an Anthony LeStrange show. The man specialized in outdoor magic, making tigers appear in Basildon High

Street, that sort of thing. Not for him a curtained stage and suspect cabinets. And he was such a dish, Sylvia realized anew. In those leather trousers, nothing false about *his* bottom.

'Mirrors,' Tiffany told her.

Sylvia looked at the girl languishing on her settee, hair wet from the shower, towelling robe wrapped around her like cotton wool.

'Oh, really?' the school nurse said.

'Miss Hussey explained it all in the Upper Fourths,' Tiffany said.

'Miss Hussey?' Sylvia checked.

'Lesbian!' Lucy chimed right on cue from the kitchen where she was making short work of a sandwich.

Tiffany's face said it all. 'And Physics teacher.'

'How's it going, by the way?' Sylvia asked. 'At Leighford High, I mean? It must be very difficult adjusting.'

'It's all right,' Tiffany said. 'And it's not for much longer.'

'Except for History, of course.' Lucy came in with a mouth full of cheese and tomato. 'Uncle Max is so weird. What do you see in him, Sylvia?'

The older woman looked at her. 'God!' Tiffany's head dropped onto the back of the settee.

'What?' Lucy looked from one to the other. 'What did I say?'

'Nothing, darling,' Sylvia said. 'Nothing at all.'

But Lucy was still staring at her big sister. 'What?' she whined, like a female Kevin out of Harry Enfield. 'You are in love with him, Sylvia, I know you are.'

'Shut up, you little shit!' Tiffany hissed through clenched teeth. 'I'm sorry, Sylvia. Dear little Lucy is a sweet child, but sometimes she just sticks both feet in her mouth and the rest of her body just naturally follows.'

'What do you mean?' Lucy had showered too and stood there with a sandwich in one hand and a hairdryer in the other, the quintessential symbol of the threshold of womanhood.

In the end it was Anthony LeStrange who answered her from the screen of the one-eyed monster in the corner. 'I mean,' he said, 'that what you just saw was a trick, an illusion.' The camera closed in on his lofty temples, his long, ringleted hair and his eyes burned into Sylvia's soul. 'Or was it?' The voice was sonorous, like a symphony in stereo, coming now from one direction, now another. 'Or was what you have just seen magic? Only I can know that. Until next week,' and his astonishing eyes merged with those of the tiger, growling deep from somewhere in the dark. Then a rather silly woman said 'This is BBC Two,' and the spell was broken.

It was broken too by a simultaneous ringing.

'I'll get it,' and Tiffany had gone like a pink streak, dashing to the hall where Sylvia Matthews kept the phone. 'Oh, hi.' The Miss Cool voice was totally at odds with the sparkling eyes, the pounding heart. Lucy wandered past her sister as she twined the phone cord around her arm and purred into the receiver. The younger girl, whose sandwich had gone, stood there staring at her sister and forced two fingers into her mouth as though to vomit. Tiffany lashed out with a powerful left leg, but Lucy had been here before. Months of telephone love affairs had taught her speed and timing. She twirled away, smirking, to tackle every thirteen-year-old girl's worst nightmare – split ends.

'I'll get the door, then, shall I?' Sylvia said to no one in particular.

No!' she heard Tiffany squeal down the phone and the girl carefully turned her back, almost whispering. 'I don't know if I can.'

Sylvia padded through on slippered feet to the frosted glass of her front door. There were no surprises there. She knew the silhouette in the faint evening sun, the glow on the cycle clips. He'd been there before, countless times. All through her divorce he'd been there, a rock in the swirling sea of failed relationships, a beacon in the darkness. She'd run out of metaphors for him years ago. He was mad, bad and dangerous to know. And she loved him for all of that.

'Yes?' He gave her his Billy Connolly take-off as she opened the door. And she reached up and kissed him quickly on the cheek, as friends do.

'Come in, Max. Take the weight off your feet.'

He doffed his shapeless tweed hat, the one he used to tell his Year 7 kids had been given to him by William Tell in that unfortunate incident with the apple and the baddie, Landberger Gessler. That was in the days of course before the National Socialist Curriculum when History teachers were allowed to tell it like it was. 'Where away are the little darlings?' he asked her.

'Lucy's doing her hair, Bedroom Two,' Sylvia led him past the shrieking Tiffany. 'Tiffany is on the dog and bone.'

Maxwell smiled at her and she blew him a kiss. 'No,' he heard her say into the receiver. 'No. Just Uncle Maxie.' She laughed. 'I'll tell him you said that.'

'Anybody I should know?' Maxwell asked, collapsing uninvited into a chair, 'or is it the usual heavy breather?'

'I've never noticed him breathing heavily,' Sylvia smiled, pouring the man a glass of his favourite tipple. 'My guess would be Mark Irwin.'

'Ah, the Rudolph Valentino of Leighford High. We'll have to watch that one, Nursie.'

'We?' Sylvia widened her eyes as she passed Maxwell his drink and closed the door on Tiffany's titterings.

'I never really thanked you, Sylv, for all this. Come here.'

Her heart jumped. An involuntary nervous reaction the nurse in her knew all about. She was the wrong side of forty, for God's sake. She wasn't Tiffany going weak at the knees at the sound of some stud's voice; or Lucy, looking for closet lesbians on the staff now that somebody had told her she was too old to climb trees any more. Sylvia knew she ought to know better. She'd been there. She'd done that. But this was Mad Max, the man she loved and she melted into his arms. He hugged her, rubbing his cheek against hers, squeezing her shoulders. Then he kissed the top of her head, as he used to kiss his sister's long years ago, on one of those rare days when they weren't trying to kill each other.

'It's just,' he let her up to sit next to him, 'What with my house and Chris's flat. I don't know . . .'

'No news on Chris?' she asked.

Maxwell shook his head. 'Not a whisper,' he said.

'Max,' she was serious suddenly, 'that policeman who interviewed you, Bartholomew . . .'

'What about him?'

'He's not going to make trouble for you, is he? You know, hurt you?'

Mr smiled at her over his glass of amber nectar. 'Me?' he said. 'Old Ironsides? Call me indestructible.'

'Oh. Max.' She squeezed his hand. 'Don't be too sure.'

The door burst open and Lucy scampered through. 'Hello, Uncle Max. Oops!' She saw the held hands. At least Sylvia couldn't be a lesbian. 'Did you see Anthony LeStrange tonight? He's brill. I missed the tiger trick though, 'cos I was making a sandwich.'

'Sylvia!' Maxwell sat bolt upright. 'This appears to be a clear example of child abuse. You're making this poor darling make her own sandwiches!'

'Oh, Lor!' Sylvia held up her hands in mock horror.

'Actually,' Maxwell sat back again, 'I'm afraid that in my capacity as burster of bubbles, I have to tell you he's not nearly so dazzling in the flesh.'

'You've met him?' Lucy had to sit down. 'Oh, wow!'

'Wow indeed,' agreed Sylvia. 'When was this?'

'Yesterday. I went to see him in his London flat.'

'Phone number,' Sylvia burbled. 'Phone number. Give me his phone number.'

'He gave me the time of day,' Maxwell was remembering.

'What?'

'His phone number was in Chris Logan's little book,' Maxwell explained. 'No name. Just a number and an address. A very upmarket place in Bloomsbury. He gave me a drink.'

'So?' Lucy had inherited some of the critical faculties of her uncle. 'He obviously knew you were an alcoholic, Uncle Maxie.'

He threw a cushion at her. 'It's an odd thing, isn't it? A relative stranger turns up unannounced on your doorstep and you greet him like an old lost buddie.'

'A relative stranger?' Sylvia asked.

'Yes, I'd met him a couple of days before at some God-awful bash to do with the school's building programme. Deirdre Lessing's idea. One of her worst.'

'Well, if he'd met you,' Sylvia reasoned, 'perhaps he was only being polite.'

'Trust me, lady, I'm a teacher,' Maxwell said. 'He was too friendly. Too open. And why, if LeStrange didn't know who he was should Chris Logan just happen to have the man's private number?'

'Mr Maxwell?'

'Thingee.' A stickler for names, was Peter Maxwell.

'There's someone to see you. A Miss Carpenter. . . Hello? Mr Maxwell?'

But Peter Maxwell had gone, hurtling down the stairs three at a time, feeling chewing gum of various ages under his hand on the stair-rail as he went. 'Keep left, Lee, you mindless dolt,' he bellowed at a passing child who was on his way up, but only in the literal sense. 'How many times must I tell you?'

She was waiting for him in Reception, that weird room where they kept the tradescantia and the Investors in People plaque. Thingee was pressing buttons like a thing possessed trying to reconnect the History Department and Thingee Too was working on the day's absentee lists to send to that nice Mr Blunkett.

'Jacquie.' He took her by the hand, nodded at both Thingees and swept her away down the corridor. 'Any news?'

'This isn't a social call, Max.' She was aware of her heels clattering on the chill of the parquet. Then they stopped as they reached flotex and they were suddenly on the stairs.

'You're timing is impeccable,' Maxwell said. 'I've got a free.'

'How quaint,' she half smiled.

'Don't give me that,' he growled, holding open his office door. 'I don't know what a rest day is.'

'Six weeks summer holiday,' she said wistfully. 'Isn't it funny the things that occur to you in your dreams?'

'What do you dream about, Jacquie?' he asked her. She was in his demesne now, on his turf. Film posters peppered the w alls, there were videos stacked on shelves along with text-books and quotations from Martin Niemoller. She blinked, the question searing into her soul. None of your damned business, you nosy old bastard, one side of her brain was idling her. You, purred the other side. It was night and day. Yin and Yang.

'May I?' and she sat down.

He took the other chair, the one under the window that looked out onto the car park below and the summer-green fields beyond the hedgerows. 'Coffee?' he asked.

She shook her head. 'Christopher Logan is dead,' she said.

He sat down heavily, having been on his feet ready to hit the switch on the kettle. 'Jesus!' he was frowning, thinking, trying to make some sense of some of this. Any of it. 'How?'

'Shot, we believe. Still waiting for the full forensics.'

'I just can't believe it. I mean, how many clichés are there in a situation like this?'

'You were at his flat two days ago.' It was a statement, based on the one he'd made. Maxwell nodded. He wasn't really listening to her. They heard through the open window the distant roar as a contract groundsman opened up the throttle and began to mow the perimeter of the field, just to make life hell for the hay-fever sufferers in the Examination Season.

'Why did you go there?'

'He'd left two messages on my answerphone,' Maxwell told her, 'saying he was on to something.'

None of this was in the Bartholomew statement. Jacquie sat straighter. This wasn't like Maxwell. He wasn't fencing with her, dummying, whatever sporting analogy came to mind. You were more likely to get an apology from the Japanese for the Burma Railroad than you were a straight answer from Peter Maxwell.

'What did that mean?'

Maxwell looked at the girl. She was wearing her official face.

'It means,' he said numbly, 'that I cost that boy his life.'

The one side of her brain rang warning bells. It was all about notebooks and cautions and closing cases with commendations. The other side, the one that held her heart, was all for crossing the room to him and cradling his head and kissing away the hurt.

And she heard a voice, her own voice as it was all those years ago, 'Mummy mend it.' But she couldn't mend Maxwell. Not unless he let her.

'You'll have to explain that,' she said.

He sat back in the mock-leather chair, staring into her face. 'Chris and I were working on the Larry Warner thing.'

'I knew *you* were . . .' she began.

'I needed his expertise. His journalist's knack of finding things quickly. Internet, car – all those little help-mates on life's Information Superhighway about which I know extremely little.'

'And?'

'Oh, Jesus.' And she saw him bury his face for an instant in his hands. 'What kind of bastard do I sound when I say he wasn't very good? He told me he'd worked on the *Sun*, but at heart he was provincial stuff; flower shows, summer fetes, that sort of thing. I got him in over his head, Jacquie. Whoever you've got in the frame, I pulled that trigger.'

'That's just it,' she shrugged. 'We haven't got anyone in the frame.'

Maxwell blinked. 'Hamlyn?' he asked.

'Still in custody,' she told him. 'He may have killed Warner, but there's no way he could have killed Logan.'

'Have you talked to LeStrange?'

'Who?'

'Ah.' Maxwell got up and crossed to the window. He could see, beyond the town, the whitecaps on the choppy sea under a churning, restless sky. 'I showed your video to Chris.'

'What?' Her eyes were wide with disbelief. 'Max, tell me that's not true.'

'When it went missing after my break-in, I assumed that perhaps he'd taken it. Then he left the messages and I couldn't reach him. I went round there and found his flat had been done too. Why? Did he help himself to my video and did someone else want it from him?'

'That doesn't make sense,' she frowned. 'Why didn't he just borrow it?'

He turned to face her. 'I said he couldn't. I didn't want to run the risk of it leaving my place. I didn't want to implicate you.'

She tried to smile at him, but it wasn't easy. He'd probably wrecked her career for ever this time.

'I did some snooping at the *Advertiser*. He had Anthony LeStrange's phone number in his book.'

'The television magic guy?'

Maxwell nodded.

'Somebody's at the *Advertiser* now,' Jacquie told him. 'They'll pick that up. Max,' she was standing next to him. 'Max, I'll do what I can – to keep you out of it, I mean. But well, it's difficult. The DCI sent me here this morning. Wants to know what you know about Chris Logan.'

Maxwell hadn't turned from the window. 'Nothing, Jacquie,' he said to his faint, blurred reflection in the glass. 'Not a goddam thing.'

It swept over her about then. The one side of her brain saw, for a fleeting instant, a little boy again, lost in a world he didn't understand, playing, out of his depth, with the grown-ups. She couldn't help herself . . .

'Oi, did you see that?' Jason of Year 10 was jogging around the athletics track, yards behind the rest of the field and was staring across at the Sixth Form Block, wondering where he'd left his fags.

'What?' Kent was looking the other way, wondering how long before that Fascist bastard who was head of PE noticed they were trailing behind the crowd.

'Some bird just kissed Mad Max.'

'Never!' Kent and Jason both stopped in their tracks, focusing on the windows of the office of the Head of Sixth Form.

'Straight up!' Jason was adamant.

'What? A snog, you mean?'

'Looked like it to me.'

'Can't be.' Kent didn't buy it. 'For a start he's as mad as all get out. Bee, he's about a million. And third, he's gay, y'know.'

'Get away!'

'As I live and breathe. Course, he's past it now, but he used to hang around the boys' showers, y'know.'

'He didn't!'

'He fucking did. I thought everybody knew that.'

'Who's the girl, then?'

'Bet it's that Mrs Lessing,' Kent suggested.

'Nah,' Jason wouldn't have it. 'She's a fucking lesbian.'

'Ovett! Coe!' roared the head of PE (who was rather long in the tooth and remembered names of famous athletes these lads had never heard of) – 'Any chance of you two finishing the lap, I wonder?'

And Kent and Jason jogged on.

Chapter Fourteen

'I remember a time when Saturday afternoons were sacrosanct,' Jim Astley muttered, turning the typed pages of the report in front of him. 'First when I was young enough to play wing three quarter for my college, more recently for a round of golf.' He looked over his glasses at Henry Hall. 'Important thing, golf, Henry. It settles the nerves, tones the buttocks and above all,' he smiled, lolling lurk in his chair, 'sorts the men from the boys. Now this boy,' he tapped the photograph of Chris Logan on page six of the report, 'was shot to death.'

Hall had said nothing for some minutes. He didn't want to be here either, sitting in a stuffy hospital office at Leighford General, discussing how a young man had died. It was his Youngest's birthday. Jeremy was thirteen. Bike or Playstation? Millennium Dad's dilemma. 'Bike?' Helen Hall had been incredulous. 'Whose thirteenth birthday are we talking about, Henry, his or yours?' So a Playstation it was.

'Tell me something, Henry,' Astley took off his glasses and sucked one end, his cognitive nipple, 'they do have the basics these days, don't they, in Her Majesty's constabularies?'

'I don't follow,' Hall said.

'Reading skills for example. I mean, you have read this or had it read to you?'

Levity didn't sit well on Henry Hall. 'Of course,' he said. 'But what's left of Christopher Logan is on a slab at the Yard morgue. In the absence of an actual body, Jim, I'd value your expertise. Basically, have the Yard got it right?'

'Oh, ye of little faith,' Astley chuckled. 'Well, I'm no gunshot expert, but I'll have a go. Look, here.' His stubby un-doctor-like fingers jabbed into the grey photographs of the dead man's throat. 'This is an entry wound, millimetres right of the sternum. The elasticity of the skin has closed over it to an extent. There's bruising here with the impact and a grease ring. Otherwise clean as a whistle. Note the hole is oval.'

Hall did.

'Oblique entry. Mr Logan was shot from the front, but at a slight angle. Whoever killed him was facing him, but to his right. There'd be very little blood.'

Hall frowned. 'But the photographs I saw showed him covered in the stuff.'

'Ah, that's because he was moved.'

'Go on.'

'The blood ran down his shirt because at some point he was carried, head downwards, probably parallel to the floor and facing it. Was he washed at the crime scene?'

'Pass.'

'Should have been. Still, that's the Met for you. Now, the exit wound.' Astley flicked several pages further on. 'Here we are.'

'My God.' Hall hadn't seen that one before. And he didn't really want to see it again.

'No, he hasn't been clubbed and stabbed as well. It's what we in the business call cavitation. Gun expert or not, I'd say you're looking for a high-velocity bullet fired from some sort of hunting rifle. See here, several wounds to the back. Looks like blunt instrument work, doesn't it? Actually, what happened was that the bullet shattered his vertebrae and blew the bone out through the back. The only consolation is that death would have been virtually instantaneous.'

'Wouldn't have known what hit him, you mean?'

Ah.' Astley waved a warning finger. 'Don't put words into my mouth, now, Chief Inspector. A high-velocity bullet sets up high-pressure waves when it hits the soft tissue of a body. Your classic is the head wound, like Kennedy.'

'JFK?'

Astley nodded. 'I don't suppose you'd cut your first tooth, but I was looking at my first murder victim, in fact. Friday, November 22nd 1963. Rather ironic, really. Oh, we'd seen cadavers before – stiffs aplenty – but never one who'd met a violent end. Cadaveric spasm he had. Hands like claws. And five thousand miles away, in Dealey Plaza – pow! For some people, life's a bitch and then somebody kills you.'

'Anything else on the bullet?'

Astley blew outwards, thinking. 'Tail-wagging possibly. A rifled gun will send a bullet spinning at two or three thousand revolutions a second. At the end of the trajectory though, it becomes unstable. Not too much sign of that.'

'Meaning?'

'Range was . . . and I'm really sticking my neck out here, Henry; it's not something I'd repeat in court . . . something like sixty metres. I'd say he was standing up. From the blood on the shirt and jacket he was fully clothed; oh . . . and this is interesting.' He'd flicked ahead to the closing pages. 'He was killed indoors. Wooden splinters in the back of the cranium, limited into the hair and skin.'

'Parquet floor?'

'God knows. I'm a police surgeon for my sins with a bit of pathology on the side. Interior designer, I ain't.'

'You've been helpfulness itself, Jim,' Hall said, collecting the file from Astley's desk.

'Tell them on the thirteenth hole,' the doctor growled.

Peter Maxwell didn't normally read the *Advertiser*. Sewage disposal along the south coast and what to do about the West Pier hardly engaged an intellect as mighty as his. He read it that Saturday though, the tribute to Chris Logan, the lad's geekish smile radiating from the front page. Maxwell was downing a last gulp of his breakfast coffee, in no mood to notice the weekend that was dawning. He stood in his sunkissed kitchen, a towel round his neck and his shirt dangling off one arm. He threw the paper down, but it landed wrong way up on the breakfast bar, Logan's face, boyish and fresh, still staring at him.

'All right, Chris,' he said quietly, 'I owe you that at least,' and he rang Sylvia to cancel his lunch date with the girls and pedalled for the station.

From his spot in the sun, Metternich tilted his head, sighing. So, the old bugger was off again. Shit. That meant hunting tonight and Metternich just wasn't in the mood for hunting. Still, better that than the endless cooing of that old bat next door, whose vocabulary consisted of something that sounded ludicrously like 'diddums'. Perhaps he'd misheard.

There were essential line repairs at Guildford and huge blokes with shoulders like wardrobes wandered the gravel and sleepers, with 'Highways' blazoned across their chests and 'Byways' across their backs. Maxwell had toyed with the crossword, opened the Stephen King he'd unaccountably bought on the platform at Leighford, closed it again and sat staring at the hurtling hedgerows, once the temporary halt was over. He had the Arches on his mind.

It was there, Logan's miserable bastard of an editor had written, dewy-eyed now that the boy was dead, that they'd found the body. Maxwell found himself walking across Waterloo Bridge in the late morning sun, passing the chattering Japanese tourists, all taking frantic photos of the Mother of Parliaments along the river. He needed to clear his head, make some sense of it all, find some answers.

'I'm on to something, Max.' He'd played Logan's answerphone message over so many times that it had played in his head all the way up on the train. 'What?' he'd shouted, much to the terror of the teenaged girl opposite, who'd slowly got up and walked away. They were letting them out into the community now. Mad as arseholes.

He cut down the concrete stairs by Somerset House, where not so long ago he could have got a copy of his birth certificate for half a crown, search fee a bob, all for a penny stamp. But it wasn't the good old days he'd come for. He moved south-west on the Embankment, following the sparkling brown of the river in the summer sun. The sun didn't shine under the Arches and he felt a chill as he crossed into the shadows. He hated it, really, laying flowers on a bare pavement. When Diana died, he'd read some of the cards they'd left at Leighford Town Hall and around the War Memorial, words of goodbye from people she'd never met. And the little mounds of flowers that always appeared where a car had left the road. Like his car. All those years ago, before flowers were fashionable and when upper lips were stiffer. Yet there it was, a single rose lying against the grey-damp curve of the Victorian brick and a card that read in a large round hand 'And we that knew the best down wonderful hours grew happier yet. I sang at heart, and talked and ate, and lived from laugh to laugh, I too, when you were there, and you, and you.'

'Nice innit?' Maxwell wasn't ready for the voice, rapt as he was in the card's message. Something stirred to his right, lifting out of a rolled mattress. It was a girl, not much older than the one on the train, than the ones he taught every day. Her eyes were cold and dead and her nose around the stud cracked and crimson.

'Yes,' he said. 'It is.'

'Did you know the bloke?' she asked. He couldn't place the accent. Walsall? West Bromwich?

'Yes,' he said, then turned, still squatting, to face her. 'Did you?'

She recoiled at that, watching him, guessing his worth. Natty jacket, bow-fucking-tie. Should be good for something. 'Got any small change?' she asked him.

'What's your name?' he sat down on the cold of the pavement, where they'd washed the debris of Chris Logan into the gutter.

'No names,' she said, pulling back further. He noticed that her jeans were tied at the ankle with rags. He couldn't see her feet.

'Did you see who left this rose?' he asked.

Nothing.

He fumbled for his wallet. Her eyes lit up for the first time. There was a tenner in his hand. 'If I give you this,' he said, 'what'll you spend it on?'

'A fix,' she said.

He shook his head. 'I'm not going to help kill you,' he said. 'I've been there, done that.' And he stood up.

'It was a woman,' she told him quickly with more power in her voice now. 'Last night. Late.'

'A woman?' Maxwell was crouching again, fingering the card with its curious verse. 'What did she look like, this woman?'

The girl's hand came out, tentatively, touching his knee, the bony fingers running along his thigh. He caught them, holding them gently. 'The woman,' he said.

'I didn't get a good look,' she pulled her hand away. 'What does it matter?'

'It matters,' he said. 'And that's all that matters. Are you going to tell me or not?'

'Small change,' she repeated.

The tenner was in his hand again. 'Promise me,' and he took her hand again, 'promise me you'll buy some food with this.'

She blinked at him in the shadows. A June lunchtime in the capital of the sun and they might as well have been on the polar icecap. 'I promise,' she said.

He opened her tightly clenched fingers gently and put the note there, closing her fist again.

'She was tall,' the girl told him, 'with dark glasses and a head-scarf. She didn't see me. She was scared. Sort of . . . sad . . but scared. I could tell that.'

'Did she have a car?'

The girl shook her head. 'She come down the hill. Over there. Went back the same way.'

'To the Strand?'

The girl nodded. 'That's all I know. Who was he, mister? The bloke what died here?'

'He was just a boy,' Maxwell said. 'Somebody sent him to do a man's work.' He stood up, looking down at the wreck of humanity at his feet. 'I sent him.'

Henry Hall didn't enjoy Incident Rooms. He'd seen too many of them and they always meant the same thing. Tragedy. Hopefully, if you got the breaks, you got the man, solved the case, tidied the whole thing up – until the next time. But the victim was just as dead, other lives just as broken. There was no mending any of that, no turning back the hands of time.

'Astley thinks the same gun,' the DCI told his team. It was a Saturday night. Blokes who should have been down the pub, out with the missus, sat in front of him, shirt sleeves rolled, eyes tired; estimated concentration span – ten minutes. 'Frank.' He motioned to Bartholomew, who got to his feet brandishing a rifle.

'This,' he said, 'if you've not seen one before, is a Ruger KM77 Vt Mark Two .308 calibre hunting rifle. Hendon have come through with the same weapon for both the Warner and Logan killings. It's a specialist weapon, people. Bolt action as you see, with a 26-inch barrel, sights and silencer. It weighs nine and a half pounds.'

'And,' Hall added, 'and, it's not available in this country and it doesn't belong to Neil Hamlyn.'

There were murmurs around the room.

'At least, he's not registered as its owner. And bearing in mind how meticulous he was about the Ruger Mini Fourteen that surprises me. Anyway, the bottom line is that Hamlyn was in custody when Christopher Logan was killed. Unless he's Harry Houdini he's in the clear.'

'Guv,' a voice came from a smoke-filled corner. 'I don't understand. Are we talking copy cat?'

'It's possible,' Hall nodded. 'The papers carried the Warner thing. And of course our friends the television people had their cameras up . . .'

'. . . our arses.' Bartholomew was quick to pinpoint their exact position. Nobody laughed.

'But we believe Logan was killed inside and since nobody has reported anything it looks as if this was a solitary hit – no witnesses. Nothing flash.'

'Different purpose then, sir?' It was Jacquie Carpenter who wanted to know.

'Sorry?' It had been a long day for them all.

'If it's the same finger on the trigger, why is one indoors and apparently in secret and the other one in front of hundreds of would-be witnesses? Is it because the killer was making a statement with Warner? A sort of exhibition kill? Whereas Logan . . .'

'Had stumbled onto something.' It was Hall's turn to finish the sentence. 'Yes, Jacquie.' He was thinking, sitting forward in his chair, staring at the rifle cradled in Bartholomew's arms. 'Yes, that's good. What did Mr Maxwell tell you?'

Jacquie felt every pair of eyes in that room burning into her. She felt naked in the spotlight. 'Not a lot,' she said, hoping that her voice was steady. She saw Frank Bartholomew sit down, resting the Ruger against a filing cabinet. 'He and Logan were working on the case.'

There was a ripple of hubbub and one or two guffaws. What's this then?' somebody wanted to know. 'Fucking Holmes and Watson?'

'Well, Watson's dead,' Bartholomew answered. 'Maybe Sherlock's next in the line of fire.' He was looking at Jacquie as he said it.

'What did Logan find out?' Hall asked.

'Maxwell doesn't know. He – Logan – intended to visit Anthony LeStrange, the magician, in London. Had his phone number.'

'Intended to?'

'He never got there. At least, that's what LeStrange says.'

'Who is this Maxwell, guv?' somebody else asked.

'Frank?' Hall glanced sideways.

'I was going to ask DC Carpenter,' Bartholomew said. There were a few sniggers.

'And I was asking you, Frank,' Hall persisted.

'He's a teacher. Up at the High School,' the Detective Sergeant did the honours. 'We caught him snooping round Logan's flat last Wednesday. Claims he taught him.'

'He did,' Jacquie confirmed, staring at Bartholomew.

'Who's been covering the *Advertiser* today?' Hall thought it best to change tack.

'That's me, guv,' Ray Sounness was on his feet. 'I can confirm the LeStrange connection. A colleague of Logan's . . .' he checked his notebook, 'Keith Kershaw . . . had the phone number. I rang it and got LeStrange's secretary. The magician himself wasn't available, but the secretary handles all appointments and had never heard of Christopher Logan.'

'Did you buy that?' Hall asked.

Sounness shrugged. 'Over the phone, guv. I don't know.'

Hall nodded. It was an unfair question. He was grasping at straws and he knew it, floundering in the sea of blood that swamped his darker dreams. 'Get back to him tomorrow, Ray, first thing. Get me an appointment with Mr LeStrange. And Jacquie . . .'

'Sir?'

'First thing tomorrow – you get me one with Mr Maxwell.'

'Well, come along, Count,' Maxwell rolled sideways a little on his bed. 'You either recognize it or you don't.' He was waving the card in the air, the one that had accompanied the rose left where they'd found Chris Logan. The rose left there by the woman in the headscarf, the woman in dark glasses.

The cat didn't even look up, just curled tighter on the television base and let a leg dangle over the video front, just in case the old bastard wanted to use his remote. Maximum annoyance; minimum support – the way of the cat.

'Well, I thought Housman,' Maxwell explained his reasoning, adjusting the pillows against the headboard. 'I even toyed with Betjeman – and that's not something many can claim. I asked Annette Richardson, though I should have known better. She's only the Head of English after all – I mean, be fair. Know what she said? "Could be Housman. Could be Betjeman. Have you thought of Philip Larkin?"' Maxwell flopped back on his pillows like the Death of Chatterton. 'Who the hell thinks of Philip Larkin? But more to the point, Count, who is the dark lady who left it? The dark lady of the sonnet? Girlfriend? He didn't seem to have one. Mother? Hardly. Wife? He wasn't married. Admirer? What, a *Sun* journalist? But that might be it, though.' The Great Man was thinking again. Metternich could always tell. The old duffer's eyes narrowed and he set his jaw, standing, or in this case lying, like an ox in the furrow. 'Tomorrow, I'll go and see Mr LeStrange again. And then, Icarus that I am, I'll go to the *Sun*.'

Monday, Monday. Hate that day. There was always something that the weekend had thrown up, some ghastly trauma that only a man like Maxwell could sort out.

'Gutteridge,' he stood looking up at the ghastly trauma in question. Six foot three of uncoordination. 'Did you or did you not encounter Mr Holton, the Head of Science, on the Seafront on Saturday?'

'Yeah.'

Well, that was something. At least Gutteridge wasn't pleading the fifth. 'And did you cross the road in order to engage him in conversation?'

'Yeah.'

'Had you or had you not been imbibing at the time?'

'Eh?'

'Having a jar?'

'Oh, yeah.'

'At an establishment of ill repute called The Coach and Horses?'

'Yeah.'

'Where you are unable to acquire alcohol legally on account of your being under-age but that didn't stop you because the bar man is either a mate or an idiot or both?'

'Uh . . . yeah.'

'And did you, having downed an unknown quantity of said alcohol, proceed to tell the aforementioned Mr Holton to – and I quote "sort out [his] fucking life" or words to that effect?'

'No.'

'Gutteridge, Gutteridge,' Maxwell circled the overgrown oaf, standing as he was in the centre of his Head of Sixth form's carpet, 'Taking a GNVQ course does not entitle you to lie through your teeth. Now would you like to reconsider that answer or do I have to put my career on the line by beating you to a pulp?'

Gutteridge looked down at the man. He was six inches taller, two stone lighter, with all the youthful advantages of reflex and speed. On the other hand, the other guy was Mad Max and you didn't push your luck with Mad Max.

'All right, yeah.' Discretion was ever the better part of Gutteridge's valour.

'Excellent!' Maxwell slapped his arm. 'A right decision if ever I heard one. Now, you will take yourself off to the Science Department, you will find Mr Holton, you will apologize to him. You will, if he so orders it, kiss his backside and above all, you will be grateful that I don't end your career here and now. Am I communicating with you, Gutteridge?'

'Yeah.'

'I'm sorry,' Maxwell frowned. 'I believe there's a word missing there. It's quaint, old-fashioned, even a little eccentric perhaps, but it is only one syllable. Try it for me, there's a good lad.'

'Yeah, sir.'

'Stout fellow.' And Maxwell saw the shambling oaf out, just before his telephone rang.

'Mr Maxwell? This is DC Jacquie Carpenter, Leighford CID.'

'Woman Policeman.' Maxwell knew that police switchboards, like walls, have ears.

'I wonder if you'd mind coming down to the station, sir. Detective Chief Inspector Hall would like a word.'

'Delighted,' Maxwell said. 'But the National Curriculum is an exacting beast, Woman Policeman. I simply cannot spare the time at the moment.'

'Shall we say the end of the day?'

'The end of the day,' Maxwell complied. 'No, 'fraid not. What about a working lunch? Neutral territory. Er . . . the Seafront, why not? Will you act as his second or mine?'

But duelling wasn't Jacquie Carpenter's bag. 'Tomorrow then?' she asked, her voice still crisp as a Brannigan's. 'Twelve thirty?'

'Better say twelve thirty-five,' he suggested.

'Twelve thirty-five,' and he could, just for a moment he landed, hear the smile in her voice.

'Irwin,' Maxwell was already unshackling White Surrey from that rusty bit of iron that jutted from the Design Block wall.

'Mr Maxwell,' the handsome lad broke away from his companion of a mile. 'If it's about the phone calls . . .'

'Phone calls?' Maxwell's eyebrow reached new heights.

'Er . . . oh, nothing.'

'Am I right in remembering that your good father is a lecturer in English at that Godless institution known as Southampton University?'

'He is indeed,' Irwin smiled.

'Excellent. If he has a moment, could he locate this for me?' He handed a transcript of the elusive poem to the boy.

'It's Rupert Brooke,' Irwin told him. '"Dining-Room Tea", I think it's called.'

Maxwell's mouth didn't hang open very often, but then he didn't hear a miracle every day. 'Is it?' he asked. 'Irwin, I'm humbled. How did you know?'

'"When you were there, and you, and you,
Happiness crowned the night; I too
Laughing and looking, one of all, I watched . . ."'

'Yes, yes, quite. But how . . . ?'

Mark Irwin laughed, hauling his holdall onto his shoulder. 'Rupert Brooke happens to be my dad's favourite poet – after Philip Larkin, of course.'

'Of course!'

'Each of us sprog Irwins had to learn bits of poetry. I got Rupert Brooke – "Dining-Room Tea" and "Kindliness". Party pieces, really – to impress aunties and make them give us money.'

'Oh, excellent young man,' beamed Maxwell. 'Were it not for the impropriety of the thing and the risk of being struck off, I'd kiss you.'

'May I say, sir,' Irwin asked, 'you're not my type.'

'Very glad to hear it. Oh, by the by . . .'

'Sir?'

'About those phone calls.'

'Um?' For an intelligent lad, Irwin did a good line in vacant.

'The ones to Tiffany – no problem. As many as you like.'

Peter Maxwell didn't like bothering Deirdre Lessing. But he needed one teensie bit of information from her and he needed it today. She wasn't in her usual lair, her office on the mezzanine floor, strewn as it was with the bleached bones of lesser men. Undeterred, Maxwell held his metaphorical polished shield in front of him and swept in, batting aside the writhing serpents she'd left there to guard her ghastly secrets. He checked her desk – little bouquet of spring flowers in a glass, cutesy bunny pen holder, a 'thank you' from some sad, deranged girl and – ah, a filofax. All right, so she'd probably wound a single mousey hair across the catch so that she'd know later if it had been opened. There was probably a CCTV camera on Maxwell as he spoke, cunningly disguised as a rubber plant. But he was so far steep'd in blood. He checked the addresses, committed the one he wanted to memory and was gone.

There was a magic about Lammas Court on Sydenham Hill. They'd moved the mighty Crystal Palace there after its debut in Hyde Park, until that fateful night when a fag-end put an end to an era. Now, as Maxwell found the place, the houses glowed in the mist-shrouded hollows and the lights that twinkled and flickered like King Henry's army before Agincourt couldn't possibly be shining from anywhere as prosaic as Penge.

'Yes?' a woman's voice sounded over the intercom, rather tired, rather world-weary.

'Peter Maxwell, from Leighford High School. We met last week.'

There was a buzz and a click and the front door opened. The house was the mockest of Tudors, but the quality was pure 'thirties and it wouldn't have surprised Maxwell at all that this building, in itself, was listed.

She met him in the hall, gliding with an elegance over the polished parquet floor. 'Mr Maxwell,' she said, extending slim, jewelled fingers. 'This is a pleasant surprise.'

'I hope I haven't come at a bad time,' he kissed her hand and surprised her with his chivalry, 'but there's a poem I'd like to discuss with you.'

'A poem?' she smiled. 'Couldn't you have phoned?'

'Oh, no,' he shook his head. 'For this poem, I needed to see you face to face.'

She frowned. 'But why?'

Only now did he let her hand fall. 'Because it's a poem you wrote.'

'One of mine?'

He twisted his lips a little. 'Let's say a collaboration, shall we? Part Amy Weston, part Rupert Brooke.'

CHAPTER FIFTEEN

'You like cats?' It was a superfluous question really. A large tortoiseshell had pinned Maxwell to the chair, a Devon Rex was curled under one armpit, a silver tabby was under the other. Only the Persian blue sat aloof, knowing exactly how gorgeous she was without Maxwell billing and cooing all over her.

'I'm a cat person,' Maxwell said. 'Although I'm not sure whether I'm a cat owner.'

'What do you have?'

'A black and white.' Maxwell buried his fingers in the bundle of fur in his lap. It was the most fun he'd had in a long time. 'I think they're called Friesian in some circles.'

She passed him a coffee, just poured from an expensive cafetiere. 'I never know whether to take you seriously or not,' she said.

'Oh, please do,' he begged her. 'Sudden death is something I never joke about.'

'Sudden death?' Amy Weston, the poetess, was sitting on an elegant chaise longue across the room from him. Everything about the woman was elegant, her long flowing kaftan, her cats, her cream-coloured decor.

'Chris Logan,' he said.

She frowned and shook her head, all in one movement.

He reached into his pocket and read the contents – 'And we that knew the best down wonderful hours grew happier yet. I sang at heart, and talked and ate, and I lived from laugh to laugh, I too, when you were there, and you, and you.'

'Yes,' she said. 'You were right, Mr Maxwell. It is Rupert Brooke. Probably written in 1910. It's called "Dining-Room Tea".'

'I know,' he said. 'What I don't know is why you should quote it on a card, left with a single rose, where the police found the dead body of a journalist.'

'Why *I* should?' That curious frown and shake of the head again.

'It is your handwriting?'

'Mr Maxwell, how did you get my address?'

'You're famous, Ms Weston, one of the country's foremost women writers.'

She arched an eyebrow. 'Do I catch a sense of limitation there? Some sexist condition?'

'Not at all,' he smiled, sipping his coffee. 'I'm merely quoting your friend Archie Godden.'

'Godden.' He thought he saw her face darken. 'He's a bastard.'

'Oh, really? I'm sorry, I naturally thought . . .'

'Neither of those words apply to Archie, Mr Maxwell. He isn't natural and he doesn't have a thought in his head, at least, not an original one.'

'I see.'

'And it's precisely because I am famous that I don't give my address away to any Tom, Dick or . . . you'll forgive me, Harry.'

'Ah,' he winked. 'But you gave it to Deirdre Lessing.'

'Who?'

'Quite!' he beamed triumphantly. 'My sentiments exactly. Her publicity team however tell me she's Senior Mistress, a sort of middle-aged concubine, at Leighford High School.'

'Whence you emanate?' she checked.

'Where I teach,' he corrected her. That in itself was bad enough, but he drew the line at emanation. 'Well, you've been very kind, Ms Weston,' and he put the coffee cup down before removing the tortoiseshell's claws from his country casuals, 'but I fear I'm wasting my time.'

'Must you go?' He sensed the routine detachment of the question.

'Yes, I have to report all this to the police. My only quandary is whether to see the Met, on whose patch poor Chris died, or Leighford CID, where the dear departed lived. Still, co-operation between the forces is excellent these days, isn't it? I've never been to Scotland Yard.'

'Wait,' the command was harsh, imperious. 'Please, Mr Maxwell. We needn't be hasty about all this. Is it, after all, such a crime to commemorate the passing of another human being?'

'No crime at all.' Maxwell sat down again and the tortoiseshell re-established his lap as her territory, shaking an erect tail at him before curling to bring her nose up her bum. 'Would you like to share it with me?'

'Before I do,' she sat upright, staring into his eyes, 'I need to know why you want to know.'

'Larry Warner's murder,' Maxwell said, watching for all the old familiar signs. 'Chris Logan was investigating it.'

'He was? Why?'

'Because he was a journalist. Because Warner died on his newspaper's doorstep . . . And because I asked him to.'

'You're involved?'

'I was at the Wild Water ride on the day Warner was killed. I didn't have any choice but be involved.'

'You could have walked away,' she said.

He looked at her. 'I'm not the walking away type,' he told her.

'Neither am I,' she said. 'I heard about Mr Logan on the local news. The Arches, the Adelphi, the Embankment – I knew these areas well. You know my *Shifting Sands* trilogy?'

'Er . . .'

'No matter. It touched a chord – I don't know why. The Arches, a futile death.'

'Futile?'

'Isn't all death futile, Mr Maxwell, unless it's in a cause?'

'A cause?'

She shifted on the chaise longue. 'Well, you know, a just war?'

'Are we talking jihad?' he asked her. 'A holy war?'

She chuckled, a soft rippling sound that rippled through his head. 'We're not Muslims, Mr Maxwell. Curiously un-English, isn't it? We British fight wars, but they're never holy. We'd be too embarrassed to admit to that. It's too emotional.'

'So you left the rose?' he asked her. 'Isn't that emotional?'

'I didn't say it wasn't,' she said. 'It's just that we aren't, as a people, as a nation.'

'Why the Rupert Brooke?'

'I told you,' she sighed, 'when we met last. He was a fine poet. Influential certainly on my earlier work.'

'And why "Dining Room Tea" in particular?'

'I don't know,' she shrugged, frowning. 'I don't know why it came to me. Mr Maxwell, you aren't really going to the police about this, are you?'

'Why?' he asked her. 'Would you rather I didn't?'

'Snoopers,' she said suddenly. 'I don't like snoopers.'

'But you're a celebrity,' he said. 'Doesn't snooping go with the territory?'

'Poetry is private,' she told him. 'No one's seen my best work. Or . . . nearly no one. What I let the public see is only a façade. Not the real me.'

'Tell me,' he said, 'about Anthony LeStrange.'

Anthony?' she frowned. 'I barely know him. We only meet via Charts. He's very well known, certainly. Quite seriously wealthy, I should think. Quite a brilliant hypnotist.'

'That's his metier?'

'Oh yes. All that tigers in the High Street and sawing people in half, that's his public persona.'

'Like the poetry you let us see?'

'Exactly. I suspect his best work is done behind the scenes. We'll never see it.'

'Why should Chris Logan want to talk to him?'

'You said it yourself,' she told him, 'but about me. Anthony is a celebrity, a television personality. Why shouldn't a journalist want to talk to him?'

'I meant,' he leaned forward as far as the cat would let him, 'in connection with the Larry Warner murder.'

'Ah,' she said, smiling. 'I'm afraid I can't help you.'

'Perhaps not,' he smiled back. 'But I think I know a man who can.'

'Yes. Hello. My name is Peter Maxwell. I'm an old friend of Chris Logan. Yes. He was found dead unfortunately, a few days ago. Yes. Well, I'm planning a memorial service for him and I believe he used to write for you. Yes. That, I don't know. Can you help? Yes. Yes. Of course.'

Maxwell waited while the *Sun* switchboard played some dreadful Muzak at him down the phone. He lolled back in the chair, waving to his littler niece across the quad from him in the science labs at Leighford High, disguised in white coat mid goggles as she was.

'Yes. Until '98. That would be right. Tell me, we've asked a celebrity to be present at the service, say a few words, you know. Er . . . Anthony LeStrange . . . Yes, the magician. Oh, brilliant, yes. No, I've no idea how it's done, no. Well, I seem to remember that Chris did a story on him for you once. Yes. Just for the record, you know. Could you? Oh, wonderful.'

And he lolled back again, watching Lucy as Ben Holton scurried round her, flapping about bunsen burners. Whoever made such a neurotic into the Head of Science? Oh, wait a minute. Maxwell remembered it was Legs Diamond, he of Bad Appointments R Us, adding fuel again to the old adage, if you want to get a Head, get a twat.

'Yes. Ah, he did. Oh, three articles. Excellent. And . . . what? Hypnosis? You're sure about that? No, thanks. I don't need that. Thank you. You've been most helpful.' And he put the phone down.

'I don't usually have lunch with strange men,' Maxwell assured Henry Hall. 'Especially Detective Chief Inspectors.'

They sat in Hall's silver Volvo under a cloudless sky, facing out to sea. Around them, sunburnt kids scampered, lobster-red. Maxwell didn't care. They should have been at school, but their semi-literate parents had other ideas. Sunstroke and stupidity – the great British summer.

'I'm glad we could find a mutual moment,' Hall said. Maxwell tackled his baguette with gusto. He'd met Henry Hall before and had learned to respect him, but he was a bland bastard, for ever hiding behind protocol and the blankness of his rimless glasses.

'I'm glad you're glad,' the Head of Sixth Form was on his precious lunch hour, that glorious window in the day when some sort of peace descended and teachers sat comatose, like cryogenic experiments in the staffroom, psyching up for the uphill battle that was the afternoon.

'I wanted a chat about Chris Logan.'

'I rather thought you might.'

'You were in his flat.'

'I was looking for him.'

'Clearly, so was someone else.'

Maxwell turned in his seat, reaching for the can of something fizzy resting on the dashboard. 'Clearly. Any idea who?'

Hall was still staring at the hazy line where the sky met the sea. 'I was just going to ask you the same question.'

Maxwell chuckled. A less humourless bastard than Hall would have joined him. 'Do I sense an offer coming on?'

Hall turned to him. 'What do you mean?'

'There are things I know,' Maxwell said, 'and things that you know. Put those things together and we might just catch Logan's killer.'

There's a distinction there,' Hall noticed. 'The things I know are police business. The things you know are being withheld and could be classed as obstruction.'

Tsk, tsk,' Maxwell shook his head. 'Mi casa, su casa, Chief Inspector. I suspect you want to nail this man more than I do.'

'And Logan makes it personal for you, does he?'

'He does,' Maxwell told him. 'It might have been me under the Arches the other night. Should have been, perhaps.'

Hall looked at him curiously. 'People with a death wish are no good to me,' he said. 'Your investigation's heading towards Anthony LeStrange.'

Yes,' Maxwell nodded. 'Policewoman Carpenter will have told you that.'

'Keith Kershaw told us that,' Hall corrected him, 'at the *Advertiser* offices.'

Jacquie was the last person Maxwell wanted to land in it. He'd have to box cleverer than this.

'Have you talked to LeStrange?'

'The Met have. He's never heard of Chris Logan and he has an alibi for the time of his death. As he does for that of Larry Warner.'

'Warner?' It was enough to make Maxwell stop chewing.

'What we haven't released yet,' Hall told him, 'is that both men were killed with the same gun. A Ruger KM 77 Vt Mark Two.'

'Jesus.'

'We know exactly when Warner died from eyewitness accounts – including yours. Logan we can ascertain to within an hour and a quarter. LeStrange was actually filming on both occasions. We've got corroboration of that from more technicians and members of the public than you and I have had hot dinners.'

'He is a magician,' Maxwell reminded the detective.

'True,' Hall nodded, 'but unless he's sussed the time-space continuum thing, I've got to rule him out.'

'Where does that leave us?' Maxwell asked.

'With loose ends,' Hall said, scanning the timeless horizon again. 'And brick walls. I'll tell you what, Mr Maxwell; are you a gambling man?'

Maxwell shrugged. 'Well, you know, the National, the Boat Race, I've even been known to buy a Lottery ticket.'

Hall fumbled in his pocket and fished out a coin, spinning it and catching it expertly. 'Heads or tails?' he asked.

'Heads,' said Maxwell. 'I've always had such respect for them.'

'Heads it is,' Hall told him. 'Do you want the loose ends or the brick walls?'

'I'm not quite sure . . .'

'Ends or walls?' Hall persisted.

'All right, then.' Maxwell was never one to chicken out in a corner. 'Walls.'

'Good,' said Hall. 'I hoped you'd say that.'

'Have you heard of the White Knights, Count?' Maxwell was adjusting the saddle of Sergeant Mitchell's mount, filing off the flash with an expert action. Naturally, the cat had not.

'Neither had I.' Maxwell applied the glue, carefully, not wishing to make his pet feel in any way inadequate by his lack of knowledge. 'But apparently, the Met's anti-terrorist squad has been aware of them for some time. They're a white supremacist group. You know, Hitler was a nice guy, the KKK collect for Barnardo's and should we really let anyone other than heterosexual Caucasians live? It's the kind of tolerance you show to Leighford's mouse population, only we humans are supposed to have the odd moral or two, mixed with a little conscience and a smattering of principles. Well, it seems that our friend Mr Hamlyn, confessor to killings, is a member of this august body, which raises all sorts of implications about his SAS credentials. Who told me this useful little snippet? That nice policeman, Mr Hall. And why did he tell me? Because he thinks I can be useful to him.'

The phone shattered his cogitation. 'Oh, bugger.' Sergeant Mitchell flew over his horse's neck and landed at an angle, the animal's ears jammed into his crotch. 'Get that, will you, Count?'

As usual, the animal ignored him.

'War Office,' he grabbed the receiver, wrestling with his plastic creation.

'Max. Oh, thank God.'

'Sylv?' Maxwell was frowning. Something was wrong.

'It's Tiffany, Max. She's gone.'

CHAPTER SIXTEEN

They sat, in the long watches of the night, huddled in Sylvia's Clio. Every now and again, Sylvia herself would glance in her driving mirror at the little girl in the back seat. Lucy's face was dark and small, shrunk in the shadows and as she turned, there was a silver trail down her left cheek.

Sylvia Matthews should have been happy. She was sitting alongside the man she loved, her fingers clasped in his. But the warmth had turned to terror and only now could she bring her courage to the sticking place and look him in the face.

Mad Max wasn't looking at either of them. His left hand rested on the door handle, his eyes fixed on the frosted window of The Grapes, the dive in Fountain Street that had been home to Leighford's lushes for generations. The elegant Victorian façades glowed with their floodlights and a thumping bass reverberated along the length of Maxwell's tether.

'I don't know,' he said. It was only a murmur, but to Lucy it sounded like a trumpet-blast and she visibly jumped, her heart jumping into her throat as he spoke. 'I'm going in.'

'No, Max,' Sylvia's hand squeezed his and she half turned. There was a shriek on the pavement behind them and a nubile lovely, tottering on fuck-me heels, clattered past chased by a zombie with a shaven head – the unspeakable in pursuit of the all-too-catchable. 'What if I'm wrong? What if he's not there?'

'If you're wrong, then we'll start again. We haven't tried Big Willy's yet or the Salamander.' He looked at her for the first time in what seemed forever. 'Don't worry,' he said, 'I've cleared bars before. Warlock, Gunfight at the OK Corral, I've seen 'em all. All you do is let fly before the other guy does. Now, you two,' he broke Sylvia's panicky grip and turned to face both his girls, 'stay put.' He was staring into their eyes, willing them to obey him. 'I won't be long. Neither of you is to move. All right, darlings?' And he winked at them, trying to lighten the moment, as much for himself as them.

They both nodded.

'Max . . .' Sylvia began.

But he'd held a finger to her lips and looked across at Lucy.

'Uncle Maxie,' she filled the empty silence. 'Will it be all right?'

He winked again, reached across Sylvia's headrests and kissed the girl's forehead. 'Trust me, lady,' he gave her his best Bruce Willis, 'I'm a teacher.' And he was gone, sidestepping the vomit by the old bootscraper, crashing through the bat-wing doors. Henry Fonda, Burt Lancaster, they'd have been proud of him. But the old joanna in the corner didn't stop playing. There was no scrape of furniture as the nervous brethren of the cowtown ducked for cover, out of the line of fire. No buffalo gal came sauntering up to him, looking like Lana Turner or Virginia Mayo, saying 'You wanna dance, mister?' And the balding barkeep didn't slide a half empty bottle of Redeye the length of the mahogany counter.

Instead, the lights continued to whirl and spray in the darkened corners and Afterbirth were loafing around a cluster of mike stands, standing sideways to the audience to disguise the weakness of their chord mastery. One of them was shouting obscenities into a mike to disguise his lack of ability as a singer. They'd got a tame orangutan with a woolly hat thumping the drums at the back, swinging at his cymbals every now and again in the hope that it vaguely resembled whatever the bassist was supposed to be doing.

'Where,' muttered Maxwell, 'are Peter, Paul and Mary when you need them?'

In other circumstances, Peter Maxwell would have moseyed to the bar, bought a Southern Comfort or failing that a pint, found a dark corner and chosen his time. But these weren't other circumstances, and he didn't have the time. He barged into the circle of raucous joke-tellers and hauled one of them upright. 'Mr Irwin,' he snarled into the young man's face. 'A shout in your ear, if I may,' and he dragged him outside.

Sylvia and Lucy saw them both tumble out, the shorter one pulling the taller by his collar. They saw the shorter one look round in the bright light from the pub's windows and then they vanished up the blackness of the alley that ran alongside.

Irwin felt his teeth crunch as the back of his head hit the wall. 'Where is she?' Maxwell wanted to know.

'Who?' Irwin asked.

Maxwell's fist still gripped his collar. Maxwell's nose was inches from his. 'You've known me, boy and boy, for seven years, Mark,' his Head of Sixth Form told him. 'A long and glorious apprenticeship. But I'm not Mr Maxwell tonight, the guy who tells you funny stories and holds your hand through all the trials of GCSE and A level. Tonight, I'm a bloke whose niece has gone missing and I'm not inclined to be reasonable and I want some answers. Now, however many you've sunk tonight, sunshine, I want you to clear your head and tell me about every breath you've taken since seven thirty. Make it so.'

There was a murmur at the lit end of the alleyway and Maxwell looked up to see a knot of silhouetted oafs blocking the light. 'You all right, Marky?' one of them asked.

'No sweat, Joe,' Irwin called. 'Just a last minute spot of revision before my History A level.'

'You what?'

'It's fine, Joe, really. You go along now. I'll be in later.'

'What did that old geezer want?' Joe was persistent, but he was a little taken aback by Maxwell looming out of the dark at him.

'The old geezer wants to be left alone.' His Greta Garbo was, as ever, lost on the younger generation.

'You what?' Joe squared up to the man, his mates around him, his dander up, his reputation on the line.

'Seen *Le Bossu*?' Maxwell asked casually. 'It's a French film, means The Hunchback. A rattling good yarn, lots of excellent swordplay.'

'What the fuck you talking about?'

'Come on, Joe,' a mate murmured. 'Leave it alone, eh?'

'Yes,' Maxwell's Biro flashed silver in the street light. 'It's all about concentration, feint, confuse. Known as the Nevers attack.'

'What?' Joe was more confused than ever.

'It's all about the fact that there's a weak point in the skull, just above the bridge of the nose.' He tapped Joe's forehead and the lad bobbed backwards.

'Come out of it, Joe, that's Mad Max. He'll fuckin' kill you.'

Joe had never been to Leighford High School. His mate had. Even so, there was something in the mate's voice, the tug on his sleeve. Maxwell threw the pen to his right hand from his left, 'Parry in Seventh, riposte.' He jerked his right arm behind his back so that the ballpoint protruded by his waist, 'Envelop in quarte, take blade as you change arm,' then hurled it back so that his left hand came out of nowhere, the Biro's business end quivering above Joe's nose. 'To the forehead.' The lad's eyes crossed, his mouth sagged open, an inky dot between his eyebrows.

'Fortunately,' Maxwell smiled, 'that's only a dummy run, with a Parker Flighter. Now, let's try it with a knife, shall we?'

But the knot of heavies had gone, legging it down the street in their Doc Martens and nobody was running faster than Joe.

'I'm sorry about them,' Mark Irwin said at Maxwell's elbow. Maxwell clicked the Biro point and slid it back into his pocket.

'Tiffany,' he said to the lad. 'You don't leave this alleyway until I know where she is.'

But Peter Maxwell didn't find out where Tiffany was, not from Mark Irwin. The boy had made his usual five-thirty phone call, from his mobile somewhere along the Front. It was his mother's birthday day after tomorrow and he'd gone in search of a present. Luck had deserted him so he thought he'd try a woman's input. Jessica wasn't talking to him at the moment, Emma had about as much feminine sense as a lock forward and it was unlikely that Hazel would know what day it was. Tiffany now was a different proposition. He'd rung for her advice and she'd told him that mothers' birthday presents required face-to-face consultation. She was free that very evening as a matter of fact.

Sylvia Matthews hadn't been too sure, but she'd given in. She knew Mark. He may have some rough diamond friends, but he was a gentleman. His old man was a University lecturer for God's sake. Surely, Tiffany was safe with him? They'd chatted for a while at Sylvia's, dashing Mark and his golden girl. Lucy had walked through the lounge an awful lot, prattling about, doing this-and-that essential something-or-other. Eventually, Sylvia had taken her away and metaphorically tied her up in the kitchen. At about seven, Mark had popped the vital question. Could he and Tiffany go to see A Bug's Life? There was a showing at 7.30, the animation was great and it would take Tiffany's mind off the appalling prospect of having Mad Max for an uncle for the rest of his life, if not hers. Sylvia hadn't been too sure, but the girl was already changing and when Sylvia saw what she'd put on, she made her change again, and they were gone into the Leighford night.

They'd watched the film – excellent fare; Maxwell would have approved. And in case the Great Man was wondering, no, Mark Irwin made it a rule never to kiss on the first date. That seemed to piss Tiffany off a little, but hey, he was a gentleman and a scholar. Maxwell doubted both, but let it pass. He'd bought her an icecream before the film started and they shared a bag of chips on the way home. He'd dropped her off at Nurse Matthew's at just after ten, thanked her for a lovely evening and headed home. He hadn't intended to nip in for a swift one, but a few mates flagged him down in a beat-up beetle and they'd gone to The Grapes. The last time he'd seen Tiffany, she'd been waiting for Nurse Matthews to let her in.

'There was nothing, Max,' Sylvia sat in the harsh neon of her kitchen, cradling a mug of coffee, wishing she could put back the hands of time. 'The bell didn't ring. Not when Mark said he'd dropped Tiffany back, not at any time. And the bell is working, I know. I've checked. You're sure Mark's right about the time?'

Maxwell nodded. 'The kid was scared,' he said, staring into the swirl of his coffee. 'I frightened him tonight, Sylv. Oh, yes, he's six foot one and he's a man of the world, but it's not every day your Head of Sixth Form goes apeshit. I'm afraid I don't feel very proud of myself.'

She reached out and took his hand. 'You don't!' she said, tears welling in her dark eyes. 'And what about me? I'm to blame. I'm the one.'

'No.' He put the cup down and held her to him, stroking her hair, kissing away the tears. 'No,' he told her. 'Look at me when I'm talking to you, Sylv.' It was an excellent Eric Morecambe, but she was too wound up to notice. 'This isn't about you at all,' he said, 'or about Tiffany. It's about me.'

'Oh, Max, where is she?'

Maxwell laid the frightened woman's head on his shoulder and felt her tears soak into his shirt. 'That's the one, Sylv,' he whispered. 'That's the sixty-four thousand dollar question. And just about now, I'd trade every scrap of useless bloody knowledge I've got for that one, single answer.'

They drove to Maxwell's that night, to lazy, winding Columbine with its blossom trees and its cosy houses. They'd got together everything that made sense for a siege. From now on, it was the three of them together, the dauntless three against the world. Maxwell's answerphone was flashing in the dim light as he reached the lounge.

'That thing's flashing again,' Metternich thought as he stretched his full length on the carpet. 'Oh, shit. Women!' and he bolted up the stairs to the Inner Sanctum where only he was welcome, along with the 387 soldiers of Maxwell's growing Light Brigade, sitting patiently in their saddles ready for the fourth order of that fateful morning long, long ago.

'Max, darling, it's Sandie.' Lucy stood in the middle of the room at the sound of her mother's voice. It was late. Very late. And it had been such a day. 'Another week, I promise. Sorry to mess you about again. Love to the girls. I'll ring again, but it's gone a bit pear-shaped out here.'

Her message's bleep was drowned out by Lucy's sobs, heavy, uncontrollable. Maxwell pulled her head into his chest and cradled it. Over the sweet-smelling brown hair he nodded Sylvia in the direction of the bedroom and Nurse Matthews, with her long years in the TLC Department, took the hint and the girl and led them both away.

But there was another voice on Maxwell's machine, a man's voice, one he didn't recognize. 'Mr Maxwell. I hope you haven't been out combing the streets and I hope you haven't contacted the police. Either way, it would be pointless. The first because she's not on the streets. The latter because Tiffany will die if you do. I will contact you again with specific instructions. Now, I don't want to sound melodramatic, but the life of your niece is in your hands.' And the line went dead.

'Shit!' Maxwell had stood frozen, rooted to the spot in fear. Now he moved himself, pressing the replay button and sitting on the edge of the seat, where his heart had been all the time.

'My God!' Sylvia Matthews's comment was barely audible. She'd left Lucy getting ready for bed and was in search of a towel when she heard the voice. She sat down heavily on the floor, suddenly not trusting her legs.

'I'm ringing Jacquie,' Maxwell had the receiver in his hand.

'No, Max,' she screamed at him, snatching the white plastic from him. 'The tape . . .'

He snatched it back, looking steadily and calmly into her eyes, brimming as they were with all the emotions of the longest night of her life. 'The tape said no police. But Jacquie isn't police, not in the literal sense, not tonight.'

'Max.'

But he was punching out the numbers, twisting the cord around his fist, chewing his lip. Come on. Come on.

'Hello?' It was a confused and bleary voice on the other end of the line.

'It's Maxwell.'

'Max? Do you know what time it is?'

'Yes, I'm sorry,' he said. 'But I know it's not time for clichés. Jacquie, we've got trouble. Can you get over here now?'

'Why?'

'Just do it!' he heard himself shouting, then calmer, 'Park around the corner, in Celandine, all right? Come in the back way, over the fence at the back. I'll be waiting.' And he rang off.

'Jacquie Carpenter?' Sylvia checked, trying to control her breathing, fighting off the panic welling like a floodtide inside her.

'Yes,' Maxwell said. 'She's good. She'll know what to do.'

'Oh. Max,' and she got up and ran to him, throwing her arms round his neck. 'Don't you know what to do?'

'I've seen it a thousand times, Sylv,' he told her. 'Up there, on the big screen. Jimmy Stewart, Michael Caine, Mel Gibson, they've all been through it. But that's a script, it's a story. It's got its own built-in safety net. This? This is real, Sylv. It's happening. And I daren't look down. I daren't look down because I know there's no safety net down there, just a black hole where they've buried Tiffany.' And he felt her body shake with sobs all over again.

'She's asleep now.' Sylvia looked pale in the lamplight. 'I gave her something. We won't see her before morning.'

'What time is it?' Maxwell asked.

'Four thirty,' Jacquie said, still holding the empty coffee cup. 'How are you feeling, Sylvia?'

The nurse shrugged, pushing her hair away from her face. Even now, with all this, she resented Jacquie Carpenter. The way she held her head, and filled her jeans and most of all the way she sat too close to Peter Maxwell.

'I'm okay,' she said.

'Try it again, Max,' Jacquie suggested. 'Play the tape.'

'It's no good, Jacquie,' he told her. 'I don't know the voice.'

'South Yorkshire, I'd say,' the detective was thinking out loud. 'I'm no expert, but I'd say South Yorkshire. We can't trace the call, unless it's on a digital exchange. He'd have dialled 141 of course. If he calls again . . . I can get a team . . .'

'He said he would,' Maxwell reminded her.

She nodded, not wanting to say what she said next. 'I know, Max. But,' and she reached out and held his hand, 'they don't always do what they say. They might intend to, but something goes wrong and they panic.'

Her voice was steady, low, kind, but matter-of-fact.

'Who are they, for Christ's sake?' Sylvia blurted. This silly bitch was just sitting there, making eyes at the man she loved, holding his hand, talking bollocks.

Jacquie sat up again, turning to the other woman. 'He hasn't mentioned money,' she said, 'so we must assume this is a pervert, a weirdo.' She saw Sylvia's lip quiver, the glint of new tears in her eyes. 'Max, did Tiffany mention anybody else apart from this Mark Irwin? A boy? A man?'

Maxwell had been racking his brains on that one. He couldn't help. 'What about a girlfriend? Sylvia, she'd been staying with you. Did she talk about anybody? At Leighford High? Elsewhere?'

Sylvia shook her head, the one that was spinning, still trying to take in the enormity of what had happened, to put the impossible into some sort of framework she could understand.

'She's at school in London,' Maxwell explained. 'Roxburgh Hall. She's certainly had no calls from there as far as I know. Sylv?'

'No, no, I don't think so.'

'We can check incomings,' Jacquie said.

'No,' Maxwell's command was curt and clear. 'No police, Jacquie. No team, no electronic gadgets. I'm not playing with Tiffany's life.'

She looked from one to the other of them, frightened, guilty, desperate people looking for a ray of hope in a darkened world where the lights had suddenly gone out. Sylvia who had stupidly agreed to let the girl go out in the first place. And Max, who had stupidly passed the buck before that. 'Max,' she said softly, 'I am what I am. We can put a trace on the next call that he makes, analyse the tape you've got, get a fix on that accent, identify background noise in aircraft, train, clock, something.'

'No,' he told her again. For a moment, she was a little girl again and her teacher had told her off.

'Then you've lost her,' Jacquie said. 'There's nothing I can do.'

Maxwell didn't want to leave his phone, but Jacquie persuaded him he had to. Business as usual. Take Lucy to school, occupy her time in the normal way – Sylvia's too. Lucy would plough through double German as though the bastards had won the war and Sylvia would talk acne to Year 9 and show the Year 10 girls how to roll a condom onto a cucumber – just one of the little life skills necessary for the twenty-first century. Maxwell held an Assembly, bawled out a child who had dared to drop some litter by his feet; and talked the Year 12 historians through Louis XVI's foreign policy as if it was the most natural thing in the world.

Al half past ten, he was in his office, pacing the floor, his mind whirling with the events of the night. His telephone rang and Thingee was there for him. 'A call for you, Mr Maxwell.'

'Hello?'

'Mr Maxwell?' It was South Yorkshire Man, smooth, sophisticated, slimy. 'How are you feeling today?'

'Who is this?' he asked.

'Oh, come now, Mr Maxwell,' the voice chuckled. 'Let's let that be my little secret, shall we? I promised I'd be in touch.'

'Where's Tiffany?'

'Safe,' the voice said, 'for the present.'

Maxwell sat down at his desk. 'What do you want?' he asked.

'I want you out of my life, Mr Maxwell,' the telephone told him. 'Out of the Larry Warner business. I said as much to Chris Logan before I killed him.'

'I want to talk to Tiffany.'

'You're not listening to me, Mr Maxwell,' the voice sounded calm, assured. 'You'll never talk to Tiffany again unless we can come to an arrangement.'

'An arrangement?' Maxwell frowned. 'Meaning what?'

'I've heard about you, Mr Maxwell. You've got a reputation for snooping. You're a latter-day Don Quixote, aren't you? Tilting at other people's windmills. Well, take care, Mr Maxwell. Remember what happened to the old knight? He got his lance caught up in the windmill's sails, didn't he? Fetched himself a nasty one. And, if you want to take the analogy further, I've got Sancho Panza.'

'I wouldn't think that analogy works too well,' Maxwell told him. 'Wasn't he a fat little squire?'

'And not at all like Tiffany, quite. No, she's rather your Nordic type, isn't she? Not at all your greasy Dago. Tell me – I haven't looked yet – is she a natural blonde?'

'You bastard . . .' Maxwell was on his feet, his knuckles white around the phone.

'Uh-huh-uh, Mr Maxwell,' the Head of Sixth Form could practically see the bastard wagging a warning finger. 'You upset me and I could make life very miserable for you. What, for instance, are you going to tell Tiffany's mother about all this? Sorry your daughter's dead, only I was rude to her kidnapper. That would never do, would it?'

'How much do you want?'

There was a chilling chuckle at the other end of the phone. 'I've told you my terms, Mr Maxwell. Please don't insult me further by mentioning money. You've already cast doubt on my parentage as it is.' And with a click, the line went dead.

He couldn't concentrate on his marking – those fumbling efforts of Year 10 to explain exactly how the Big Three had got it wrong at Versailles. His Number Two in the Sixth Form, known to generations as The Fridge because of her bulk and her preference for white, recognized the symptoms and left well alone. When Mad Max looked preoccupied, with a glint in his eye and an iron ridge in his jaw, you stepped aside, walked away.

'Max,' Sylvia popped her head around the door as the bell that tolls the knell of parting day rang and the Leighford herds made their way slowly o'er the car park. 'Any news?'

He waved her to a seat and closed the door. 'Another call,' he said. 'He wants me off the Larry Warner thing.'

'What about Tiffany?'

'He's got her. Knows about Sandie, knows she's blonde. That's enough for me. It's genuine all right.'

'Max, you've got to get back to Jacquie.'

'No.' He shook his head. 'Sylv, I can't take the chance.'

'Here,' she said. 'Sit down and have some of this.'

'What is it?' He hadn't seen her slip something out of her pocket.

'Brandy.'

He held his fingers in the sign of the cross, as he usually did when he sighted Deirdre Lessing.

'It won't kill you,' she said. 'It'll calm you down.'

'Where's Lucy?' He took a reluctant swig while she clattered about with his kettle and coffee mugs.

'Drama Club. I checked.' She caught his look. 'It's all right, Max. She's with the others. David's there.'

'Oh, good,' he snarled. Somehow, the information didn't reassure him. He didn't trust his own shadow at the moment.

'Would it help,' she asked him, 'if we talked it through, twist by twist?'

He looked at his watch. 'Mrs B. will be here in ten minutes, sprinkling more fag ash than she hoovers up. Have we got time?'

'Of course,' Sylvia Matthews should have been a public schoolboy. In the shipwreck that was Maxwell's life at the moment, she was indispensable. 'Here,' she passed him a mug, designed to cheer. 'That'll take away the horrid taste of the brandy.' It comforted him that he was still able to smile.

He leaned back on his soft, black, plastic chair, the one that came with the Sixth Form territory, provided by County. 'All right,' he said. 'Larry Warner, shot dead at an indeterminable distance – let's say three hundred yards – by a high-powered hunting rifle, to whit, a Ruger KM 77 Vt Mark II. The question is, why?'

'A professional hit?' Sylvia was thinking aloud. 'Is there such a thing? It all sounds a bit far-fetched.'

'Some murders are,' Maxwell nodded, his face wreathed in the coffee steam.

'But it's fiction, isn't it? Hit men aren't real, surely, not in Britain?'

'Neil Hamlyn?' Maxwell reminded her.

'But Jacquie said he couldn't have done it. He was in custody when Chris Logan was killed.'

'And she also told us he was killed with the same gun. Right. But Chris was an afterthought. The Yorkshire tyke said so – or hinted at it. Chris, bless him, got too close. Found out something he shouldn't. The Yorkshireman killed him as a result.'

'And where did Chris go?'

'To see Anthony LeStrange, who denies seeing him. And who has an alibi for the time Chris was murdered.'

Sylvia shook her head, cradling her coffee mug. 'I'm not a very clever person, Max,' she said, 'Give me a sprained ankle and period pains, I'm fine. But this . . . everywhere you turn, there's a brick wall.'

'Yes,' Maxwell said. 'Brick walls. That's what DCI Hall said.'

'When?'

'Yesterday. I had lunch with him. He was buying.'

'You didn't tell me that.'

'Sorry,' he said. 'What with one thing and another, it slipped my mind. He gave me a rather curious option brick walls or loose ends. Then he started talking about the White Knights.'

'Who?'

'Quite. They're a racist group, a little to the right of the old National Front, I believe. Genghis Khan is their patron saint.'

'What's the connection?'

'Neil Hamlyn is a member.'

Sylvia was lost. 'You mean Warner was killed for racial motives? What was he? Jewish?'

Maxwell shrugged. 'But Hamlyn didn't do it. We've established that. Warner was a homosexual and our friends on the Right don't usually go a bundle on them either. Remember the London bombings? Bangladeshis in Brick Lane, Afro-Caribbeans in Brixton, gays in Soho. There's a pattern of a kind, warped as it is.'

'Where does that take us?'

'It takes us,' Maxwell was sitting up now, the germ of an idea in his head, 'to a brick wall that I believe has a chink in it. O sweet and lovely wall. Show my thy chink, to blink through with mine eyne. Sylv, I need to be out of here for a day, perhaps two.'

'Where?'

'I'll tell you when I get there. If anybody asks, I've got flu. I'm not telling a soul about the real reason. Not Diamond, not his idiot deputies, not that sadist who does the supply cover. Sylv,' he picked her up and held her shoulders, 'Sylv, are you going to be all right with Lucy? At my place?'

'Your place?'

He nodded. 'They took Tiffany from outside yours . . .'

'I don't need reminding, Max,' she said.

'Here are the keys,' he passed them to her. 'For what it's worth, I had a new lock fitted. How do you buy a moveable telephone machine?'

The door crashed open and Mrs B. stood there, half a mile of fag ash dribbling down her chin. 'Bleedin' kids. You'd think they'd get tired of chuckin' their cheese and tomato sandwiches down the bleedin' staircase, wouldn't you? Course, I blame the government, you know. It's that bleedin' blind bloke. Might as well let his dog do the job.'

CHAPTER SEVENTEEN

'Lucy, darling, how goes it? God, how do you young things cope with these?' Maxwell was talking into Sylvia's mobile, shaking it, rattling it. No point in buying one of the damned things when one's School Nurse has one.

'I'm fine, Uncle Maxie, but I wish you were here.'

The kid sounded like an ancient seaside postcard with two fat ladies and a tiny bloke, but Maxwell wanted to hug her. How many little girls can one man lose in a lifetime? 'I won't be long, sweetheart, I promise. Put Sylvia on, will you?'

'Love you, Uncle Maxie.' And she was gone.

'Love you, darling.'

'Max,' Sylvia was there. 'You say the nicest things. Where are you?'

'On a train, somewhere north of Guildford.'

'Where are you going?'

'To the Library for some answers. Sorry to be so cryptic, Sylv, but it's better you don't know. Has he called again, the Yorkshireman?'

'No, but an Irishman has.'

What?' There was a horrible crackling and an intermittence down his ear. 'You're breaking up, Sylv. What are you talking about?'

'An Irishman, Max. Don't ask me which part. North, I think. Ulster. Sounded like Ian Paisley. Max, I'm scared. I'm trying not to let Lucy know, but where is he? Where's he calling from? Where are you? Oh, God, this is hopeless.'

'Sylv? I can't hear you. Did you say Irishman?' Maxwell was shouting so that the whole carriage heard. 'Get Jacquie. Nothing official. But you need protection. If the bastard rings again, give him this number. I need to talk to him myself. Sylv? Are you there?'

But Sylvia wasn't there. She was stabbing out Jacquie Carpenter's private number, the one Maxwell had scrawled on the cover of the phone book aeons ago. Before his world had turned upside down.

Amy Weston looked tired and old. Not that Maxwell habitually went around guessing the ages of ladies, especially poetesses. After all, he'd been to a good school. She stood in the hall of her Mock Tudor home, more than a little surprised to see him. And certainly more than a little surprised to see him suddenly crouch and feel her parquet flooring.

'It's a bitch, this stuff, isn't it? Endless scuffing. What caused this particular bit, I wonder? One of the cats? The stiletto heels of an autograph-hunting fan – or Chris Logan's head as it hit the deck, a split-second after you put a bullet into him?'

He was standing again now, his eyes on a level with hers, watching for the tell-tale signs. 'Let's talk you through it,' he said, edging forward to close the front door. 'Your throat's gone dry, you're experiencing tunnel vision. All you can see is me, no right, no left. You can barely hear what I'm saying, can you? That's because of the noise of your heart thumping in your head. Your chest – forgive my bluntness – feels tight, compressed. Your hair is detaching itself from your head. And, my, aren't those hands heavy? What'll go first, I wonder, your knees or your bladder?'

Amy was blinking, walking backwards, trying to cope with the verbal battery he was giving her. 'What are you talking about?' The voice was thick, strangled.

'I'm talking about guilt, Ms Weston; more specifically, I'm talking about murder, Ms Weston. I'm talking about shooting a man, right here, I'd say, in the hallway.' He looked around him. 'I must say, your repairman has done an excellent job. No splintered woodwork, no torn wallpaper. How did you explain a bullet in the doorframe to the handyman? Unless of course,' he had circled the space, sliding his fingers reflectively over the surface, 'your handyman speaks with a genteel Yorkshire accent and has a reasonable grasp of Cervantes. You know, Don Quixote? And then, of course, there's that other little matter – which one of you has my niece?' He wasn't smiling now, but standing, head to head, staring hard.

'I'm going to call the police.' Amy Weston snapped out of the hold his eyes had on her and made for the lounge.

'Excellent!' Maxwell's strides were longer and the Devon Rex leapt a mile as he snatched up the receiver. 'Allow me to dial for you. What's the number? Or shall I cut out the middle man and just ring 999?'

She grabbed the phone from him and put it down, breathing heavily, fighting for calm, desperately seeking composure.

'All right,' he said. 'Citizen's arrest. I don't know the form of words. "You're not obliged to say anything"? No, they've changed that now, haven't they? And for the worse in my opinion. Worse than the New English Bible. How about "You're nicked"? That packs a certain punch, even when it's not delivered by the long arm of the law.'

'Please,' she said, both hands in the air in supplication, both hands trembling. 'Please, I'm frightened enough.' And she sat down on the chintz settee, taking breaths, feeling her heart-beat slow towards simple hysteria.

'Why did you leave the rose and poem at the Arches?'

'Mr Maxwell,' she looked at him through pale, sad eyes. 'Will you let me make a phone call?'

'To Mr LeStrange? I think not.'

'No,' she shook her head. 'Not Anthony. Someone else.'

Maxwell hadn't really paid much attention to Robert Hart at the Garrick the week before last. He'd never met a Booker prizewinner before, but he wasn't impressed. It had been an hour or so before he arrived at the Mock Tudor house at Lammas Green, and he looked older, scruffier – a tank top and deck shoes; but perhaps that's what the literati were wearing these days.

'Bob.' She threw her arms around his neck, clinging there as though to the wreckage of her life. 'I think we have to talk to Mr Maxwell.'

'Amy . . .' he began. Then he saw Maxwell leaning on the lounge doorframe. 'What's all this about?'

'That,' Maxwell said, 'is what I hoped you were going to tell me.'

'Bob. I think we've found an ally in Mr Maxwell.' She led the writer into the lounge and they sat down together. 'Drink, darling?'

'I think I might need one,' Hart said.

She filled two glasses with fingers of gin and splashed in the tonic. 'Mr Maxwell?'

'No thanks,' he shook his head. 'But I'd like some answers.'

'Bob?' she sat down again and laced her fingers through his.

Hart took a swig and faced his man. 'All right, Mr Maxwell, what do you know about Archie Godden?'

'Basically, only what he told me when I met him. Music critic for the *Observer*. Clearly a member of the Garrick Club. Something of a BOF, I gather.'

'Bof?' That wasn't an acronym Hart knew.

'Boring Old Fart.'

'Yes, well, he's certainly that. But that's not all. Mr Maxwell, have you heard of an organization called the White Knights?'

Maxwell looked at them both. 'As a matter of fact, I have,' he said.

'And what do you know about them?'

'Not much, I'm afraid. They're a right-wing group, opposed to ethnic minorities various. That's about it.'

'They were formed back in the 'sixties,' Hart told him, leaning back in the settee and savouring his g 'n' t. 'A rather exclusive club at Oxford.'

'Oxford?' sneered Maxwell. 'I might have known.'

'I won't embarrass the particular college in question, although, to be fair, they came from everywhere, cross-faculty sort of thing. They did a great deal of damage in the 'seventies. Remember the winter of discontent? The three day week?'

'That's what I still work in honour of,' Maxwell told him.

'What about the miners' strike? Scargill?'

'Arthur Scargill is a member of the White Knights?'

'No, no,' Hart shook his head. 'You're missing the point. Wherever two or three hundred are gathered together, Mr Maxwell, you're going to find the White Knights. I detest the word arcane, but it's the only one that fits these people. Working behind the scenes, faceless. Never in the crowd, never caught on security cameras. Scargill, Tariq Ali, Danny Cohn-Bendit, they were the names we knew, the faces the media showed us. They had their agendas, some of it laughable, some of it laudable. No, I'm talking about the puppeteers, the string pullers. What we saw, what the media ranted about – and still does – are Rent-a-Mob. We're talking about the brains behind.'

'Archie Godden?'

Hart was warming to his theme now. 'Think about it. Godden was at Oxford in the early 'sixties. They held a party on the day Kennedy was killed.'

'Really?'

'Sick, wasn't it? They were celebrating the fall of a Good Guy. All right, so he wasn't quite King Arthur, we know that now, but he had time and respect for the blacks, the underdog. There was a killing in Oxford the next day. A Jamaican was found beaten to death in an alley.'

'Godden?'

Hart managed a laugh. 'Oh, not personally, no. But he was there, organizing, planning, holding coats. The police interviewed him, but of course, got nowhere. That man could lie for England.'

'And often has,' Amy added. 'We believe that since his Oxford days, Godden has been orchestrating every bit of mayhem he can. He despises the left, obviously, but he now also despises every government since the war. The only politician who made any sense to him, after Oswald Mosley, was Enoch Powell.'

'Rivers of blood, hmm?' Maxwell asked.

'Of course.' Hart got up to freshen his glass. Amy declined. 'He's moved with the times. He was never your front man. No dire warning speeches from him, not even irate, loony letters to *The Times*. Just quiet control of money and people.'

'Money?'

'Charts,' Amy said. 'As far as we can tell, it's a front.'

'A front?'

'Money laundering.' Hart winced as the gin hit his tonsils. 'We don't know the mechanics of it yet, but under the guise of a charity, backing worthy causes like your school, he's stashing away a fortune for whatever the next little anti-social spree's going to be. What would be your guess, Amy? The Millennium Dome? Jesus, the damage doesn't bear thinking about.'

'And Warner?' Maxwell wanted to know.

'Ah,' Hart raised a finger, 'now that I can only guess at. The man's a forensic auditor – was, sorry – and about the best in his field. We think he'd got a sniff of something, what Godden was up to with the money – really, that is. I'll lay you odds the law haven't got a clue about any of this.'

'It's the first place they'd look,' Amy said. 'An auditor dies suspiciously – you assume a financial motive. Except they haven't, as far as we know, been able to find one.'

'What about Neil Hamlyn?' Maxwell asked.

'Who?'

'The man helping police with their inquiries and currently, I presume, in Leighford Nick. Ex-SAS I understand.'

Hart shrugged. 'I told you,' he said. 'Godden's never the front man. He couldn't shoot his way out of a paper bag. This Hamlyn is Rent-a-Mob. If he's ex-SAS he'd have been drummed out for instability. Classic, isn't it, the government trains a man to kill and then become alarmed when he does. Whatever happened to common sense in the world?'

'Now, Bob,' Amy scolded gently. 'We aren't here to sermonize.'

'You're right,' Hart smiled at her and held her hand.

'And Logan?'

'Logan found something out,' Amy said. 'We don't know what.'

'About Godden?'

'We don't know.' Hart shook his head. 'But we know a man who might.'

'Who?'

'Hilary St John.'

'The fashion photographer?'

Hart nodded. 'He was at Oxford with Godden. They used to be close, but I gather there's been something of a rift.'

'Much more to the point, people,' Maxwell said, 'my niece.'

'What?' Hart asked.

Amy turned to him. 'Mr Maxwell was telling me about it before you got here, darling. Someone's kidnapped his niece . . . er . . . Tiffany.'

Maxwell nodded.

'My God,' Hart growled. 'This is intolerable. Mr Maxwell, you must be beside yourself. What can we do?'

'Find her,' said Maxwell.

'If Godden's got her . . .'

'Yes?'

'Well, he lives in Oxford. Got a town house not far from the Radcliffe Camera. Look, I've got an idea.'

The others looked at Bob Hart. Even the Devon Rex seemed interested.

'It's going to take some nerve on your part, Mr Maxwell. Are you game?'

Maxwell leaned forward. 'If it'll get my niece back in one piece, Mr Hart,' he said, 'I'm a brace of pheasant.'

Working, Hilary St John looked even more dissolute than when relaxing at the Garrick. Leaving Amy near a phone, Hart had driven Maxwell up to town. It may have been mid-evening, but Fashion Photography in general and Hilary St John in particular took no notice of office hours.

St John was lying on the floor when Hart and Maxwell arrived, lights and white umbrellas in all directions, pointing a ludicrously expensive camera at a slim, naked girl gyrating in front of him.

'That's it, sweetheart.' The camera whirred with a life of its own, 'Give me more of that. Yes, pout. Excellent. Back. And again.

Great. Just move . . .' He suddenly saw them out of the corner of his trained eye. 'Fuck!'

The mood was broken, the magic gone. The girl stood limply, then threw both hands on her hips in resignation. She was used to this. St John rolled upright and hung the second of two cameras around his neck. 'I can't say I like your timing, Bob,' he growled, a tad gruffer than when Maxwell had met him last.

Maxwell, for all his sang-froid, found himself staring at the girl.

'What's the matter with you?' she asked, snatching up a cigarette packet. 'Never seen a pair of tits before?'

Maxwell went into his coy routine. 'Not since dear Mama's,' he said.

'Weirdo!' she muttered and stomped off to find a robe.

'You'll have to forgive Jessica,' St John said. 'It's been a long session.'

'What particular fashion are you photographing at the moment, Mr St John?' Maxwell felt bound to ask.

'Do I come into a classroom and tell you how to teach?' the camera man asked.

'Touché,' Maxwell bowed.

'We've got a problem, Hilary,' Hart said. 'I gather you remember Mr Maxwell.'

St John nodded sullenly while Maxwell began fiddling with a light gadget. Deftly, the photographer removed it from him.

'Yes,' he said pointedly, 'I do.'

'It's Archie,' Hart said.

St John looked at them both. 'Is this something I'm going to need a drink for?' he asked.

'Better make that three,' Hart suggested and found a low, soft chair out of the circle of lights.

'That's a wrap, Jess,' St John called to a room beyond a curtain. 'Same time tomorrow.'

The reply was a slammed door.

'Tart!' St John growled. 'Now,' he fussed with three Scotches. 'What of Archie?'

'Mr Maxwell thinks he's involved with the murder of Larry Warner.'

St John stopped in mid soda squirt. 'Does he, now?'

'Not to mention Chris Logan,' Maxwell added.

'Bob,' St John sat down on the little leather stool, perched, vulnerable. 'Can I have a word?'

'Hilary,' Hart frowned, 'anything you have to say to me you can say to Mr Maxwell.'

St John looked from one to the other, gnawing his lip, looking for space to manoeuvre. There wasn't any. 'Archie and I go a long way back,' he said.

'Hilary,' Hart said. 'You can't hide behind old loyalties for ever. Two people are dead. And we think Archie's got Mr Maxwell's niece.'

'What?' the photographer gaped. 'No, no,' he chuckled, 'that's not Archie's style. Why should he have your niece, Maxwell?'

'To shut me out, shut me down. I was asking questions about Larry Warner. So was Chris Logan. I think that's why he died.'

'I've told Maxwell about Archie, Hilary,' Hart explained. 'It's time. What do you know?'

'Oh, God,' St John sighed and drained his glass, feeling the searing on his tonsils. 'When we were at Oxford, it was all a bit of a giggle. A laugh. There were Leftist groups and Rightist groups. All indulging in debate. Just average schoolboys – and girls – really. Intoxicated with the sound of our own voices. But Archie? Well, Archie took it all seriously. There was a black lad, not a student, a local. Archie paid some thugs to beat him up. He died.'

'You were involved?' Maxwell asked.

'No,' St John sighed. 'No, I wasn't, and I've often asked myself what I'd have done if I'd been there. Would I have tried to save the boy, waded in? Or would I have helped to kick the shit out of him.' He reached across for another Scotch. 'I'll never know.'

'And Godden?'

'We went our different ways,' St John said. 'I took pictures. Good ones. I make an awful lot of money, Maxwell. Exhibitions from the

Palace to as far as the eye can see. Archie . . Archie is more your philosopher.'

'Philosopher?' Maxwell echoed.

'Oh, yes, here,' and the photographer passed him a book. 'Only the author's name has been changed to protect the guilty.'

Maxwell read the title aloud. '*Nietzsche Now.*'

'It's a sort of brave new world,' St John said, 'in which the British Empire is restored, handed over with a generous helping of neo-Nazi race hate. Tony Blair is publicly burned, I believe and the letters t, u and c are removed from the alphabet.'

'Really?'

St John laughed. 'All right, I'm being flippant, Mr Maxwell. I'm being flippant because actually it's all so bloody frightening. Archie's not talking about some fantastic Never-Never, he's talking about tomorrow. Christ, he's talking about today.'

'What about my niece?' Maxwell closed to the man.

'I don't know,' St John told him. 'Maxwell, if I had any idea, I'd tell you. As I said, it's not Archie's style. He isn't the muscle, he just buys it.'

'Is that what he did?' Maxwell asked. 'Bought the muscle to hit Warner and Logan?'

'That's his style,' St John nodded.

'Tell him about the phone call,' Hart said.

'What phone call?' Maxwell asked.

'Archie and I only meet occasionally,' St John told him. 'Charts meetings, the odd media bash. Last week he rang me, out of the blue, asked me about the Warner business.'

'Asked you what?'

'Whether anyone had been snooping. He mentioned this Chris Logan.'

'He did?'

St John nodded. 'Archie liked to think I was still his, still loyal to the cause. I wasn't. Christ knows I'd told him that often enough. He wouldn't let it alone. He told me this journalist, this Logan, was pestering him, asking questions.'

'The next we heard,' Hart butted in, 'Logan was dead. It was all over the *Evening Standard* and the local news. We put two and two together.'

'But you've no proof?' Maxwell asked.

'I told you,' St John said, 'Godden's style. He'll have distanced himself. Alibis coming out of his arsehole. There'll be nothing to link him with Logan at all.'

Something of a silence fell. 'I rather think,' Hart said, 'that that's going to be Mr Maxwell's aim in life, establishing that link. Am I right, Mr Maxwell?'

Maxwell had been to the Bodleian before. Several times. But now, it was for research of a different kind. He sat in Duke Humphrey's Library, the sun gilding the magnificent fan vaulting of the low ceiling. Learned tomes gathered dust in the rarefied air and assorted students, such culture wasted on their callow youth, were dotted around, poring over faded manuscripts. Maxwell was delighted to see there wasn't a computer in sight.

It was nearly eleven before his target arrived and Maxwell had been up since shortly after dawn, having availed himself of Robert Hart's spare room. The author had driven him up to town and he'd caught the seven forty-eight from Paddington. Archie Godden appeared to be wearing the same bow tie he'd worn at the Garrick, obviously a sort of uniform for the music critics' society or that of the White Knights. Maxwell waited until the man had found a seat and had settled himself with a pile of volumes and a notepad.

'Rattling good yarn,' Maxwell whispered and placed another book on top of the pile.

Godden started. He read the title '*Nietszche Now*' and the name of the author 'Hans Welt'.

Maxwell sat down next to him. 'Good morning, Mr Welt,' he said. A frowsty old spinster, comatose and cobwebbed, rustled into life in the far corner. She looked as if she'd been here since Duke Humphrey bought his first book, waiting for someone to cast her as

Miss Havisham. 'Sshh,' was her highly original contribution to the proceedings.

'How did you find me?' Godden ignored the warning.

'How did I discover you were Hans Welt or how did I know you'd be here at this hour?' Maxwell asked.

'Either,' Godden would settle for.

'Bob Hart and Hilary St John,' he told him.

'Sshh,' the old girl hissed louder.

Godden looked up, interested. 'Let me buy you a cup of coffee, Mr Maxwell.' And he swept out past the ancient reader. 'If you can read that, madam,' he growled at her, 'thank a man.'

Her mouth fell open.

'And a teacher,' Maxwell echoed. And they were gone.

Roger Garrett was First Deputy at Leighford High. Like all Deputy Heads his insecurity complex could more accurately be described as a conurbation. He also had a brown nose from all his years of being up somebody else's bottom. 'Well, where is he?' he asked all and sundry. 'It's not like Max to be off. And there's no answer from his answerphone.'

Sylvia Matthews swept past him, dithering in the Hall as he was, being roundly ignored by multitudes of children. It wasn't like Sylvia Matthews, who was good and loyal and true. She'd given fifteen years of her life to Leighford High School, but suddenly, today, she'd had enough. 'Roger,' she said, 'Get a life.'

Maxwell was mother in the Crypt Tearooms. He poured for them both as Godden eyed him suspiciously. He still didn't like the man's bow tie and without that charming lady Deirdre Lessing, he was afraid that Maxwell would probably be even more of an oaf. It came as something of a surprise to him that Maxwell didn't actually drink coffee from his saucer or pick his nose with his elbow.

'I must admit,' Maxwell was saying, sparkling at his man, 'I underestimated you.'

'You did?'

'Well, you're not going to believe this, but I'd just bought *Nietzsche Now* when we met at the Garrick.'

'Really?'

'I was particularly interested in the Ethnic Cleansing section.'

'Well, it seems to be in vogue, doesn't it?' Godden asked. 'Africa, the Balkans. The bottom line is that coffee-coloured people won't do.'

'Well, quite,' Maxwell sipped his Earl Grey. 'I had a ticklish situation the other day. One of our brown brethren caught stealing from the School Tuck Shop.'

'Well, there you are. Breeding will out, you see, Mr Maxwell. But I had no idea you were of . . . shall we say, like mind?'

'Oh, my dear fellow. It all started when I was at Cambridge.'

'Oh dear!' Godden crowed. He sounded as if he'd swallowed an even bigger plum than usual.

'I know,' Maxwell chuckled. 'But we'll have to agree to differ on the Varsity front.'

'Well, we're white men all,' Godden smiled at him.

'We're of an age, you and I. Good school. Good college.' Maxwell felt the skin on his back crawling. He wasn't sure how much more of this he could keep up. 'Then, suddenly, I looked around my college and there were Americans and Jamaicans and Lord knows what else.'

'Tell me about it, dear boy,' Godden nodded. 'I tell you, the day we lowered the Union Jack in India . . . well, that's only the tip of the iceberg, of course.'

'Of course,' Maxwell nodded, attacking his Danish. 'But what can be done?'

'Done?'

'About it all. The situation. I'm not just talking corner shops here, Mr Godden . . .'

'Oh, Archie, please.'

'Archie, I'm talking about politics, medicine, the media, for God's sake.'

Godden leaned forward. 'Queers and Jewboys,' he said. 'In the Beeb of course, it used to be Queers and Catholics. Give me your honest moronic nigger any day. At least they have a history of slavery – knowing their place.'

'Well, quite.'

'But the Yids, well – God's chosen people!' He almost spat his Genoa the length of the table. 'The arrogance of it. The unadulterated nerve.'

'Homosexuality.' Maxwell shook his head despairingly. He thought that if he spread his arms it would look too Jewish.

'Cabinet's riddled with it,' Godden assured him. 'Riddled. And as for the Church, well . . .'

'Oh, appalling,' Maxwell concurred. 'Absolutely appalling.'

'So what can be done?'

'I asked you that.'

'Well,' Godden sat back so that his stomach never parted company with the table rim. 'One or two things, actually.'

'I'm all ears.'

Godden looked at him, then glanced around, mostly, Maxwell noticed, to the right. 'How well do you know Tony LeStrange?'

'The magician? Not at all.'

'Mm,' Godden munched on his Genoa. Other than that, the silence was deafening. 'There are things to be done, Mr Maxwell

'Oh, Max, please.'

Godden smiled. 'Max. But there's a little fly in the ointment.'

'A nigger in the woodpile?' Maxwell twinkled.

For a second Godden was silent, then he roared with laughter, pounding the table with the flat of his hand. '*Nietzsche Now* is doing rather well,' he said, suddenly quiet and sitting closer to his man. 'You know how some books are world-shakers – the Bible, of course, *Mein Kampf,* John Hackett's *Third World War* – there's no doubt that the groundswell of opinion is changing. Stephen Lawrence is only the beginning.'

'Stephen Lawrence? Were you involved . . . ?'

'No, no,' Godden beamed as though delighted by the notion. 'No, that case is just symptomatic. Joe Public are just sick and tired of being dictated to and milked by every *Untermenschen* group from here to eternity. There's a reckoning coming, Max, you mark my words – a great reckoning.'

'Marlowe,' said Maxwell. '"A great reckoning in a little room" – Shakespeare's description of Marlowe's death.'

'Pooftah, wasn't he?'

'And a Cambridge man,' Maxwell nudged the great critic, who roared with laughter once again. 'What's the little fly in the ointment?'

'Oh, that?' Godden was suddenly serious again. 'Look, Max, I have to be somewhere in half an hour. Can you hang around, do the sights or something? Come and see me tonight, say, eight? Have a spot of dinner.' And he passed Maxwell his card.

'Thanks,' Maxwell smiled. 'Dinner it is,' and he raised his Earl Grey. 'Here's to Nietzsche,' he toasted, 'and to flies in ointment.'

The other women in Maxwell's life looked at him, each unsure of the other.

'When was this taken?' Jacquie asked. The photograph showed Maxwell under the slouch hat of a Confederate general, all dim and flaring lamps. Around him, a group of other uniformed gallants and their Southern belles stared back from the sepia.

'A History Department dinner,' Sylvia told her. 'They always have them at Leighford – the outgoing Year Thirteen historians and the staff meet to celebrate or drown their sorrows, whichever.'

'In fancy dress?'

Sylvia closed the album and put it back on Maxwell's bookcase. 'Historical period, I think he'd call it,' she said. 'Takes it all very seriously. Notice nobody's smiling. They all had a whale of a time, but apparently nobody in the Civil War smiled very much. Something to do with exposure time.'

Jacquie crossed to the settee and curled up on it, wrapping her hands around a cup of coffee that said 'Get the Max taste'. She already had. And so had the woman who sat opposite her now, idly stirring her cocoa.

'How long have you loved him?' Jacquie suddenly asked.

Sylvia looked up just as suddenly, scalding her top lip. 'I didn't know it showed,' she winced. 'How about you?'

Jacquie was going to deny it, but she saw there was little point. 'I don't know,' she said. 'I couldn't tell you how long.'

'Fifteen years in my case,' Sylvia said. 'Ever since I've been at Leighford High. I was going through a pretty messy divorce then. And no, before you ask, Max wasn't involved in that. He was funny, he was kind. He was . . . there. Sometimes that's all it takes, isn't it?'

Jacquie nodded. It was like looking into a mirror.

'What do we do?' Sylvia asked. 'Draw lots? Claw each other's eyes out? I expect Max would suggest pistols at dawn or something like that.'

'We go on,' Jacquie said. 'We go on doing what we are doing. It's up to him.'

'Up to him?' Sylvia's eyes widened in disbelief. 'My dear girl, I could give you fourteen years. I'm supposed to be the resigned one, the little woman generation. I thought you lot were all Greenham Common and It's My Body Right Or Wrong.'

Jacquie chuckled. 'It was your generation who discovered female orgasm,' she said.

Sylvia found herself laughing in spite of herself. 'And the only reason I didn't burn my bra was that I couldn't afford to.'

It was odd. Two women in the house of the bachelor they loved, his niece upstairs asleep, his soldiers saddled in the attic, his cat out on the tiles and the two of them laughing together like old friends. Then the phone rang.

'Hello?' Sylvia answered it under silent, nodded instructions from Jacquie.

'Sylv, is that you?'

'Max, where are you?'

'Never mind. How's Lucy?'

'She's fine. Sleeping.'

'Any more calls?'

'Nothing.'

'Are you all right?'

'Fine. Jacquie's here.'

'Jacquie. Put her on.'

Sylvia held the cold receiver to her heart for a moment, then passed it across.

'Max. Where are you?'

'It doesn't matter, Jacquie. I'm making headway.'

'What sort of headway?'

'White Knights. Tell Hall I'm on to something. I'll be in touch.'

'Max . . .'

But the line had died.

'Come to think of it,' Jacquie was thumping 1471, 'he's the most stubborn, cantankerous, awkward bastard on God's earth.'

'Isn't that what we can't resist, either of us?' Sylvia asked.

'Oxford,' Jacquie said. 'He's in Oxford.'

'Why?'

'Let's find out.' She was dialling again. 'Pauline? It's Jacquie Carpenter. Look, can you check a number for me please? Oxford. Yes, I'll wait.' She cupped her hand over the receiver. 'Do you mind if I stay tonight?' she asked. 'Keep an eye on Lucy?'

Sylvia nodded, smiling. 'That's what Max would want,' she said. 'I do too.'

'Great.'

I'll tell you what,' Sylvia was already crossing Maxwell's carpet, 'while the Great Man is away, doing whatever he's doing in Oxford, what say you and I make inroads into his drinks cabinet? Unless, of course, you're on duty?'

'Bollocks!' snorted Jacquie. 'You're on!'

Elegant Georgian houses didn't bother Peter Maxwell. The fact that his modest abode in Columbine Avenue could fit into Archie Godden's place several times over didn't discomfit him one jot. Not for Mad Max the politics of envy. He put the phone down on Jacquie, the one in Archie Godden's hall, and dialled his next number, using this time the mobile that had been snuggling in his inside pocket.

'You've reached me, but I'm not available at the moment.' Amy Weston's voice came back at him. 'Please leave a message after the tone.'

He waited. 'Amy, it's Maxwell. I'm at Archie Godden's. He's kindly asked me to stay over. We're going somewhere tomorrow, but I'm not sure where. I'll keep you and Bob posted. Bye.'

'Max!' the great critic's stentorian tones echoed through from the hall. 'Nightcap?'

'You're spoiling me, Archie.' All evening, Maxwell had found this bonhomie increasingly difficult. His natural inclinations were to wring the fat racist bastard's neck.

'Southern Comfort, I think you said.'

'Oh,' Maxwell took it. 'Now this really is too much. Thank you again by the way for dinner. I didn't really equate you with Thai food, but those butterfly duck breasts! Marvellous!'

Godden led him into the library, where wall-to-wall leather filled the eye and, via the music system piped throughout the house, Wagner filled the ear. 'You mustn't jump to conclusions,' Godden said. 'I wouldn't want my daughter to marry one, but the Thais do a good line in cuisine, I'd be the first to admit. We're not all roast beef and Yorkshire, you know.'

'That's funny.' Maxwell paused by the Adam fireplace, catching his reflection in the huge, plain mirror over it.

'What?' Godden sprawled on the vast settee that a languid wolf hound had just vacated.

'Accents. It's a hobby of mine. Trying to place them. Now I'd say yours was Yorkshire. South Yorkshire, to be precise.'

Godden bellowed his mirthless laugh. 'Well, there, I'm afraid, you'd be way off. Pain me to admit it though it does, my people are Irish originally. County Mayo.'

'Irish,' Maxwell tutted and shook his head. 'Well, I never.'

'Tomorrow.' Godden sat up and leaned forward as his guest perched on the arm of the other settee. 'Pastures new.'

'Where away?'

'I want you to meet Tony again.'

'LeStrange?'

Godden nodded. 'Remember the fly in the ointment?' he asked. Maxwell nodded.

'There is a need in our business, Max, for trust. Total. Absolute. There can be no backsliding, no shilly-shallying. It's all about faith too. You have it – or you don't.'

'Are you talking about the *Observer*, Archie?' Maxwell raised an eyebrow.

A silence, then an explosion of mirth. 'The *Observer!* What dear, kind souls. If only they knew. No. I'm talking about the other business. The cleansing business, if you get my drift. Larry Warner, now. Poor Larry I'm afraid was not of the order. Oh, he was homosexual of course, I think we all knew that. I even suspected him of being Jewish, but the reason he had to die was this trust thing. His professionalism kicked in, the poor, sad bastard. Ethics, I suppose. He discovered the true purpose of Charts, where the money was eventually going. He couldn't be trusted. He had to be eliminated.'

'Why are you telling me all this, Archie?' Maxwell wanted to know.

'I told you,' Godden said. 'Trust. As soon as I met you, I knew you were different,' he looked him earnestly in the lace. 'One of us, so to speak. Tell me I'm wrong . . .'

'Well . . .'

Godden laughed. 'Exactly.' He stood up. 'Tell me, Max. What's your view on murder?'

'On Murder As One of the Fine Arts?' Maxwell checked.

'Yes,' Godden chuckled. 'I'm not sure de Quincy was being quite upfront there, was he? No, I mean, personally. Could you kill someone? Would you? Given a cause?'

'It depends,' Maxwell said.

'On the cause?'

'Something like that.'

Godden closed to his man. 'Our cause?' he said.

'What about you?' Both men's words had dropped almost to a whisper. 'Did you kill Larry Warner?'

'Me?' Godden exploded with laughter. 'My dear boy, my days of crawling through the undergrowth undetected by thousands of rubber-neckers are over, I can assure you. In fact, they never began. As for shooting, I can't hit a barn door. But, as the old advertisement had it, I know a man who can.'

'Who?'

'Tony LeStrange.'

'LeStrange? I thought he had an alibi . . .'

'Really?' It was Godden's turn to raise an eyebrow. 'Who told you that?'

Shit! Maxwell's repartee had led him too far down Godden's garden path and there was no way out now. 'The police told me.'

'The police?' Was it the late evening light or had Archie Godden turned a little pale?

'I was there,' Maxwell told him. 'Riding the Wild Water when Larry Warner was killed. That's how I got caught up in all this in the first place. As a witness, the police obviously talked to me. And my nieces.'

'How did LeStrange figure?'

'He was questioned too. So were you, weren't you? As a member of Charts, I mean?'

'Oh, yes,' Godden confirmed.

'Don't ask me how it all came out in conversation. I seemed to be at the station for bloody hours. I think I said, as a joke, really, it was probably done by magic. I think I said "I bet Anthony LeStrange could do it." And the DCI said "No, he's got an alibi" or something like that.'

Godden relaxed and laughed. 'Well,' he said. 'More fool the DCI. Doesn't he realize a magician can be in two places at once?'

CHAPTER EIGHTEEN

Rummaging through other people's fol-de-rols wasn't Maxwell's idea of a good time. Still, there were only so many places you could hide a five-foot-five-inch blonde girl who was fifteen, going on forty. He waited long enough for Archie Godden to reach the land of nod, then started on the ground floor. To his left was a cellar, like the one where Norman Bates occasionally kept his mother. There was nothing there, once Maxwell's eyes became accustomed to the dark, but some rather upmarket wines, the dust of which he was careful not to disturb, and spiders as big as your head. And they were far too big to be disturbed by anything as insignificant as Peter Maxwell.

He'd already combed the kitchen, the sitting-room, the library, the usual offices on the ground floor. He'd quizzed Archie Godden over dinner on the history of the house. It wasn't old enough for priest holes and it was too old for breeze blocks. He'd never believed in secret panels – they belonged to the spooky old house matinees usually starring Bob Hope or the ones in which Abbott and Costello meet Loaf. Which left the bedrooms and, if he could find the way up, the attic.

As he crept, Raffles-like, into each room in turn, grateful for the soft carpet and the fact that the dog slept outside in a kennel, he toyed with using Sylvia's mobile again, this time to call the police or at least talk to Jacquie. But what, in the end, did he have? Archie Godden might be a reincarnation of Attila the Hun. He might even be a psychopath. But they didn't put you away for either of those things in Tony Blair's Britain. He could expect a few sucked-lemon lips from the Politically Correct lobby, perhaps even a letter from the Race Relations Board, but that was about as heavy as it would get. And the murder of Larry Warner? Well, that was Godden's word against Maxwell's, the one, a sophisticated bon viveur with an international reputation; the other a teacher in a third-rate comprehensive and one who had been in trouble with the police before. Even if they read *Nietzsche Now* as an example of Godden's right-wing ideology, it was hardly evidence he was a murderer. After all, Adolf Hitler read Nietzsche, yet he never pulled a trigger at close quarters in his life, excluding a little thing called World War Two of course.

No, Maxwell's best bet was to stick like glue to Archie Godden, waiting for a slip, the offer of some tangible evidence rather than the hot air the man spouted. Bugger and poo! The attic was empty, apart from tea chests various and a rocking chair under a drugget that glowed ghostly in the early morning clouds that broke through the skylight.

'Christopher Logan.' Maxwell had just demolished the most devilish kidneys he'd ever sampled.

'Who?' Godden was already on the toast.

'Cub reporter on my local, the *Leighford Advertiser.*"

'What of him?'

'He's dead,' Maxwell said. 'Shot dead, in fact. Found under the Arches, near the Embankment.'

'Hm. Fancy.' Godden sank his teeth into a mound of marmalade.

'Not the White Knights.'

'The White Knights?' Godden paused in mid-mouthful.

'Your organization,' Maxwell smiled. 'The one I believe I'm on the brink of joining.'

'How did you know we were called that?'

'Er . . . didn't you mention it?'

'No,' Godden shifted a little uneasily in his seal.

Maxwell couldn't afford to blow it now. 'Come to think of it,' he said, 'it was Bob Hart.'

'Bob?' Godden's mood lightened a little. Then he flicked his napkin up from his lap and wiped his mouth. 'What did you make of him? And our Amy?'

'Charming couple,' Maxwell beamed, 'assuming they are a couple?'

'Oh, I expect so,' he said. 'Seem to be all over each other recently. I find that sort of thing rather sordid.'

'You never . . . er . . . ?'

'Married? Lord, no. Far too busy being who I am and what I am. They just get in the way, women. It's just that that's the problem. Oh, I think Bob is sound enough. And Hilary too, by his lights. It's her . . . it's Amy. Can be something of a renegade at times. One to watch, I think. Come on, finish your coffee. We've got places to be.'

Henry Hall was taking a calculated risk. Another one, that is. The first was telling Maxwell about the White Knights in the first place. Quite a departure, he kept reminding himself, for a man who'd always done things by the book. He switched off the tape recorder and sat back in his chair. He'd got used, over the past week, to sitting in this position facing Neil Hamlyn. Bartlett, the psychiatrist, had given his all. A schizoid psychosis was all he was prepared to say. The Crown Prosecution Service had pulled a rather wry face at what the police had to offer. There was no bullet from the corpse of Larry Warner, lying in frozen limbo in one of Jim Astley's cold drawers. Scores of coppers had simply failed to find it. The wound was consistent with a missile fired from a gun that Neil Hamlyn did not possess. Yes, he could have thrown said gun into the sea, the nearest river, an adjacent wheelie bin. But why, if he'd actually killed the man, as he said he had, didn't he admit to owning the gun? It made no sense. And the Crown Prosecution Service, anxious as ever to achieve a result, knew it didn't. Mr Hamlyn's counsel for the defence would have a field day.

'I'm letting you go, Mr Hamlyn,' Hall said.

The soldier blinked. 'Why?'

'Because you didn't kill anybody,' Hall sighed.

'I killed Larry Warner,' Hamlyn protested. 'I've told you . . .'

'Yes, you have,' Hall nodded. 'I've lost count of the times. But you see, Mr Hamlyn, we have this little thing called forensic science. A gentleman called Christopher Logan was killed with the same gun that killed Larry Warner – at the moment we are making the assumption by the same perpetrator. And you, Mr Hamlyn, have one of the best alibis I can think of for the murder of Mr Logan – you were with us, in police custody, at the time.'

'Look,' Hamlyn was leaning forward, into the pool of light from the table lamp, 'I don't understand this. Any of it. I've never heard of this Logan bloke. All I know is I killed Larry Warner. I don't give a fuck about your forensics. I did it, okay?'

Frank Bartholomew bristled as the man's voice grew louder, his tether shorter. He was half out of his chair when Hall defused the situation. 'Whatever you say, Mr Hamlyn,' he said, one hand in the air as a gesture of reconciliation. 'But I must warn you that I am considering charging you with wasting police time. Let me sleep on that. In the meantime, Sergeant Bartholomew will take you to the front desk and see that your belongings are returned to you. All except the Ruger KM 77. That we'll keep and it will be sawn up into two-inch sections, just in case temptation comes your way.'

For a moment, Hamlyn stood there, swaying, uncertain what to do. He didn't understand this. Didn't know what was happening to him. The whole thing was like a dream, a waking nightmare. Bartholomew crossed to the door and opened it, ushering the man out. Hall clicked the intercom on his desk. 'Jacquie, a word please?'

'Archie?' Anthony LeStrange was sitting in front of a mirror in his dressing room at the Lyceum, the light of the two dozen bulbs shining in his eyes. 'Not the best of times, I'm afraid.'

'Sorry, Tony.' Godden ushered Maxwell into the presence. 'We have a slight problem.'

LeStrange paused in mid-application of his five and nine, staring at Maxwell in the mirror. 'I spy strangers,' he murmured.

'I believe you two have met.' Godden stood about, looking large and rather uncomfortable amidst the sequinned glitter of the stage green room.

'More than once,' LeStrange turned, rose and shook Maxwell's hand in a deft movement.

'He knows,' Godden said.

LeStrange's hand froze in Maxwell's. 'Knows what?'

'About Larry Warner,' Godden said.

'Archie,' LeStrange fumed. 'I'm due on stage in ten minutes, for God's sake. What's the matter with you?'

'Couldn't be helped,' Godden shrugged. 'Mr Maxwell – Max – wants to join us.'

LeStrange looked at his man. 'Mr Maxwell,' he said. 'You'll forgive me if this sounds rude, but we are not the WI. Being a dab hand at whist and being able to sing "Jerusalem" cuts no ice here, you know.'

'Give him some credit, Tony.' Godden found a chair somewhere under a velvet cloak. 'And me too, for that matter. Mr Maxwell's been talking to Bob, Amy and Hilary. He's sound.'

LeStrange stared at the Head of Sixth Form. 'Mr Maxwell,' he said, 'you'll forgive me again, but what proof have we of your affiliation to our cause?'

'What would you like?' Maxwell asked him. 'Recitation of a few pages of *Mein Kampf*? My solemn promise not to eat another Chicken Vindaloo?'

LeStrange's face fell. 'Archie,' he said. 'I thought you said he was sound.'

'Seeing is believing,' Godden said.

'Ah, yes,' LeStrange smiled. 'How do you feel, Mr Maxwell, about a little initiation ceremony?'

'A sort of Bar mitzvah?' Maxwell beamed.

LeStrange ignored him. 'I think you'll find this one a little more taxing, Mr Maxwell. Chanting slabs of the Talmud won't do it, I'm afraid.'

'I'll give it a whirl,' Maxwell said. 'What do I do?'

'Enjoy the show,' LeStrange grinned. 'Archie, see the fellow on the door, will you? You and Mr Maxwell relax. I'll see you afterwards. Mr Maxwell, are you by any chance carrying a mobile phone?'

'Yes, I am, as a matter of fact,' Maxwell confessed.

'Could you hand it in at the door for me? They aren't allowed in the auditorium and anyway they interfere with the electronics of my act.'

'Delighted,' Maxwell said and swung the thing out of his pocket, spinning the loop around his finger like Robocop. Nothing. Clearly this pair of White Knights were not film buffs. What sort of organization was Maxwell joining?

'Follow him, sir?' Jacquie Carpenter repeated.

DCI Hall nodded. 'Is there a problem?' he asked her.

'No, it's just that . . .'

'Then get to it. I can't spare a partner for you and anyway, SAS or not, I get the impression this is one observant cookie. He doesn't know you and he might not be expecting a woman tail.'

'I hope he's not expecting a tail at all, guv,' she said.

Hall nodded again. 'Jacquie,' he said, looking her in the face, 'I don't like doing this. Tails are always risky. We both know that. But there's something not quite right about our Mr Hamlyn.'

'What? You mean he's a psycho?'

'Well, that's just it. I don't think he is. At least he's not a killer. But that doesn't mean you can afford to turn your back on him. Watch yourself, Jacquie. Keep in contact with us all the time. If this man so much as scratches himself, I want to be kept informed. Understand?'

Jacquie nodded. 'Guv . . .'

'Yes?'

'Nothing,' she told him. 'It'll keep.'

All the way along the corridor and down the cold concrete lairs she rehearsed what she *should* have said. She should have told him that the man she loved was in this thing up to his neck. That she had broken every rule in the book by copying the tape of Hamlyn's interview with Dr Bartlett. And she should have told Hall that every nerve in her body was twisted with worry. He'd gone, she didn't know where. But she'd been a policewoman now for nine years. Some things became instinct, reflex. You didn't analyse, didn't rationalize, you just knew. There was a smell about some things, a tangible odour. Jacquie Carpenter knew the smell of danger. And she smelt it now.

It *was* a brilliant show, all the razzle-dazzle of the world of make-believe, the world of magic. And it was only afterwards that things turned a little sour. It was as Maxwell retrieved Sylvia's mobile from the man at the door, he was barged into by the exiting crowd. Before he could stoop to pick it up, Archie Godden, never a man for a tight space, trod backwards and the sound of crunching plastic said it all.

'Sorry, Max,' Godden smiled sheepishly. 'Get you a new one tomorrow, eh?'

Neil Hamlyn took a cab to the station. Bugger! That meant Jacquie abandoning her car and going with him. He caught the ten forty-three to Bournemouth. She hung around the platform, careful to keep her back to him as far as possible and her shades on. He talked to no one, nodded to no one. Why should he? She couldn't believe Leighford was his home town. How, she wondered, had he got to Magicworld in the first place? A man in flak jacket and full combat gear, carrying a high-powered hunting rifle. Had he caught a train? A bus? Hailed a cab? No, someone would have dropped him off. But who? All the Incident Room had met was brick walls. Neil Hamlyn had no past and no present. He'd given them his address, in Leighford, but the squalid little flat he lived in was as anonymous as the man himself. It was as though Neil Hamlyn had chosen a street and house number at random and placed a few basics there, fastidiously, painstakingly, antiseptically. She'd seen him on that bloody video tape, the one stolen from Maxwell's. She'd seen him in the flesh, though always from a distance. What was it about those cold, dead eyes? The eyes of a killer? Perhaps. But there was some-thing more.

A harsh and largely incomprehensible voice barked over the tannoy. She caught the relevant bit about the destination and waited for Hamlyn to make his move. Once he was safely on board, she waited for the conductor's whistle, then hauled open a door of the end carriage and hopped up.

He'd positioned himself with his back to the engine, his holdall beside him, his combat gear on, his flak jacket and beret in the bag. He stared out of the window, silent, unseeing, as the train lurched into motion and Jacquie found a seat. She flicked open her Danielle Steele and sat midway from the window, checking over her shades every now and then that he was still there.

A funny little Asian buffet attendant rolled the trolley past her, enquiring whether she'd like any teas or coffees, cold drinks or sandwiches.

She smiled up at him, shaking her head. By the time he'd gone, so had Neil Hamlyn. She found herself staring at an empty seat. Shit! She half stood, checking ahead and back. He couldn't have got past her. He could only have gone forward, to the front of the train.

She grabbed her bag, the one with the telescopic night stick and the can of mace and hurtled down the aisle, buffeted as the train rattled on its brave curve west. The first loo she came to was occu-pied, so she waited, as casually as she could, until a drunk lurched towards her, crimson-faced and swaying.

'Hello, darling. Oh, hello, hello, a queue I see, I hate to queue before I pee.' And he doubled up with laughter. 'You going to Bournemouth, then?'

'Perhaps,' she said. He was unaware of her stony face or the anxious glances she sent to the toilet door.

'Well, that's where I'm going,' he said. 'Look, the bloke with the drinks cabinet's back there. I'm going to have a little one for the road – or should I say the rail. Ha, ha,' and he steadied himself against the rattling wall as his own sense of humour overtook him again. 'Won't you join me? G 'n' t or something? Scotch?' He put his arm around her.

She inched away.

'No, now come on,' he slurred. 'Do you know, you remind me of a girl I once knew. Yep. Corker, she was. Went like a train. Ha, ha.'

She closed to the idiot, staring steadily up at him, her mouth set, her jaw firm. 'Are you going to fuck off or am I going to plant my knee in your nuts?'

'Wha . . . ?' The drunk had had some rebuffs in his time, but this was a new experience. Even in his less than vertical state, he noticed the girl's determination and pretty powerful thighs. Maybe he'd just find another loo somewhere and pester somebody else. They heard a flush and the narrow door clicked open. A little old lady stood there, with a Mary Whitehouse hairdo and somebody else's teeth that parted company with her gums as she spoke.

'Excuse me,' she said. 'My dear, is this man bothering you?'

'Er . . . no, no,' Jacquie said. 'Not at all.'

'It's good of you to cover for him, my dear, but I'm all too familiar with his wretched habits, I'm afraid. Lionel, get back to your seat – and give me that hip flask, you dreadful boy.'

'Oh, Mother!' Lionel had turned more crimson than ever, fumbling in his pockets to comply, but Jacquie had gone, hurtling along the aisles, batting aside the doors, fighting her way through buggies and their attendant toddlers and young mothers. Christ! If she'd lost him . . . Then, suddenly, there he was, moved to a no-smoker and sitting patiently, his arms clasped in his lap, still staring out of the window. This time she carried on past him, then swung round and tucked in three seats back, head down, book out, her heart back in its place.

The lights burned blue. Peter Maxwell sat up in his bed. This was his second night away from home. His second night of borrowing pyjamas and bath robes and he realized again that he was in fact a prisoner. The only phone he could use now was the prison's own and he didn't feel safe enough to use it. The prison this time was Anthony LeStrange's unpretentious little pad in Gordon Square. He'd been here before, of course, in the pursuance of his enquiries, but that was then. Now, Chris Logan was dead and Tiffany was missing and Maxwell had the uneasy feeling of a man with his head in a tiger's mouth. And the man who made tigers appear and vanish slept across the corridor from him now, his oppo of the Wagnerian leanings one down from that. Maxwell's head was reeling, his heart pounding as he padded down the landing. It was three days since he'd seen Tiffany, since someone had snatched her from Sylvia's front door. He was seething about that. Seething and terrified for her at the same time. She wasn't at Archie Godden's. But Archie Godden had a friend, a like-minded fascist bastard whose house was even bigger.

He tried the spare rooms, empty and abandoned. Some of them were unfinished, all of them cold. The carpets were plush under his toes and a grandfather clock ticked in the still watches of the night. Nothing. A barn of a place with no heart, no soul, no golden girl called Tiffany. He went back to bed and tried to sleep.

It must have been nearly three when he heard the rattle of the door. For a magician's house, this one creaked and groaned and he remembered the Toby Twirl books of his childhood, where the brave personified little pig was always landing himself in the most appalling danger and Professor Bison was the magician in question. 'Toby' sat upright in bed now, wishing for that little cow-catchered train called the Dilly-Puff which would whisk him away to safety. A shadow crossed the room, huge on the walls, gigantic on the ceiling.

'Max?'

He switched on the bedside lamp and breathed again.

'For fuck's sake, Archie, don't tell me you've come for a bed-time story.'

'Actually,' the critic slumped heavily into the peacock chair in the corner. 'I've come to tell you one.'

'Do you know what time it is?'

'Yes. Look, Max, we've got a problem . . .'

'The fly in the ointment, yes, I know.'

'No, no. That's taken care of. It's Tony. He's . . . well, I know it sounds melodramatic, but I think he's gone mad.'

'Really?' Maxwell was beginning to wonder just who ran the asylum.

'I think he killed Larry Warner.'

'Yes,' Maxwell nodded. 'Archie, it's late. We've already had this conversation.'

'No, we haven't, Max.' Godden was no longer the opinionated bastard, with a conceit to match his waist measurement. This was a man running scared. A man on the edge. 'Look, it takes a lot to rattle me. Oh, I'm like most people, I suppose, deep down, a bloody hypocrite. No, I don't like blacks and Jews and queers and yes, I do my bit to keep the bastards in their places. But I'm a philosopher, Max, a man of words. A man of music . . .'

Maxwell wondered if there was anything under his bed he could vomit into.

'I'm not Action Man. I confess I've done a few illegal things in my time, but murder? No, my God, no – I draw the line at that.'

'But you said . . . All right,' Maxwell corrected himself, 'you implied, that Tony LeStrange had killed Larry Warner.'

'I was trying you out,' Godden told him, pale and shaking in the lamplight. 'I had to know if I could trust you. If you recoiled at that prospect, well, a quick change of subject and forget it. But you wanted to know more. I'll admit I was using Charts as a front, to route funds in a certain direction. When Warner found out, I was all for buying him off . . . Tony had other ideas.'

'Who else is involved in this, Archie?' Maxwell asked.

'Just me and Tony,' Godden said, burying his face in his hands. 'The mountebank and his zany. I never thought he'd actually do it, Max. The fucking maniac killed him, shot him on that idiotic Water ride.'

'How?' Maxwell asked.

'What?'

'Archie,' Maxwell sat on the edge of the bed, knee to knee with his man, suddenly, unaccountably, feeling oddly sorry for him. 'When we talked about this before, you came out with some line . . . er . . . about magicians being in two places at once.'

'I was fishing, Max,' Godden blurted. 'I wanted to know how much you know. You were there with Deirdre Lessing. You went to see Tony. You even went to Amy Weston and Bob Hart – what the fuck possessed you to do that? They'll blab. Honest bloody Bob. Some sort of crypto-socialist and Miss Poet Laureate of the Bleeding Heart. They'll crucify us. And I haven't the first bloody idea what Hilary St John will do – he's always blown hot and cold. They'll go to the police.'

'No, they won't,' Maxwell assured him.

'How do you know?'

'Because LeStrange has got my niece. And I told them he had. They won't go to the police.'

Godden sat bolt upright. 'What?'

'She was taken from outside a friend's house three days ago.'

'Jesus! Is she here?'

'No, I've looked. Anyway, I'd smell her.'

'What?'

'Calvin Klein.'

'That's quite common, isn't it?'

'I'd know it on my niece, believe me.'

'Well, there we are.' Godden was shaking his head, 'Max, I'm sorry. For you. For her. But it just proves my point. Tony LeStrange is insane. He's killed once. And now he's kidnapped . . . God, this is impossible.'

'He's killed twice,' Maxwell corrected him. 'He killed Chris Logan too – though I've got to carry a share of that particular blame. The point is, Archie, how do we stop him?'

'Harold Wiseman.'

'Who?'

'Another member of Charts. Another honest one, thank God, along with Amy and Bob.'

'The impresario,' Maxwell clicked his fingers. 'Got a theatre in Bournemouth.'

'That's right. But, wait a minute. He wasn't at the Garrick when you and Deirdre met us all for tea over that wretched little theatre of yours. He couldn't make it, if I remember rightly.'

'I'd already met him at Leighford High,' Maxwell said. 'Now it's my turn to confess. As well as being Superteacher who could have put Socrates in the shade, a historian's historian par excellence, and a thunderingly good Head of Sixth Form, I am also infuriatingly modest and a bit of a sleuth in my spare time. I knew Warner knew Wiseman, so I went asking questions. He couldn't help.'

'Perhaps not then,' Godden mused, 'but I think he can this time. Max, can you play along tomorrow? I'm going to suggest to Tony that we all go to Harold's theatre. I'll think of a reason. Once we're there . . . well, trust me, will you?'

'I don't have much choice, do I? Not if I want to see my niece again.'

Godden nodded. 'You know, Max, I want to thank you,' and he held out a chubby hand.

'Me? Why?' Max took it.

'Because you've helped me find myself. Oh, it's a cliché I know and a columnist should know better, but . . . well, I'm bound to do time for all this. The fraud. The embezzlement. But at least you've kept me out of murder. I knew your heart wasn't in the White Knights.'

'God, was I that obvious?' Maxwell chuckled.

'Goodnight, Max,' Godden smiled, getting to his feet. 'And don't worry about young Tiffany. She'll be fine.'

Sylvia Matthews stood at the window, the one that looked out onto the street. She couldn't sleep anyway and a little before four, she'd got out of bed, popped her head around the door to check on Lucy and wrestled with a Tom Clancy. It was no good – her heart wasn't in it and she threw the thriller aside. She never knew what it was that made her look out of the window. But when she did, she saw

him, standing in the dappled shadows of the street lamp. A silhouette with head and shoulders and a heavy coat. Just standing there.
Looking. Looking, she knew, at the house. And at her. Most especially at her.

She dashed across to the phone, punching out Jacquie's number
and waiting in an agony of silence, heart pounding, throat dry, waiting, waiting.

'Come on,' she hissed. 'Be there, for God's sake.'

'Hello,' a recorded voice clicked in. 'I'm afraid I can't come
to the phone at the moment . . .' And she slammed the receiver
down. In her rising, blinding panic, she checked the security in her
head. All doors were locked. All window catches fastened, exactly
as Jacquie had told her. No lights anywhere in the house. Curtains
on the ground floor drawn. But windows were only glass. Doors
only ply and sawdust. If that bastard wanted to get in, he could. She
ducked across to the wrought-iron Punch doorstop that kept the
bathroom door ajar and carried it back to the window. He was still
out there. With difficulty, she hauled the chair into place, where
she could still watch him, arms on the sill, and kept her feet on Mr
Punch.

What did the bastard want? Was he real, that he stood there,
so still, so unmoving? Was he an extension of her own worn out,
jangled nerves? 'Where are you, Jacquie?' she found herself wondering. And she heard herself saying, softly, in the shadows, 'Where
are you. Max?'

Robert de Niro was waiting.

CHAPTER NINETEEN

The sun was shining on the sandstone cliffs of Hengistbury as LeStrange's Range Rover crested the hill. No one was talking as it joined the steady trickle of traffic winding its way west where Alfred the Great's fortress once stood in the killing ground between the Avon and the Stour. Maxwell saw the dazzling white tower of Christchurch priory and the huge signs that welcomed a marvelling world to Tucktonia, four acres of replica buildings on a 1:24 scale (for anybody who was interested).

Breakfast had been coffee. Godden had managed some toast. Conversation on the way down, along the M3 and beyond the Ringwood Interchange, had been minimal, each of them alone with his own conscience. The Wyndham, that Saturday morning, was festooned with posters advertising its current show, *The Duchess of Malfi*. Not bad that a work written four hundred years ago by a carter from Cow Lane should still be wowing them to packed houses. But then, the play was all about murder and death loves a crowd.

'Right,' LeStrange was first out of the Range Rover, looking up at the building's facade. 'Ready for your initiation then, Mr Maxwell? Archie, you seemed very keen to do it all here, so you'd better lead the way. I just hope Harold's in.'

He was. The impresario was crossing the plush-carpeted foyer as the three got there.

'Gentlemen?' Wiseman took off his glasses and let them dangle from the little gilt chain around his neck. 'I'm afraid you're a little early for the matinee.'

'I believe you know Mr Maxwell, Harold,' LeStrange said.

'Indeed,' Wiseman nodded, but made no attempt to accept the Head of Sixth Form's outstretched hand.

'Mr Maxwell is a novitiate, Harold,' LeStrange walked with the ex-thespian into the darkened auditorium. Wiseman glanced back. 'Is he now?' he smiled. 'Well, then, Tony, centre stage, d'you think?'

'Centre stage, Mr Maxwell?' LeStrange asked.

'I wouldn't be anywhere else,' Maxwell beamed.

Wiseman disappeared through a side door and the maroon curtains slid back. There was a series of thuds and the stage flooded with light. The set was Jacobean, with gnarled old wood trestle tables and joint stools.

'All right, Tony?' Wiseman's voice bellowed around his theatre, coming in stereo from the wooden O and bouncing back to the balcony and beyond.

'Mr Maxwell,' LeStrange held out his right arm and Maxwell mounted the steps.

Halfway up he stopped as the floorboards creaked. '"I pray you," he said to LeStrange, "see me safe up, and as for my coming down let me shift for my self."'

'Thomas More,' Wiseman's voice boomed across the stage. 'One of my favourite lines. It's an honour to welcome a fellow intellectual, Mr Maxwell.'

But Maxwell wasn't listening to the compliment. He was listening to the voice. It was a gentle, sonorous Northern accent. It was South Yorkshire. He was on the stage now, bathed in light and he turned back. From the footlights he could make out Godden, making himself comfortable three rows back, aisle seat. Wiseman emerged from the wings, smiling, licking his lips in that way that luvvies do.

'Look at me,' LeStrange was suddenly in front of him, waving his hands in space like a virtuoso. 'Watch.' From nowhere, the magician had produced a coin. 'Hold that.'

Maxwell did. It was a twopenny piece, complete with princely feathers and the head of the Queen, God bless her.

'A perfectly conventional coin of the realm, you'll agree?'

'Yes.' Maxwell nodded, not quite sure where any of this was leading.

'Bite it.'

'Sorry?'

'Bite it.'

'All right.' Maxwell was still game. Follow instructions was what Godden had said. 'Once we get to the theatre, play along.' Maxwell was playing. Calcium met metal and he stood there, holding the coin. 'Seems genuine,' he said.

LeStrange took it from him, spun it in the air, as DCI Hall had done days before when he offered Maxwell the choice of brick walls or loose ends. The magician caught it in his teeth with a reptilian jerk of the head and handed it back to Maxwell. There was a jagged piece missing from the rim. Despite himself, Maxwell shouted out 'How did you do that?'

LeStrange smiled slowly, then took the coin back and spun it again. 'Catch it,' he shouted. Instinctively, Maxwell did. The coin was whole again. 'How did you do that?' he shouted again.

'Magic,' growled LeStrange and he wandered towards the wings.

'I was hoping for something more spectacular, Tony,' Maxwell stopped him. 'Say, hypnosis?'

Wiseman chuckled, busying himself with his set.

'Hypnosis?' LeStrange came back. 'Mr Maxwell, you've been hypnotized ever since you nearly got in the way of the bullet that killed Larry Warner. Murder is a form of hypnosis in itself, isn't it? And you are one of the most easily hypnotized subjects I've ever met. It doesn't take me to draw you in. Archie did it perfectly.'

Maxwell glanced down to where the fat critic sat. He could see his sides wobbling with self-gratification. 'You fell for it, Max,' he said. 'My hysteria, my conscience. Harold, you'd have been proud of me. I was magnificent.'

Maxwell smiled too and crossed to the set, straddling a particularly painful bench. 'You were pretty good,' he admitted, 'except for three things.'

'Oh?' Godden, the critic, didn't really care for criticism.

'First, you were a little too ready to trust me. It was obvious at the Garrick it was loathe at first sight, yet in Oxford, among the dreaming spires, you were chumminess itself. It was all Maxie and Archie and I'll show you mine if you show me yours. Now, nobody involved in an organization as vile and clever as yours is so easily persuaded to drop their guard. Take my word for it, Harold, you wouldn't have been proud at all.'

'And the second little thing?' Godden roared, his anger rising.

'Mentioning my niece by name. I hadn't, you see. And you, overly solicitous, overly concerned, told me not to worry "little Tiffany" would be all right. Where is she, Harold? Where've you got her?'

Wiseman was standing now, glancing nervously at LeStrange across the stage from him.

'The third thing was putting your bloody great foot on my mobile so that I couldn't ring out of the nice little web of deceit you were spinning for me. You owe a dear friend of mine about seventy quid for that, by the way.'

'You want to see some real magic, Maxwell?' LeStrange asked him. He pointed to the rafters, where pulleys and weights and beams cluttered the ceiling. 'There's magic.'

Maxwell didn't know he was rising from his seat. He couldn't see the glaring lights or the silhouettes forming at the back of the auditorium. All he could see was Tiffany, floating across the tangle of wires, her arms by her sides, her eyes closed, her trainers dangling with loose laces. She was lit from below and looked, Maxwell imagined as the Angel of Mons must have appeared to the exhausted, terrified troops of 1914.

'Jesus,' he whispered, not daring to move, not daring to breathe. 'How do you do that?'

'Maxwell,' LeStrange snarled, his arm outstretched, his finger pointing. 'If you want your little Tiffany to live, don't say another word. Don't breathe.'

Maxwell turned to face the girl, passing directly over the stage as though caught in a current, a shaft of light. He had never seen anything like it. Suddenly, the light went out and Maxwell stood alone, centre stage, staring up into the dark and silent rafters.

'A little to the left,' a voice commanded over the intercom. It was LeStrange's voice this time. 'To the left, Maxwell.'

Maxwell hadn't seen it before, but he did now. There was a red light, about the size of a twenty-pence piece on his chest. As he obeyed the voice and moved left, it moved with him.

'Stop.' He heard another voice, coming this time from the back of the auditorium.

He turned to face front, arms outstretched. 'How's that, Bob?' he asked.

A figure emerged into the creeping light along the rows of empty seats. 'Well, well, well.' Maxwell brought his arms down slowly. 'The second gunman on the grassy knoll. You know, you almost convinced me, Bob.'

'Really?' Robert Hart was looking along the barrel of a idle, his face half hidden by the sights. 'And what was my mistake? You've demolished Archie pretty effectively.'

'Bastard!' the critic growled, turning casually in his seat.

'Oh, the general chain of events,' Maxwell rested his hands on his hips. 'Would you like to hear about it?'

'Finish it,' Godden grunted. 'We're all here.'

'Yes,' Maxwell shouted. 'I can just about make you out. At the back there.' He lapsed into his Marine Sergeant, straight out of Full Metal Jacket. 'Front and centre, mister.'

A solitary figure wandered down the far aisle, careful not to get further forward than Hart.

'Hilary,' Maxwell began a slow hand clap. 'How nice.'

And another figure, slim, hesitant, came out of the shadows on the left. 'And Amy,' Maxwell stopped clapping. 'The circle's complete. The magic circle of course, Tony.'

'Get it over with, Hart,' Godden snapped. 'We don't have time for all this.'

'No,' LeStrange's voice boomed around the theatre like the Wizard of Oz. 'We owe Mr Maxwell his moment in the spotlight.'

'Go on, then, Max.' Hart's muzzle hadn't wavered a millimetre. That damned red spot was still nudging Maxwell's bow tie. 'But I must warn you, my trigger finger gets tired eventually.'

'All right.' Maxwell hadn't moved. 'The chain of events. Back in the 'sixties . . .'

'Don't try our patience, Maxwell,' LeStrange warned. 'There's no Seventh Cavalry on its way for you, I assure you.'

'All right,' Maxwell licked his lips. They felt like sandpaper. 'Archie had a little right-wing club going at Oxford. A few fashionable Fascists. They organized a little Paki-bashing, that good old British sport of yesteryear, but then Archie grew up. He got famous writing bollocks about classical music and even more famous writing unsupportable political claptrap under an assumed – dare I say, Nazi – name. He's not an Action Man – he told me that himself. So instead, he started to fund those who were; soccer hooligans, National Front, British National Party. Toxteth, Broadwater Farm, little happy-go-lucky killings like that, all funded by our Mi Godden. Of course, he wasn't made of money. He needed some support, so he recruited the rest of you one by one. The Arty Farty circle whose racism is all the more sick because it's overlaid with a dollop of political correctness as long as your arm. But there was a fly in the ointment, wasn't there? You needed a legitimate front for funding right-wing activities and you called it Charts – isn't the Prince of Wales himself your patron? Gala bashes, celebrity knees-ups, Garrick Club, royal approval. You'd got the lot. And sad, innocent dupes like Deirdre Lessing were sucked right in, delighted to receive the odd crumb from top table. But you'd all reckoned without Larry Warner, hadn't you? Look, Bob, do you mind if I sit down?'

'For fuck's sake, Hart,' Godden screamed, 'kill the sonofabitch.'

'Tut, tut, Archie,' Maxwell still had the nerve to scold. 'I'm not sure the *Observer* would print anything quite so direct. Or, if I may say so, quite so American.'

'Tony?' It was Hart's voice.

'Do you have a problem with a sitting target?' the magician's voice boomed.

'What do you think? On the table, Maxwell. The one behind you. Nothing extreme now, nothing sudden. Or it's your head all over the stage.'

'Ah, the head shot.' Maxwell smiled. 'Glad you're back on track now.'

'What?'

'Just a little something, a little intellectual problem my niece was chewing over recently. The killing of JFK. Six shots, at least five in Dealey Plaza, but only three did the damage. The shot to the back – Larry Warner. The one to the throat, Chris Logan. That leaves the head shot; me.'

Maxwell lowered his arms to his sides his hands drifting from his hips. Every move now was crucial. He was rattling them, slowly, picking them off one by one, but he had a fair way to go and death followed him. He eased himself backwards, his shoes creaking leather on the planks. He felt the table rim against his bum and hoisted himself up. Hart had not moved. Neither had the red spot.

'Where was I?' Maxwell gave them his best Frankie Howerd. 'Just get comfy. Ah, that's better. Ah, yes, the prologue.' He was Maxwell again. 'Dear old Larry. Just a threat Jewish, just a tad of a left footer. I wonder any of you could stomach him for long. But the real bitch of the thing was that he'd sussed you, hadn't he? Found out where the Charity Arts group was really sending its cash donations. That's when you played this little charade of yours. I have to admire you, Harold,' Maxwell called. He couldn't see Wiseman and that bothered him a little. 'You coached them all bloody well. Such improvisation. Such ability to think on their feet. Whichever one of you was probed by a busybody – Larry Warner, Chris Logan, Peter Maxwell – you'd string them along with a load of guff and draw us all the deeper. I've seen it done before of course – the Tottingleigh Players are dab hands – but never for real,' and he swept off his hat in acknowledgement.

'That's enough now,' St John said. Maxwell could see the photographer beginning to fidget at the far side.

'Now here I'm guessing,' Maxwell was on a roll, one that he still hoped would save his life. 'Amy's the soft one, aren't you darling?' he smiled broadly, teeth dazzling in the spotlights. 'You went to see Larry I would imagine, unbeknownst to his secretary or his housekeeper, who made no mention of any female visitors.' The poetess was chewing her nails, pacing backwards and forwards, her eyes now on the gunman, now on his target. 'Or it could have been you, Bob, calling yourself Jeff. I suppose with hair as short as yours you could pass for the army man Warner's secretary supposed Jeff was. Anyway, one of you blabbed – as you did to me. As perhaps you did to poor old Chris Logan, I don't know. You suckered Warner in. Yes, it was terrible. Archie Godden was an unscrupulous bastard and you'd only just discovered it yourself. You had hard evidence of his financial chicanery and you'd gladly give it to Warner, only the meeting place was tricky. Not his office, not the Garrick. Not here, Harold, because you told me you had the builders in. The post was far too risky. And phones have ears. What about Magicworld? Ideal. Thousands of punters. Open air. The perfect place.'

'This is getting tedious,' Godden yawned ostentatiously.

'Oh, bear with me, Archie,' Maxwell put his head on one side cutely. 'This is better than a play, isn't it, Harold?' Where the fuck was he? 'Where was I? Oh, yes. So Bob puts on his technician's overalls and packs his Ruger into his tool bag and off he goes. Warner had instructions to take certain rides and to sit by himself in a car. Number Four, I believe it was. What did you do, tell him there was a brown paper package under the seat?'

'Bravo,' said Hart.

'That's why – and I shall be grateful to him for ever – he had to be alone in the car, so that he could find it and take possession. He kept my girls away. You were in the rocks, high to the left. If anyone had seen you, you were a repair man, just doing your job. You probably assembled the Ruger in seconds and pow! Goodbye Larry. And this is where dear Hilary came in.'

'I was waiting for my cue,' the photographer mumbled.

'Tiffany was looking that way down the Wild Water,' Maxwell went on. 'She saw a flash. She's a bit sensitive, my Tiff,' and he wondered where she was now, perching in the beams over his head. 'Got thoroughly hooked on the Kennedy killing at school. Up there on your grassy knoll, you got the back shot in. Clean and fatal. And you did it precisely how only a physicist could tell me, with that natty gadget on your sights that's glowing red on my shirt now. Some ultra beam of some kind. Invented, I believe, by Hilary St John. Or so it says in the Great Book of Unbelievable Inventions I consulted in the library on my way to Amy's a few days ago. You're not a bad shot, Bob, but you're no Annie Oakley. With that gadget on board, however, even Archie couldn't have missed.'

'Thank you so much,' Godden grunted.

'So,' Maxwell leaned back, cradling his knee in both hands. 'White Knights, One. Larry Warner, Nil. Then I got involved. Oh, forgive me, I know it sounds a little arrogant. So did the boys in blue, but then, you expected that. Me, you didn't expect. Harold tipped you off when I came a-sleuthing, on this very spot, in fact. It must have been a bit of a facer when dear old Deirdre brought me into your lair, so to speak, at the Garrick. For one brief, delicious moment, I thought she might be in on the whole thing, but alas, no. But I was a problem because I brought Chris Logan into it – and I shall regret that to my dying . . . well.' He smiled ruefully. 'Because Chris remembered something. I got hold of a police video – which of you has that, by the way?'

There was silence.

'Very well,' Maxwell lapsed into his schoolmaster, 'you will all be staying behind until the culprit owns up. The video was of Tony's "creature" – Neil Hamlyn. He appeared to be on drugs, except he never used drugs. Chris recognized it straight away because of the series of articles he'd once written on Anthony LeStrange. But he made a mistake, did Chris – he tried to go it alone. It was hypnosis, Tony, wasn't it? That was where the library was helpful yet again. I never thought it was possible to persuade someone to do what they didn't want to do – you know, drop their trousers in the Albert Hall, that sort of thing. But an ex-SAS man who has been trained to kill. And a hypnotist of Tony LeStrange's calibre . . . Yes, it's possible. Amy said it – "I suspect his best work is done behind the scenes.'"

'I thank you,' LeStrange boomed over the speakers.

'Let's get on with it!' Amy Weston spoke for the first time, her voice brittle, her eyes bright in the auditorium's dim light. 'I can't stand any more of this. It's got out of hand, for God's sake. I'm not a murderer!'

'Get a grip on yourself,' Godden growled at her.

'Yes, a bit of a weak link, aren't you, Amy, my dear? The token woman. You know, I'm a little disappointed. I hoped you might turn out to be the brains behind all this, but no. One of you bastards got Chris to talk, you, Tony, I suspect – by hypnosis would be poetic, wouldn't it? You found out about the tape and you needed to know what else Logan knew. One of you, Bob would be my guess, broke into Chris's flat and then my house to get the tape. You needed to know what Hamlyn had told the police. You were safe there, of course. He'd given nothing away. But Logan? Well, Logan had to die.'

'Precisely where you are now,' Hart said, the rifle lifting just a threat in his hands. Maxwell saw the red glow slide up his chin and along his nose. It must have been resting between his eyes about now.

'Of course,' Maxwell said, not daring to move, 'the wooden splinters in his hair. From dear Harold's stage. You dumped him like so much rubbish under the Arches, somewhere winos die every day. But Amy cracked. Felt sorry for him. Amy?' She didn't answer. 'Well, I'd like to think so. Hence the rose and the Rupert Brooke. That was the clincher, of course.'

'It was?' her voice was steadier now, but he sensed she was inches away from snapping. 'Why?'

'You couldn't help yourself. You gave it all away. That last line – "And lived from laugh to laugh, I too, when you were there, and you, and you." You were confessing, weren't you, Amy? Trying desperately to salve your conscience with as little pain as possible. You were there,' he pointed at her, 'and you,' he jabbed a finger at

Hilary St John, 'and you,' he pointed at Hart's cold muzzle that was pointing back at him. 'It's some sort of schoolboy ritual – I expect Archie invented it back at Oxford. That's the sort of puerile bollocks I'd expect from the dark blues. You all had to be there to witness punishment, like some bloody deranged regiment parading in hollow square. I expect I walked past you all at Magicworld, didn't I? And I didn't even notice.'

'Two flies in the ointment,' Godden said. 'Drowned. You're the third, Maxwell.'

'Ah, yes,' the Head of Sixth Form nodded. 'My turn. After Logan you hoped I'd lay off, frightened away by it all. Well you played that badly, children. Because I'm Mad Max, for fuck's sake. I have a reputation to maintain. If I didn't round you bastards up, I couldn't look Year Seven in the eye again.'

Godden was on his feet now, shaking. 'That's enough, for Christ's sake. Hart, are you going to pull that fucking trigger or am I?'

Maxwell roared with laughter as Hart blinked, trying to steady his nerve, hold the red spot centre-forehead. 'That,' Maxwell was suddenly serious again, 'is when you snatched Tiffany. And that really had to be you, didn't it, Amy? Tiff's a bit silly, a bit soppy, a bit of a romantic. But she's a Maxwell deep down and no Maxwell in living memory has gone off with a strange man. Oh, except Great Uncle Piers, but we all made allowances for him. Now that was clever. You knew by now I wouldn't go away, so you guessed, rightly, I'd come looking. And you were good, all of you, stringing me along, shopping each other like it was going out of fashion. Harold, wherever he is, breathing heavily down the phone to Sylvia Matthews, one minute a Yorkshireman, the next . . . you going to give us your Ian Paisley then, Harold? I remember your Terry Wogan was legendary when you gave us a talk at dear old Leighford.' Maxwell was in full Ulster by now. 'You know, teeth will be provided!' and he rolled sideways, off the table with a thud, rolling in the dust of the Duchess of Malfi. He heard the ping of Hart's bullet hit metal behind him. A second thud from the silencer and splinters ripped into his hand.

Then he was gone, into the darkness of the wings, listening to the rising panic of the White Knights.

'You stupid bastard!' That was Godden.

'He's there, in the wings.' That was LeStrange, his voice less echoing as he ducked back from the intercom mike to peer into the bowels of the stage.

'He can't get out,' the luvvy tones of Wiseman. 'Every door's locked.'

'Maxwell,' LeStrange was back at the speakers again, commanding, imperious, like the voice of God. 'Give it up. You know you're finished.'

The Head of Sixth Form left his hat where it had fallen and eased himself backwards, crawling over coiled leads and edging towards the door he could just make out behind him. To his left was the floodlit stage, naked now and abandoned; to his right, a breeze-block wall. He raised himself up on one knee, careful to keep the Malfi flats between himself and the sniper in the auditorium. Please God, Maxwell thought, don't let Bob Hart have seen *Magnum Force*, where dear old Clint Eastwood puts two bullets of his legendary .44 through an aircraft fuselage. The Wyndham woodwork was flimsy enough, God knew.

He trusted to luck. He'd have one hit at the back door before Hart's sights found him. He saw the red spot wandering over the flats next to his shoulder, next to his head. No one spoke. No one, except for Hart and Maxwell, moved. He felt like Billy Bones in Treasure Island, that rattling good yarn of his youth. Only the spot had changed colour. The message was the same. He was upright now, crouching like a naked ape, exposed, alone. Then he rammed his bum backwards and bounced off the door. Damn. It opened outwards. There was a splintering of wood and a shattering of glass as the Ruger bullet hit the door and demolished a light beyond it. Maxwell was scrabbling at the handle and out of the wings before Hart could realign his shot.

He was in a corridor now and the lights went out with a thud as he stood up.

'Wiseman?' he heard LeStrange's voice still near the mike. 'Where's he gone?'

He couldn't hear the reply, but he knew he had options. There were doors to his left, costume stores, green rooms, who knew? He tried the first one. Locked. Each step was silent. Each step an agony of indecision. Where was she? The golden girl. She couldn't actually be in the rafters. Magic or no magic, that wasn't possible. He tried the second door and it clicked open under his weight.

'Green Room Two.' It was Wiseman's voice, loud, sharp, near. And it was followed by a thudding of feet. Maxwell's heart thumped, his pulse pounding in his head. He jumped four, five steps down, managed to catch his balance at the bottom and look around. There was light here, the morning sun filtering through slatted windows. He ran to it, cutting his fingers on the shutter's edge, ripping it from its hinges. Shit! Bars. There was no way out there. He doubled back, throwing himself in the crawl space under the stairs and he waited.

Above him in the half light, the door crashed back.

'He's here.' It was Wiseman again. Then all Maxwell heard was whispering. Two voices? Or was it three? He heard the steps creak with someone's weight. Only one of them had a gun. Only one of them was a danger. Archie Godden was no threat. He'd probably already keeled over with a coronary watching the action upstairs. Unless Maxwell had the worst luck in the world and Amy Weston added black belt karate to her poetic skills, he could handle her. Wiseman? Too old, too frail (Maxwell hoped). St John and LeStrange were younger men, leaner, hungrier than the creaking Head of Sixth Form. He'd have to trust to luck with them. But his real problem was Bob Hart and more importantly Bob Hart's bullet. Nothing could outrun that.

He heard footsteps hit the bottom. Flat, silent, concrete ground. His hand flailed in the darkness of the curtain he'd slipped behind, desperate for a weapon of some kind. His mind froze and his heart stopped as he saw the red spot creep upwards along the curtain's folds.

'Here's some light,' he heard Wiseman say and the spot wavered as Hart's concentration broke. A stage light, heavy, black and metal hurtled across the room as Maxwell launched it, followed by his own body and they both crashed into Hart. The Ruger came up, the bullet thudding through the ceiling and the two men scrabbled on the floor, both of them gripping the rifle and trying to pull the other one off. Neither of them heard Wiseman at the bottom of the stairs, but Maxwell was first to see his feet. He rolled sideways, dragging the lighter Hart with him and sending Wiseman tumbling back against the wall. Maxwell broke free of Hart's grip and was up the stairs again, the door crashing back as Hilary St John stood there, poised and ready. But Maxwell was in full flight. A bullet behind or a fashion photographer in front and it was no contest really. What was it his old rugger master had said? 'Get him low, Maxwell.' So he did, driving his shoulder into the man's groin and cracking his cranium on the corridor wall. The man just groaned and lay there, all fight and consciousness gone.

Then Maxwell was off, running left along the darkness, twisting right into the stores. He stopped, panting, trying to catch his breath, trying to get his bearings. He was next to the stage again now, facing the auditorium but on the intercom side of the wings. There was no noise of breathing from that, so LeStrange had gone. He heard by the mutterings and swearings behind him that Hart and Wiseman had disentangled themselves and were back on the scent.

Scent. That was it. Calvin Klein. It hit Maxwell's nostrils like a wall. She was here. Somewhere. Tiff was here. He edged his way, groping through flats and furniture, catching himself a nasty one as he ducked under a bar.

'Uncle Maxie?' It was Tiff's voice, suddenly, in that enormous silence, very much afraid. He reached out in the darkness and felt her hair, her face and he pulled her to him. He buried her mouth in his shoulder, feeling her whole body go limp. Not now, he willed her. Don't fall apart on me now, Tiff. Not now. Remember you're a Maxwell. He gingerly eased her away, trying to see her face in the darkness, feeling her cheeks wet with tears. He kissed them away and put his finger vertically against her lips. She nodded. She understood.

They crouched together in the darkness.

'Props Store Two.' LeStrange's voice boomed in the stillness, back at the mike again and Maxwell felt Tiffany jump in his arms. A neon strip pinged on overhead, bleak, bright. Maxwell dragged the girl into a corner, surrounded by black curtains and nets. This time his finger was to his own lips.

'Maxwell.' It was Hart's voice, not over the intercom but nearby and getting closer. 'You may have found one niece, but I've got the other.' Maxwell's heart stopped again. 'And that bitch Sylvia Matthews. You didn't seriously think we'd risk our little enterprise without all the aces, did you?'

Maxwell could see in the dim light Tiffany's eyes, wide with fear, staring up at him. What now, knight errant? Eat your heart out, Don Quixote.

'I went down there,' Hart was making his way steadily towards the corner, not anxious to tangle again with a lantern. Blood was trickling from his head and it felt as if it was bursting. 'Down to Leighford, that god-awful place you call home. Now, I'm tired of this crap. You come out now and finish this. Or the little girl dies. And what's going to happen to your little nursie friend, you don't want to know.'

'Lucy told you, Uncle Maxie,' Tiffany hissed, tears streaming down her cheeks. 'She told you. Robert de Niro's waiting He's got her.'

Maxwell hadn't seen it before, but now he could by ducking his head under the bar and craning uncomfortably to the left, he had a clear view of the lit stage and the wings to its left. Amy Weston and Archie Godden were still m the auditorium, flapping around like spare parts, panic rising in their hissing voices. What happened next was like a dream Anthony LeStrange was standing with his mouth near the mike. 'Maxwell, if you want Tiffany and Lucy to live, come out now. Don't make Hart come in and get you . . .' His voice tailed away and there was suddenly a character on stage, a lean, powerfully built man with cropped hair and the combat jacket and trousers of Desert Storm.

'Neil,' LeStrange's voice sounded brittle, near to breaking. 'Hello, Neil,' softer, coaxing, disarming.

'What's the matter with me?' Hamlyn's voice was picking up on the intercom. 'What have you done?'

'Now, Neil,' LeStrange was backing slowly away from the mike, testing his options, assessing the distance. 'Hart. Where the fuck are you?'

There was a rattle and crash backstage and the sniper doubled back from Maxwell, colliding with the flats as he went. He tumbled onto the stage as Maxwell watched, spellbound, from his hiding place. Hamlyn stood square on, his hands loose at his side, facing both men.

'Wiseman,' LeStrange snapped. 'Hamlyn worked for you. Come out here and call him off, for God's sake.'

'It's all going tits up!' was Godden's helpful contribution from the floor. 'I warned you. I warned all of you.'

'Shut up, Godden, you pathetic misfit,' LeStrange snarled. 'Fighting among ourselves is exactly what he wants.' He dashed back to the mike. 'Isn't it, Maxwell?'

'What have you done to me?' Hamlyn's voice was rising now and he was staring hard at LeStrange.

'He hypnotized you,' Godden spat with contempt. 'Said it was easy. It would wipe your feeble little mind of everything but the idea that you'd killed Larry Warner. Well, eminence grise, it hasn't bloody well worked, has it?'

'Kill him!' LeStrange growled, but he'd reckoned without Neil Hamlyn. Hart's rifle was barely up to the level when the SAS man had snatched LeStrange and spun him round, gripping his neck in the vice of both arms. The magician's mouth hung open and his arms flailed uselessly, his body a human shield between Hamlyn and Hart's bullet.

'My God,' Maxwell muttered. 'The head shot.'

There was a scream and a shout of 'No!' from who could tell how many mouths. But Maxwell heard the crack as Hamlyn broke LeStrange's neck with a single twist and the great magician's head hung at an improbable angle in the soldier's arms.

'Put the gun down! Armed police!' It was a barked order, followed by thudding feet and pandemonium. Maxwell craned to see what seemed an army of uniforms crashing through the auditorium, enveloping Godden and Amy Weston and thundering onto the stage to grab the gun and the gunman. In a second, Hart was on the stage where he'd killed Chris Logan, face down as someone put the bracelets on him.

Maxwell hauled Tiffany upright and she threw her arms around him.

'Lucy was right,' she sobbed into his neck. 'You are Nick Nolte, Uncle Max. You've saved us from Robert de Niro.'

Maxwell patted the matted hair, glancing back through the slit that showed him the stage. Neil Hamlyn was being gently unwrapped from the corpse of Anthony LeStrange and the handcuffs flashed silver in the light. He saw Jacquie Carpenter, centre stage, with DS Bartholomew and DCI Hall.

'Yes,' he said. 'Me and the SAS and the Leighford Constabulary – oh, and the Seventh Cavalry.'

Chapter Twenty

'Well, are you going to ask him, Sylvia?' Lucy was sitting next to Nurse Matthews, belted up and braced for another day at Leighford High.

She swung right along the flyover, the sea silver and silent to their left. 'Am I going to ask who what?'

'You know,' Lucy said, grinning, but looking straight ahead. 'Are you going to ask Uncle Maxie to marry you?'

'Uncle Maxie wouldn't like that,' Sylvia said, looking at her own eyes in the driving mirror. 'He belongs to the generation when the man always asked the lady.'

'Actually . . .' Lucy was particularly irritating that morning. 'Uncle Maxie told us in History the other day that the man always asked the lady's dad. What do you think your dad would say if Uncle Maxie asked him?'

'My dad,' Sylvia sighed, 'would probably think he was being proposed to and would run a mile, muttering things about the youth of today.'

They purred around the corner to catch the central tower of Leighford High in all its morning glory. Sylvia pushed the Clio's electric window button as she passed through the gate. 'Janice,' she called to a passing Year 12 smoker trying desperately to hide the fag behind her hand and not to exhale. 'I'll tell you later how many people those things kill every year. In the meantime, report to Mr Maxwell to give you a damn good thrashing.'

Sylvia parked, perhaps a little erratically, in the space reserved under the birches for the School Nurse.

'No, Lucy,' she switched off the engine and unbuckled her seat belt, 'I won't be asking your Uncle Maxie to marry me and he won't be asking me to marry him.'

'But why not?' Even at her ripe old age, Lucy still had the power to be disappointed. It showed in every inch of her face, every droop of her shoulders.

'Because,' Sylvia sighed, the door half open, 'he won't ask me because he doesn't love me. And I won't ask him because . . .' There was a sudden tap at the window and she spun round.

'Excuse me.' A rather dishy young man stood there, straddling thirty-five, with a rucksack and curly, dark hair. 'I'm sorry to bother you. My name's Guy Morley, supply teacher for Mrs . . . Grafton, is it?'

'Yes,' Sylvia cleared her throat and he stood back as she got out of the car. 'Helen Grafton, yes. Maternity leave. I'm Sylvia Matthews, School Nurse.'

'Sylvia . . .' She stood there astonished as he bowed and kissed her hand. 'Delighted to meet you. Er . . . your daughter?'

Lucy was leaning on the car bonnet, looking through slitted eyes at the interloper.

'No,' said Sylvia, perhaps a shade too quickly. 'Niece of a friend.'

'Ah.'

'Er . . . do you have children, Guy?'

'Me? No,' he smiled. 'I like them of course, but I couldn't eat a whole one. Anyway,' he waved his left hand in the air, 'nobody's caught me yet. I move too fast.'

Lucy shook her head and wandered off in disgust in search of another seven hours' savage amusement. God, the older generation.

'Do you?' Sylvia gave Guy her best Eddie Izzard, the one she'd learned from Peter Maxwell 'Do you really? Let me show you around.'

'Response time,' DCI Henry Hall was standing in the West Meon Incident Room at the end of another day, 'was slow

He looked at the tired faces in front of him, the smoke strained eyes. '*But*,' and he held his head up again, 'we got a result!' There were whoops and cheers and whistles all round, back-slapping and winks. Hall's hands were in the air for quiet. 'Joe Public will just have to get used to missing Anthony LeStrange. I doubt any of the others will be missed.'

'Sir?' It was Jacquie Carpenter on her feet. 'What about Neil Hamlyn?'

All eyes turned to Henry Hall. Where they always were. He was the boss, the guv'nor. He called the shots, whistled the tune, whatever analogy you chose. The main man. 'Hospital,' Hall said. 'Apparently, it's all going to take a little time.'

The room had fallen silent. 'People,' Hall broke it, 'a good job, all of you. But there's one person I want to single out because without her, we'd still all be working tonight.'

'I thought we were,' somebody shouted, to guffaws and chuckles.

'Jacquie,' Hall said. 'You followed your man, you made the right moves.'

'I lost him at the theatre,' she shook her head. 'Couldn't see at first how he'd got in.'

'We all missed that,' Hall told her. 'Looks as though he was SAS all along. Let's close this place down.'

And the back-slapping and the partying began.

Henry Hall crossed to Jacquie Carpenter and pulled a video tape from his jacket pocket. 'What I don't understand,' he said, 'is how this ended up in Bob Hart's flat. You do know what it is?'

She felt her throat iron hard, her blood pounding in her ears. 'Yes,' she nodded. 'It's Neil Hamlyn's interview with Dr Bartlett. I . . .'

And his raised hand stopped her. 'Bin it, will you, Jacquie? I can't see any evidential value in it. After all, we've got the original.' And he laid it into her hand.

'Well,' Frank Bartholomew was at her elbow as the guv'nor got lost in the melee, 'who's the blue-eyed girl, then?'

She gazed after Hall for a moment, her eyes wet. Then she turned to the man. 'I am, Sergeant Bartholomew,' she said, 'I am.' And she turned on her heel and marched away.

'I am just so relieved,' Maxwell stood in his Sixth Form office, smiling down at Tiffany standing under the limes by the bike sheds, holding hands with Mark Irwin and staring into his eyes.

Jacquie crossed to him, nodding. 'She'll be okay,' she said softly. 'They're very resilient, you know.'

'I know,' he sighed, turning to her. 'They're Maxwells, you see, deep down. No, it's Lucy and Sylvia I meant. That bastard Hart trying to con me he'd snatched them too.'

'He was there,' Jacquie said, 'Sylvia told us. Perhaps he thought better of it. More complications, more baggage. I want to thank you, Peter Maxwell.'

'Me?' he blinked. 'Why?'

'Because you put your life on the line to get the White Knights. That's a pretty rare thing to do.'

'Well,' he shuffled awkwardly, kicking the furniture and lapsing into hill-billy, 'Aw, shucks, Ms Carpenter, it ain't nothin' that any good ol' boy wouldn't do.' He was Maxwell again. 'Or did I put too many negatives in there? And Henry Hall did ask me nicely, with reference to brick walls and so on.'

'Will you do something else for me?' she asked.

'Name it, dear heart,' he said.

'Will you take me to the pictures tonight? If you can get a sitter for the girls, that is?'

'Sitter?' Maxwell repeated. 'What do they need a sitter for? What's on?'

'*Shakespeare in Love*,' she smiled.

'Rattling good yarn,' he smiled back. 'I'll ask Sylv . . .' and his voice trailed away. Crossing the car park below his window as the summer sun began to lend that magic glow to the world of Leighford High, strolled one person he knew very well and the other he'd nodded to in the corridor early in the day. One was a good-looking, curly headed supply teacher. The other was the School Nurse. They were chatting and laughing, lost in each other's company.

'There again,' said Maxwell, 'perhaps I won't. He held out his arm, bent at the elbow. 'What the Hell?' he said '*Shakespeare in Love* it is. But . . . the treat's mine.'

'Oh, no,' and she placed her arm on his. 'No, it's mine. Max.'

'Max, darling,' the voice sounded less distant than usual over Maxwell's answerphone, 'Sandie. We're flying home tomorrow. Heathrow. Sorry it's been such a dreadful bore for you all, darlings, but never mind. Tiffany and Lucy, back to a real school next week and you can give your poor uncle a bit of a break. Bye.'

CPSIA information can be obtained at www.ICGtesting.com
Printed in the USA
LVOW04s1508220115

423936LV00022B/1396/P